BULL'S-EYE

As if suddenly realizing someone was watching him from behind, Frank Penta turned around, smoking rifle in hand, and looked at Rochenbach through a haze of gun smoke. Seeing that Rochenbach had him cold, the rifle in Rock's hands pointed, aimed and cocked at him, Penta gave him a strange, tight grin.

"Some fight, huh, Rock?" he called out above the roar of gunfire, sounding as if the two of them had been close friends.

"Yes, it is," Rock agreed. His right eye fixed down the rifle sights; he squeezed the trigger. . . .

MIDNIGHT RIDER

Ralph Cotton

A SIGNET BOOK

SIGNET
Published by New American Library, a division of
Penguin Group (USA) Inc., 375 Hudson Street,
New York, New York 10014, USA
Penguin Group (Canada), 90 Eglinton Avenue East, Suite 700, Toronto,
Ontario M4P 2Y3, Canada (a division of Pearson Penguin Canada Inc.)
Penguin Books Ltd., 80 Strand, London WC2R 0RL, England
Penguin Ireland, 25 St. Stephen's Green, Dublin 2,
Ireland (a division of Penguin Books Ltd.)
Penguin Group (Australia), 250 Camberwell Road, Camberwell, Victoria 3124,
Australia (a division of Pearson Australia Group Pty. Ltd.)
Penguin Books India Pvt. Ltd., 11 Community Centre, Panchsheel Park,
New Delhi - 110 017, India
Penguin Group (NZ), 67 Apollo Drive, Rosedale, Auckland 0632,
New Zealand (a division of Pearson New Zealand Ltd.)
Penguin Books (South Africa) (Pty.) Ltd., 24 Sturdee Avenue,
Rosebank, Johannesburg 2196, South Africa

Penguin Books Ltd., Registered Offices:
80 Strand, London WC2R 0RL, England

First published by Signet, an imprint of New American Library,
a division of Penguin Group (USA) Inc.

First Printing, April 2012
10 9 8 7 6 5 4 3 2 1

For Mary Lynn . . . *of course*

PART 1

Chapter 1

———

Denver City, Colorado Territory

In the silvery light of dawn, U.S. Secret Service agent Avrial Rochenbach stepped down from his big dun out in front of the seedy Great Westerner Hotel, located on the outskirts of Denver City. He unwrapped a wool muffler from around his bare head and left it hanging from his shoulders. He looked back and forth along the street, which had just started coming to life for the day. A curl of steam wafted in his breath.

Scabbed onto the right side of the hotel beneath a shed roof stood Andrew Grolin's Lucky Nut Saloon. On a faded, hand-painted sign above the saloon, a large nut—of a variety Rochenbach was unfamiliar with—stood upright between a large, frothy mug of beer and two large, tumbling dice.

Rochenbach spun his reins around an iron hitch rail, stepped onto the boardwalk and inside the Lucky Nut. Before he'd made three steps across the stone-tiled floor, two gunmen at the bar turned toward him quickly.

"Whoa! Stop yourself right there," one called out, a Henry rifle in his hand, leveled at Rochenbach. "Did you hear anybody say we're open for business yet?"

Rochenbach made no reply; he didn't stop either. He continued across the floor, his forearm carelessly shoving back the right side of his long wool coat, where a black-handled Remington stood across his lower belly.

On the other side of the bar, Andrew Grolin looked up from counting a thick stack of money, a big black cigar in his teeth. He stalled for a second before saying anything, observing how everyone handled themselves.

"Hey, sumbitch! Are you deaf or something?" the same gunman called out to Rochenbach, he and the other gunman spreading a few feet apart, ready for whatever came next.

Grolin already saw what was coming if he didn't do something to stop it. A belly rig like this? The slightest move of either of his men, this newcomer would pivot left a half turn. The big Remington would slip out of its holster as if his body had moved away from it and left it hanging in midair. It would come up arm's length slick and fast. *Bang, you're dead!* Grolin thought.

"It's all right, Spiller. I've been expecting this man," he said at the last second, before the scene he'd played out in his head began acting itself out on the floor.

"Whatever you say, boss," said Denton Spiller.

The two men backed up a step; Spiller eyed the bareheaded newcomer up and down as Rochenbach stopped and returned his stare, his long wool coat still pushed back out of the way on his right side. The wool muffler hung from his shoulders.

"You need to be more careful how you enter a room, mister," the gunman cautioned him, lowering his rifle barrel almost grudgingly.

"Obliged," Rochenbach said flatly. "I've been working on it." He let his coat fall back into place now that the rifle barrel wasn't pointed at him.

Rochenbach held the gunman's stare until Andrew Grolin took his cigar from his mouth and looked back and forth between the two, still appraising, still gauging the tensile of each man's will.

"Spiller," he said, "you and Pres meet Avrial Rochenbach." He turned his eyes to Rochenbach. "Rock, this is Denton Spiller and Preston Casings. Two of my best damn men."

Rochenbach nodded; the two nodded in return. None of the men raised their hands from gun level.

"I heard of you, Rochenbach," said Casings. "You're the Midnight Rider, the fellow who prefers working in the dark of night." He looked Rock up and down. "Also the fellow who got himself chased out of the Pinkertons."

"Really?" said Spiller to Rochenbach with a cold stare. "How does that feel, getting chased out?"

"I can show you," Rochenbach said.

Spiller started to bristle.

"Easy, men," Andrew Grolin said with a short, dark chuckle. He gestured to Spiller and said, "You and Pres take a walk. I want to talk to Rock here in private. He's going to be riding with us."

"Come on, Dent," said Pres, half turning toward the front door.

"*Rock*, huh? That's the name you go by?" Spiller asked, not giving it up yet.

Rock stared at him. So did Andrew Grolin. Ordinarily Grolin would have had none of this—a man not doing what he was told right away. But he knew this was good. It showed him who he could count on when the going got tight.

"*Friends* call me that," Rochenbach said.

"Yeah? What do them who are *not your friends* call you?" Spiller asked, his contempt for this newcomer showing clearly in his eyes, his voice.

"Nothing, for long," said Rochenbach.

The threat was there, but it took a second for Denton Spiller to catch it, and that second was all Grolin needed to decide the better of the two—at least when it came to showing their fangs. It might be a different story when it came to hard testing. But for now he'd seen enough. So far Rochenbach was living up to everything Grolin had heard about him.

"How's that walk coming along?" he asked Spiller in a stronger tone.

Spiller didn't answer. He jerked a nod toward the front door.

Grolin and Rochenbach watched as Casings followed Spiller out of the saloon.

After the two had moved along the street and out of sight, beyond reach of the large front window, Rock turned to face Grolin behind the bar.

"'Cowboy' Pres Casings . . . ," he said.

"Yep," said Grolin. He eyed Rockenbach. "Used to

be, a man who called him 'Cowboy' would be warming his feet in hell before he got the words out of his mouth."

"I didn't name him," said Rock.

"I know," said Grolin, sweeping up the cash from atop the bar. "Call it friendly advice."

"Taken as such," Rock said.

"I was surprised you heard of him at first," Grolin said, eyeing Rochenbach. "Then I remembered you must know lots about us ol' boys who drop gun hammers for a living."

"I do," said Rock. "Does it bother you, my having worked for the law?"

"I don't *bother* easily," said Grolin. "Not to piss on your hoecake, but I don't figure you worked for the rightful law. You worked for the *Allen Pinkerton law*. I see a vast difference between the two."

"See it how it suits you," said Rock. "It makes me no difference. Whatever I was, I'm a long rider now." He gave a slight shrug. "I figure Juan Sodorez and some of his pistoleros must've vouched for me, else we wouldn't be standing here talking all tough and friendly to each other."

Grolin chuckled under his breath and seemed to relax a little.

"I expected you three weeks ago," he said. "Wondered if I ought to come looking for you."

"You wouldn't have wanted to be where I was three weeks ago," Rochenbach said.

"Oh?" Grolin said. "Is that where your forehead ran into a rifle butt?"

Rochenbach touched his fingers deftly to his

forehead, his dark-circled eyes, and his mending nose.

"It's a long story," said Rock. "But yes, I did stop a rifle butt up at Gunn Point."

"I see," said Grolin. "Was it over a whore, or over a card game?"

"Does it matter?" Rock asked.

Grolin grinned. "I'd like to think you were late for a good reason."

Rochenbach could tell by the look in his eyes that he had already heard what had happened in Gunn Point. He wasn't going to offer any more than he had to on the matter.

"I don't remember," he said. "It might have been both."

"But nothing you want to talk about," Grolin concluded.

"Right," Rochenbach said. "Nothing *worth* talking about, that is." He nodded at a coffeepot sitting on a tray behind the polished bar. "Not as important as a hot mug of coffee—and hearing what you've got in mind for us." He kept his gaze on Grolin.

Outside on the street, Denton Spiller and Preston Casings walked along in the grainy dawn light and stopped at a public fire burning out in front of a blacksmith and ironmongering shop. They stared at a ragged old man until he stopped warming his rough, calloused hands and walked away from the fire. They stood in his place and warmed their hands as a two-pound forging hammer rang against an anvil in the background.

Spiller rolled himself a smoke and lit it carefully on a licking flame. Behind them on the street, steam wafted in the breath of passing wagon horses pulling their loads.

"What do you think?" he asked Pres Casings. He blew out a stream of gray smoke.

"About what?" Casings replied, wringing his gloved hands near the flames.

Spiller stared at him with a no-nonsense look and took another draw.

"Oh, you mean Rochenbach," Casings said.

"Yeah, I mean Rochenbach," Spiller said in a short tone. "What the hell else would I be talking about?"

"How would I know?" said Casings, his voice equally testy. "Any number of things, I reckon."

Spiller shook his head and stared back toward the Lucky Nut. He drew on the thin cigarette between his lips.

"Anyway, I don't trust the sumbitch. I don't trust any man who once wore a badge," he added.

"You can't hold it against a man," said Casings. "A lot of lawmen get tangled up in things and go afoul of the law."

Spiller took a breath and let it out, considering Casings' words.

"Yeah," he said, "that's true enough. Still, I can't trust one. I believe there's a peculiar, gnawing little animal lives inside a man that makes him want to work for the law."

"I can see that," said Casings, nodding, warming his hands. "But a man can change his mind, decide *to hell with the law* and go his own way."

"Yeah," said Spiller, looking back from the saloon and into the fire. "But once he turns outlaw, I wonder what's become of that gnawing little animal. It still has to be fed, don't it?"

Casings didn't try to answer. He shook his head slowly and stared into the fire.

"I expect if Grolin wants Rochenbach with us, he's *with us*, like it or not," he said. He paused reflectively, then added, "Everything I've heard of him, he's a straight-up outlaw, no doubt about it. Maybe you just worry too much."

"Get this straight, Pres," Spiller said in a strong tone. "I don't worry about a *damn thing*." He coughed and blew smoke around the cigarette. "The only thing that worries me about hanging is that they tie the knot wrong."

"That would worry me too," said Casings. "Maybe they'd let me tie it myself."

"Naw, they won't let you do it," said Spiller. "I asked around."

The two chuckled darkly and warmed their hands.

"Still, I'm going to watch this Rochenbach sumbitch like a hawk," Spiller said, staring back toward the saloon in dawn's light.

Inside the saloon, Rochenbach sipped the steaming coffee and watched Andrew Grolin pour his mug half full. He tipped a bottle of rye and filled the mug close to its brim.

Before Grolin corked the whiskey bottle, Rock slid his mug forward, on the outside chance that Grolin was just checking him out.

"Where are my manners?" Grolin chastised himself. He gave him a thin smile and topped off Rochenbach's mug with whiskey.

Rochenbach nodded his thanks and sipped the hot, fiery coffee.

"Let's get down to it," Grolin said, leaning a little closer across the bar. "Arnold the Swede tells me you're a man who knows his way around safe locks, explosives and such. That's why I told him to send you to me." He watched Rochenbach's eyes as he sipped his whiskey-laced coffee. "Did he tell me right?"

"The Swede knows my work," said Rochenbach. "If he says I'm good, I won't argue with him."

Here it was, Rock thought, studying Grolin's eyes, knowing he was being tested and weighed with every word, every gesture. If he asked too much too soon, it would raise suspicion. If he didn't ask enough, it would raise suspicion too—it was all about finding the right balance.

"So, what do you feel like robbing?" he asked, raising the steaming mug to his lips.

Grolin smiled appraisingly. "Just like that?" he said, snapping his thick fingers above the bar top.

"I didn't ride all this way for the scenery," Rock said. "If you don't trust me, let's stop here before we hurt each other's feelings."

"It's a train that looks to be any ordinary freight car," Grolin said, the slight smile vanishing from his face, "except, inside, one whole end of it is a big fat safe. It's got the new permutation dial lock on it."

Rock let out a breath.

"A combination safe," said Rochencbach. "That's

good for starters. But I'll need to know what's inside this safe. Is this going to be a blasting job—will I need nitro? Or will I be opening it with a trumpet?"

"A trumpet sounds better to me. But let's talk about it some," Grolin said. "I want to hear what you say about it."

"What can I tell you?" Rock asked.

Chapter 2

Rochenbach allowed himself to relax and drink the laced coffee. He listened as Andrew Grolin leaned against the inside of the bar and spoke in a guarded voice.

"Do you know anything about the U.S. Mint and Assay Office in Denver City?" he asked.

"Not very much," said Rochenbach, lying straight-faced. "I rode past it one night the last time I was here. I remember wishing they had left a basement window open."

"How long ago was that?" Grolin asked, studying Rochenbach as he spoke.

"A year, maybe longer," Rock replied.

"In that case, you would have been sorely disappointed," said Grolin. "There was nothing in the basement there but minting equipment left behind after the government bought out the Clark Gruber Mint back during the war. The fact is, after the government bought out Clark Gruber, equipment and all, they've yet to strike a single coin there, silver or gold."

"No kidding?" said Rochenbach, already knowing it, but feigning mild surprise. "Why is that?

Grolin shrugged a thick shoulder and poured more whiskey into his coffee.

"Hell, if we're going to talk about why the government does or doesn't do what they say they're going to, we're in for a long, sad conversation," he chuffed, stirring the whiskey and coffee around with the tip of his finger.

"Yeah, I suppose so," Rock agreed, raising his warm mug and taking a sip from it.

"My notion, Honest Abe and his gang couldn't stand the thought that a commercial business was conducting banking and striking coins without getting their greasy noses stuck into the mix." He raised his cigar with his thick fingers and stuck it into his mouth. "That's usually what happens, right?"

Rochenbach saw Grolin stare at him, searchingly, for a reply. But he wasn't going to give one. There was such a thing as him knowing *too* much.

"If you say so," he said. "I don't keep up much on banking practices—government either, for that matter."

"Yeah?" Grolin looked at him closely. "I figured in your time as a detective, you had the chance to learn quite a lot about both."

"Maybe I *should* have," said Rock. "I spent most my time figuring the best way to get bank money to follow me out the door." He sipped the last of his whiskey-laced coffee.

Grolin gave a short laugh. He puffed his cigar and considered it for a moment.

"The reason I asked how long ago since you'd ridden past there," he said, "is that the past eight months, there's been smoke seen rising from the smelt furnace in that basement." He paused, then added, "Always, it's been seen late at night."

Rochenbach gave him a curious look. "But you just said they've yet to strike the first coin—?"

"That's right, I did," said Grolin, cutting him off. "And they still haven't. But they do melt down gold and ship it back East, all the way to Philadelphia. They don't do it all the time, and they try to keep it under their hats when they do." He gave him an oily, crooked grin, the black cigar still in his mouth. "But I've got eyes in Denver City. Nothing gets past me."

"Smelting gold, huh?" Rochenbach straightened a little against the bar, looking even more attentive. He set the mug on the bar in front of him.

Noting the empty mug, Grolin started to reach out and fill it with more whiskey, but Rochenbach put his hand between the bottle and the coffee mug, stopping him.

"Thanks, but I'm good for now," he said. "We're starting to talk about money."

Grolin nodded and set the bottle down. He liked that, he told himself—Rochenbach, cool and even, facing up to Spiller and Casings, knocking back a little whiskey before breakfast, but turning strictly business, now that business was at hand.

"Yes, we are, and big money at that," he said, still watching Rochenbach's eyes closely. "Only, this is not cash money."

Rochenbach kept quiet, listening.

"This is all in bullion, three-and-a-half-inch gold ingots," said Grolin, another oily grin around his black cigar. "Got anything against taking your pay in gold, Rock? My extra men I pay off in cash, out of my pocket. But my regular men get paid more, so they'll take their pay in gold, convert it to cash themselves, if they know somebody who'll convert it."

"Nothing against gold, unless I have to dig it up first," Rochenbach replied. "I know plenty of folks who can touch bullion gold and turn it into cash. They don't care what stamping is on it."

Grolin grinned and bit down on his cigar.

"I like those kinds of folks. I know some myself," he said. "But these are shipping ingots. They have no stamping on them."

"Even better," said Rochenbach. "You mentioned a big safe built inside a rail car?" he asked.

"Yes, I did," said Grolin, and he offered nothing more. Instead he gazed steadily at Rochenbach, seeing what he had to offer on the matter.

"I take it we're talking about the freight car specially made by Lomack Car and Foundry," said Rochenbach, "the one Kennedy's Detective Agency had made for the U.S. Treasury Department."

"You're right," said Grolin. He cocked his head and gave Rock a bemused look. "How'd you come by that? It's not something widely known."

"No, it's not," Rochenbach said. "But Allen Pinkerton had his men keep a close eye on anything the Kennedy detectives were up to. Kennedy started out working for Pinkerton. He went home to Ohio and started Kennedy's Secret Service. Allen Pinkerton has never forgiven him for it. When he heard about the special Treasury car being built, he offered a bonus to any agent who could get his hands on the design drawings. Guess who that agent turned out to be?" he added with a level gaze.

"Well, well," said Grolin, pouring himself more whiskey. "I'm impressed all to hell by this. So you know all about this rail car we're discussing?"

"*All about it*, no," said Rock. "But I know more about it than most people would." Now it was his turn to give Grolin a curious look. "Why is it I think you already knew this? Maybe this is why Arnold the Swede looked me up."

Grolin didn't reply. Instead his sipped his whiskey and puffed his cigar.

"So, you have held the design to this Treasury car in your hands?" he asked.

Rock only nodded.

"Tell me how it's built," said Grolin.

Rochenbach decided this cagey thief leader already knew how the big freight car was built. *One more little test . . .* , Rock told himself. So he would lay it all out for him just the same.

"When you look at it, you can't tell it from any other freight car," he said. "When they finished building it, they weathered it and beat it up, made it look years older than it really is."

"Go on," Grolin said, seeming mildly interested so far.

"The entire car itself is heavily armored," said Rock. "It's been fabricated four inches thick—three and a half inches of diagonal cross layers of wood and a half inch of boilerplate steel. Getting into the car alone is like getting into a safe. So there's no way into the actual safe from outside the car, unless you have a field cannon and all day to keep loading and firing it. If we did, we really would be digging what's left of the bars and ingots out of the hillsides." He looked at Grolin expectantly.

"I'm listening," Grolin said, smoke curling up from the cigar in his mouth. "Tell me how we rob it."

Rochenbach knew Grolin had it all worked out. He was still testing him, seeing if he knew enough to be worth cutting in on a robbery this size.

Rochenbach continued, saying, "Being an Ohioan, Kennedy turned the actual construction over to the Diebold Bahmann Company—safe builders out of Cincinnati. They're the ones who turned one end of the freight car into a rolling safe."

Grolin sipped his whiskey and grinned knowingly.

"Pretty smart for the Yankee government," he said. "Most thieves don't even know about the car. Them that do know about it wouldn't recognize it if it was staring at them."

"And then there's some of us who wouldn't touch it if it was sitting in front of us," Rochenbach continued. "Without the right information, how would anybody know when to hit it, or where?" He shook his head. "Only a fool would risk getting himself killed over opening a safe that just might be sitting empty."

"That's my part," said Grolin. "I'll know when to hit it, where to hit it and how much gold it's going to be holding. Otherwise I'd put the whole thing out of my mind."

"I hope this information of yours is as reliable as the morning sun," Rochenbach said, not about to ask where it came from right then.

"Don't concern yourself with that," Grolin said. "If I put you inside the rail car, will you put me inside the safe, without blowing it to hell and gone?"

"If it's a Diebold Bahmann experimental permutation safe, I'll walk you in it quiet as a mouse."

"What makes you so cocksure of yourself?" Grolin said. "These experimental safes are not widely known."

"I know them," Rock said.

"From having been a detective . . . ," Grolin murmured.

"Yes," said Rock. "Every brand of these new permutation safes has its own sound. So, let's just say I speak this safe's language." He returned the saloon owner's stare.

Grolin weighed his words, then nodded slightly.

"All right," he said, "I believe you."

If Grolin really had the information he purported to have, it meant he had himself a spy inside either the mint or the Treasury Department. It had to be somebody powerful enough to access the scheduling, date of gold shipments and amounts being shipped.

Rochenbach wanted that person—wanted him bad, he told himself. But that would have to wait until later.

"How much do you believe me?" Rochenbach asked flatly.

"Fifty thousand in gold bullion," Grolin returned in a like tone.

Rock allowed a gleam of excitement to come into his eyes.

"For fifty thousand gold, you're inside it," he said.

At the rear of the saloon, a door opened and a large man wearing a plaid wool coat stepped inside the Lucky Nut.

"One of my bartenders," Grolin said in a lowered voice. "We're through talking for now." He looked Rochenbach up and down. "Now that you know my play, stick close to Spiller and Casings. I hate a man who'd change his mind and try to skin out of town."

"I'll stick close. Once I'm in on a job, there's no turning back until my pockets are lined," Rock said.

"Done," said Grolin. "Go next door, tell my desk clerk I said to give you a room. Get yourself some grub down the street and get some rest. I'll send Spiller and Casings by later. You ride with them."

"Where are we going?" Rock asked, not really curious, but just curious if Grolin would tell him.

"Don't worry about it. They'll tell you," Grolin said.

He looked at Rochenbach's bare head. "The kind of money you've got coming, you might think about getting yourself a hat."

"I already am," Rochenbach said, turning toward the front door.

After a breakfast of elk steak, eggs, gravy and biscuits, Rochenbach walked back to the Great Westerner Hotel, where he'd stopped long enough to get a room for himself on his way to the restaurant.

"I had your horse taken to the livery barn like you

asked," said a young, thin desk clerk, "and there are your bags and rifle." He nodded toward a saddle-bag and a Spencer rifle standing in a corner near the stairs. He laid the key to Rochenbach's room on the counter with a wide smile.

"Obliged," said Rock, picking up the key. "Please see to it I'm not disturbed before noon."

"Yes, sir," said the clerk, the wide smile still stamped on his face.

Inside his dusty room overlooking the main street, Rochenbach took a wooden chair and tipped it back beneath the door handle, wedging it into place. He sat down on the edge of a lumpy mattress, pulled off his ill-fitting boots and stood them beside the bed. He stared at the boots in dark reflection as he wiggled his stiff toes inside his dingy gray socks.

He had taken the boots off one of two dead men he'd left lying in a livery barn in Gunn Point. He'd also taken the black-handled Remington, holster and all, and one of the dead men's coats. Neither of their blood-soaked hats had been fit to wear, he recalled.

He loosened his gun belt and hung the belly rig on a bedpost. Sliding the big Remington from its holster, he turned it in his hand, looked at it and slid it under his pillow.

The two gunmen had led him from his cell coat-less and in his stockinged feet, despite the snow that was on the ground.

"What about my coat?" he had asked.

"You won't need it," came a reply.

Their intentions had been clear enough; they'd escorted him to the livery barn to kill him, plain and simple. But they were both dead now, and here's where he'd landed, on the outskirts of Denver City, right back on the job. He let out a breath. There was no shortage of work in his profession. *Working for the government* . . .

He collapsed back onto a long, neglected feather mattress, coat and all, and stared up at two bullet holes in the pine plank ceiling. He watched a small brown spider zigzag across the ceiling and crawl into one of the dark holes. *All right, then, back to work. . . .*

A train job, he recounted to himself. Grolin had asked all the right questions, and he was certain he'd given the right answers. As for his ability to open a Diebold Bahmann, that much was true. He could open one.

He'd been taught how to listen to these new combination safes' inner mechanism through an ear trumpet by the best in the business: Quick Charlie Simms, a reformed Roma Gypsy safecracker who turned lawman and now worked for Judge Isaac Parker's court. How Simms had learned about the safes so quickly, he had no idea. *The innovation of a master thief* . . . , he mused to himself.

But he'd learned on his own that for the Diebold safe, he would need more than an ear trumpet; he would need the Cammann stethoscope he'd picked up in Boulder City and carried here with him.

The rest of the story he'd given Grolin had been a lie that he'd made up on the spot. He picked up the threads of what Grolin wanted to hear and he'd pieced together a story that suited the situation. As for the Treasury car, he'd never seen it, but he'd heard of it. He'd never held its design in his hands, but he'd heard talk. As for Allen Pinkerton offering a bonus for information on the construction of the car—*huh-uh, all a lie.* . . .

But it was close to what he'd shared with Arnold the Swede three months ago in a gambling hall in San Antonio. Two days earlier, a condemned prisoner named Vernal Tooney had told him the Treasury car was a target of a robbery in the works.

"I don't expect telling you all this could keep me from swinging, could it, Rock?" Tooney had asked him.

"Not a chance," Rochenbach replied.

"Then why am I telling you, knowing you're the law dog who put me here?" Tooney said.

"Beats me," Rock said. *"Maybe just to get it off your chest? Do something decent?"*

"Decent, ha. I hate every sumbicth I ever rode with, north or south, that's why," Tooney said.

"I understand," Rochenbach had replied.

No sooner had the rope snapped tight around Tooney's neck than Rochenbach had looked up the Swede. He'd spent a few days drinking, gambling with him, reliving the couple of times they'd ridden together—a bank job, a counterfeiting spree. Then he'd let the Swede know he was available. Reminded him how handy he was at opening safes.

He smiled and closed his eyes. That was enough to get himself into the game, he thought, drifting, catching flashes of the long ride he'd made from Gunn Point, almost nonstop, down from the Medicine Bow

Range, along the mountain line to Boulder City, a dozen plank towns and mining camps in between and now finally to Denver City.

Three weeks late, according to Grolin.

But right on time, as far as he was concerned, considering he'd lost almost a week in the Gunn Point jail—not to mention he'd burned down part of a counterfeiting ring run by the Golden Circle and killed the man running it. But he was here now, ready to get to work, he thought, rubbing the sore but nearly healed wounds of two separate bullet fragments he'd taken in his shoulder—souvenirs. . . .

He was fit enough now, he thought, taking stock of himself. He'd have to get some better boots—a hat of some sort, some gloves . . . but all that in good time. Right now he needed sleep. After he'd rested, he thought, *Let the game begin.*

Chapter 3

Rochenbach awoke at midday to the sound of a key turning inside the door lock. Almost before he'd opened his eyes, his hand streaked from beneath his pillow and raised the Remington, cocking it on the upswing. He rose quietly from the bed and stood in his stockinged feet, still dressed, his wool coat still on. He saw someone try the door against the chair back wedged beneath it. He lowered his big pistol a little as he watched the doorknob ease back around into place. He waited; a knock came.

He stepped over to the door and listened for the second knock before reaching out and taking hold of the chair.

"Who's there?" he asked. He heard cursing on the other side of the door. Then he heard Denton Spiller's gruff voice.

"It's us, damn it!" Spiller said. "Spiller and Pres Casings. Open the damned door. What are you so scared of?"

Rock uncocked the Remington, bent his arm at the

elbow and raised the gun upright beside him, poised. He pulled the chair from beneath the doorknob and set it back out of the way.

"Jesus, Rochenbach, come on," Spiller grumbled.

But Rock still took his time. He stood to the edge of the door frame, twisted the knob and shoved the door open, leaving the two gunmen staring at an empty room for just a second before he appeared at the right edge of the door.

The two looked at the wooden chair and at the Remington in Rochenbach's hand.

"Damn," said Spiller, "a man takes all this precaution, you must be guilty as sin."

Rochenbach took his thumb off the Remington's hammer and lowered the gun to his side as he gestured for the two to come inside.

"That's in case somebody had a key to my room," Rock said flatly, staring at Spiller.

"Oh. Well . . . ," said Spiller, holding a big skeleton key in his hand. He looked a little put off. But then he collected himself quickly and said, "Grolin told us to come get you and take you with us. It is *his* hotel." He pitched the key up; Rochenbach caught it in his left hand without taking his eyes off Spiller.

"Where we going?" he asked.

Spiller grinned at Casings, then turned back to Rochenbach.

"If Mr. Grolin wanted you to know, he'd have already told you," said Spiller. "Get your gun belt and boots—hurry the hell up." He gestured toward the belly rig hanging from the bedpost.

"Grolin said you'd tell me," Rochenbach replied without moving an inch. It didn't matter to him. But he wasn't going to let Spiller get started telling him what to do.

"Yeah, but I'm not going to *tell you*," Spiller said with a cold expression.

"I understand," Rock said. "So, now you can go tell Grolin."

Spiller looked at him curiously. "Tell him what?" he asked.

"Tell him that you weren't able to make me leave this room," said Rochenbach with finality.

"Now, listen, *damn it*!" said Spiller in a threatening tone. He took a step toward Rochenbach.

The Remington cocked at Rock's side.

Spiller stopped.

"I'm listening," said Rock.

Casings stood watching intently. This man was hard to deal with. But that didn't bother him.

Spiller froze for a tense second, weighing his chances. Then he let out a breath of exasperation.

"All right, Rochenbach," he said, "if this is how you're going to be." He spread his hands in a show of peace. "Mr. Grolin wants you to ride out with us, collect a debt for him."

"I'm a *debt collector*?" questioned Rochenbach, feigning offense.

"Don't get piqued. He just wants to see how you handle yourself," Pres Casings cut in.

Rock shook his head. Without another word on the matter, he walked over beside the bed and pulled on his ill-fitting boots. The two gunmen watched as he put on his gun belt beneath his long wool coat and shoved the Remington into the belly holster.

"You always sleep with your coat on, Rock?" Casings asked. He gave him a half-friendly smile.

Rock, huh? Rochenbach noted to himself.

"Doesn't everybody?" he replied, half friendly himself now that Casings had made the first gesture. He picked up his Spencer rifle and saddlebags from against the wall, slung the saddlebags over his shoulder and walked back to the two gunmen, rifle in hand. "After you, gentlemen," he said, sweeping a hand toward the open door.

"Meaning, he doesn't want us behind his back," Casings said to Spiller, turning toward the door.

"I know what the hell he means," Spiller said in an angry tone, turning behind him.

After getting his horse from the livery barn, Rochenbach left the two gunmen waiting atop their horses at a hitch rail while he walked inside a trading post.

"What the hell is this? He leaves us sitting here while he *browses*?" Spiller grumbled to Casings, watching through the open doorway as Rochenbach moved among the stacks of men's hats and clothing.

"Said he needs a hat and gloves," Casings replied. He liked the way Rochenbach handled himself—cool, calm, no hurry.

"A sumbitch should already have a hat and gloves when he shows up," Spiller said. "This is no child's game."

"Jesus. Why don't you take it easy, Dent?" said

Casings. "The man is no rube when it comes to this business. Grolin brought him in because he's a good safe man. That means we must have something big in the works."

"Did you just tell me to *take it easy*?" Spiller said, his face lit red with anger and disbelief. His right hand moved up onto the butt of a Colt standing in his tied-down holster.

Casings saw the threat, but he didn't back an inch.

"You heard me right," he said. His thumb slid over the hammer of his Winchester lying across his lap, barrel leveled in Spiller's direction. "Is any of this worth us going to the iron over?"

Spiller cooled a little, but his hand stayed on the butt of the Colt.

"I don't give a damn about his hat and gloves!" he said, switching the subject of the conversation back to Rochenbach. "Once we get back, maybe you and him would like to explain to Grolin why this trip took so damn long."

Casings tossed a glance up at the gray afternoon sky. "I didn't blame a man wanting gloves and a hat in this kind of weather."

They sat for a moment longer, Spiller's temper swelling.

"To hell with this!" he said, swinging down from his saddle, and headed inside the trading post. But he stopped as Rochenbach stepped out through the door, putting on a new pair of snug-fitting black leather gloves, which he'd cut the thumbs and fingers off of. He'd shoved the scraps down into his coat pocket.

"Ready to go?" Rochenbach asked quietly. "We'll be running out of daylight."

Along with the fingerless gloves, he wore a new black slouch-style hat and a pair of black high-welled miner's boots. He'd purchased a pair of warm wool socks and wasted no time putting them on. His wool pin-striped trouser legs were tucked inside his boot wells.

Spiller stared at him coldly.

Casings lowered his head and hid a thin smile. He managed to compose himself when Spiller stepped into his saddle beside him and jerked his horse around toward the dirt street.

"Let's ride," Spiller said over his shoulder. "The sooner we get this over with, the better."

They rode west in silence for over an hour until they stopped atop a rocky rise overlooking a short stretch of dried grassland. In the center of the grass stood a stone and weathered-plank shack, badly tilted to one side. Thirty yards from the shack, a flock of vultures were feasting and bickering on the carcass of a dead cow. Spiller drew his rifle from his saddle boot, checked it and stood it on his thigh.

"I'll be damned," he said to himself, seeing smoke curl from the chimney of the weathered shack.

Rochenbach and Casings eased their horses up on either side of Spiller.

"Here's the deal," Spiller said. "The man living there is Edmund Bell. He owes Grolin over three hundred dollars in old gambling markers. Grolin said if we can't collect payment, do whatever we think needs doing. Make an example of him. He's tired of fooling with this beefer."

"Meaning?" said Rock.

"Meaning kill him, far as Grolin cares. He holds the marker against this shack and acreage," said Spiller. He turned his face to Rochenbach. "He can go to court, take this place and resell it if he's a mind to. Do you have any qualms with killing a losing beefer?"

"Yes, I do," said Rock. "I wasn't hired to kill a man over a gambling debt. That's not where I saw my future headed."

"Your future, huh?" Spiller said with contempt. "Then you best lag back out of our way. If we don't get the money, I'd rather kill him than have to ride back out here." He nudged his horse forward at a loose gallop.

"Don't worry about it, Rock," said Casings, the two falling in behind Spiller. "Most times we put a scare into these beefers and miners, they usually offer up some money—enough to buy themselves more time. That's all Grolin is after anyway."

Rochenbach didn't reply. They galloped along in the afternoon gloom.

From the front window of the shack, a young dark-haired woman named Mira Bell looked out and saw three men ride down onto the grassland. Cupping both hands beneath a belly heavy with child, she turned from the window and looked at her husband, who was roasting a slab of beef on an iron rod over an open-hearth fire.

"Sonny, there's riders coming!" she said, her dark eyes showing her fear. "It looks like the same men as last time—from the Lucky Nut!"

"Oh no! It's too soon for them to be coming back here!" said the young man, standing, laying the sizzling meat in a tin pan on the stone hearth. "Pa said they'd be coming back, but I figured we'd have time to clear out!"

"What are we going to do, Sonny?" she cried out, near tears. "We don't have any money for them."

"I don't know, Mira," said Sonny. He jerked up a shotgun that stood leaning against a wall beside the hearth and hurried to the front door. He turned around toward her and leaned back against the door for a moment as if preparing himself to face an impossible task. "Whatever happens out there, you keep this door locked. Don't come outside for nothing."

Slowing their horses into an easy lope the last twenty yards toward the weathered shack, the three riders looked over at the feasting buzzards, then toward the scent of roasted beef wafting in the gray smoke from the chimney.

"Looks like we've caught ol' Edmund sitting down to supper," said Spiller with a laugh.

"Hey, what do we have here?" Casings asked, veering his horse over toward a grave marker standing in fresh-turned soil.

Rochenbach and Spiller turned their horses with him, rode over, jerked their horses to a halt and looked down.

"I'll be damned," said Spiller, reading the name

Edmund Bell carved on the grave board. "This sumbitch has gone and died on us."

Spiller turned his horse back toward the house and booted it forward as Sonny Bell stepped out the door, shotgun in hand. Rochenbach and Casings followed, booting their horses up, flanking him.

Sonny Bell took a stand between the coming riders and the shack, gripping the shotgun with both hands.

"That's close enough," he called out, cocking the single-barreled shotgun. "My pa's dead. He said we had time to clear out of here. Grolin can have this place soon as my woman and I—"

"*Close enough?*" Spiller said, cutting him off. He pushed his horse closer, then stopped with a cruel, bemused smile. The other two stopped beside him. "I'll tell you what's *close enough,*" he said, his Colt coming up fast, firing on the upswing. "Point a scattergun at me!"

The bullet grazed Sonny Bell's upper arm and twisted him sideways. The shotgun flew from his hands and hit the ground. Rochenbach saw the shotgun hammer drop as the gun hit the ground. But no shot exploded from the barrel.

Empty . . . ?

"Hold up, Spiller!" Rock said, seeing the gunman ready to fire again, this time taking close aim.

Spiller stared at Rochenbach as Rock nudged his horse forward, dropped from his saddle, picked up the shotgun and checked it. *Yep, empty,* he told himself, looking up at the young man.

"That's either awfully brave or awfully foolish," he said between the two of them.

"What the hell choice did I have, mister?" the young man said through clenched teeth, gripping his bleeding arm. "My pa said I'd have time to get us out of here before you men came back."

"How long has that been?" Rock asked.

But the young man didn't answer.

Mira Bell, who had seen her husband get shot, threw open the door and rushed outside screaming, her hands supporting her large, round belly.

"Get back in that house, Mira!" the young man shouted at her, but she ignored him.

"This is starting to look like fun," Spiller said to Casings. "Come on, Pres, let's get acquainted with this little filly."

"Jesus! Are you crazy, Dent?" said Casings. "She looks ready to foal any minute."

"I don't have time for this," Rochenbach said under his breath, watching Spiller and Casings swing down from their saddles. He asked Sonny Bell, "How much money can you give them, get them out of here?"

"I don't have a penny, mister," said young Bell. "We're sharing dead cow with buzzards. That's the God's honest truth."

With his back to the other two, Rochenbach fished a fold of dollars from inside his coat. Sonny's eyes widened as he watched Rochenbach riffle through the money.

"Mister, my wife is not for sale," Sonny said to Rock.

"Take this," Rock said, stuffing eighty dollars down into one of the young man's shirt pockets. He shoved thirty dollars more down into his other pocket.

Sonny reached for his shirt pocket with his bloody hand. "Mister, I told you, my wife ain't for—"

His words were cut short as Rock's fist nailed his jaw and sent him sprawling on the ground.

The young woman screamed and tried to run to her husband's side, but Spiller caught her by her arm.

"Hey, little filly, you ain't going nowhere," Spiller said, "unless it's back inside that shack with me."

Rochenbach stooped down over an unconscious Sonny, jerked the money back out of his shirt pocket in a way that allowed the two gunmen to see it.

"Here we go," he called out, standing, holding the money toward Spiller and Casings. "Eighty dollars. Turn her loose, Spiller."

The two gunmen looked surprised at the money; so did Mira Bell.

But Spiller kept a firm grip on the young woman's thin arm.

"Too late," he said. "This will teach them not to hold out on us next time we come to collect."

Rochenbach calmly stooped down and shoved thirty dollars of the money back into Sonny's shirt pocket. Sonny shook his head, trying to regain consciousness.

"Take the rest, and you and your woman clear out of here before they come back," he whispered under his breath. "Do you hear me?"

"Ye-yes, but—" Sonny stammered.

"Shut up," Rochenbach said in a firm tone. "Next time you pull that shotgun, have it loaded."

"My—my wife," Sonny said, trying to struggle up onto his feet.

Rochenbach didn't answer. Instead he walked over to where Spiller held the sobbing woman by her arm.

"Turn her loose, Spiller," Rock said again. He held the money up. "We came here for money. We got it."

"Huh-uh," said Spiller, "I'm taking a little taste for my trouble. Don't even think about trying to stop me."

Rochenbach looked away and let out a breath as if in submission. But then he turned back in a flash; his stiff new boot came up hard and fast and buried itself in Spiller's crotch. The gunman jackknifed at the waist with a terrible sound and seemed to freeze there, both hands grasping himself.

Rochenbach's Remington streaked out of his belly holster and made a hard swipe across the side of Spiller's forehead. Spiller's hat flew away.

"My God, Rock, you've ruined him!" said Casings as Spiller fell to his side on the cold, hard ground.

The woman stood staring wide-eyed, her mouth agape.

"Go to your husband," Rochenbach said to her, making her snap back to her senses. "Both of you get inside."

Turning the Remington toward Casings, Rock asked him, "Anything you need to add?"

"Huh-uh, not a thing," said Casings, instinctively taking a step back, fighting the urge to cup his hands and protect his crotch.

On the ground, Spiller let out a strained, pain-filled groan. Blood poured from a long welt running down the side of head, along his jawline.

"Throw some water on him. Let's get him in his saddle and get out of here," Rock said calmly. "We've interrupted these folks' supper long enough."

Chapter 4

——————

Two pairs of gleaming red eyes flashed in the darkness above the three riders as they rounded a sunken boulder on the trail back toward Denver City. In the pale light of a rising half-moon, Rochenbach and Casings rode along, Spiller slumped and silent in his saddle a few feet ahead of them. As the brush of padded paws swept down the side of the boulder and sprinted away into the greater darkness, Casings took his hand off his rifle stock and dropped it to his side.

"Coyotes . . . ," he said sidelong to Rochenbach.

Rochenbach didn't answer. The horses plodded on at a walk.

A few yards farther along, Casings said quietly to Rochenbach, "We had no idea Edmund Bell was dead. Our job was to collect something from him, that's all."

Rochenbach didn't answer, knowing that the less he spoke, the more Casings felt he had to.

"I mean, I wasn't going to do anything to that girl,"

he said. He nodded at Spiller riding ahead of them. "That was all his idea."

"You didn't try to stop him," Rochenbach said quietly.

Casings stared at him.

"No, I didn't," he said. "Why did you?"

"Because I was told we came here to collect money. So that's what I did," said Rock. "Sure, I had to rough the fellow up a little, but just enough to get the job done. What Spiller was about to do to the woman was stupid."

"Yeah, I have to admit, you got what we came for," said Casings, looking him up and down. "I call getting money from that ragged-ass kid nothing short of a miracle."

Rock cut him a sidelong glance.

"What are you saying, Casings?" Rock asked.

Casings shrugged and said, "Nothing, just that it was a miracle."

"A *miracle*?" said Rock. "So you're expressing a religious view?"

"No," Casings said, sounding embarrassed. "I'm just saying it's not likely that Sonny Bell or his pa, either one, would have any money. That's all."

"Then why did we waste our time riding out here?" Rock asked, sounding irritated. "Is this some kind of kid's game?"

"Whoa," said Casings. "I'm just saying we've had a hard time shaking any money out of Edmund Bell."

"Really?" Rochenbach stopped his horse and stared at Casings. "You're the one who said 'Put a scare into these beefers and miners, they come up with some money.' I put a scare into him and he *came up* with some money." He turned his horse back to the trail, seeing Spiller get farther ahead of them. "Maybe you two haven't been trying hard enough."

Casings stayed beside him.

"We tried hard," he said, "damned hard. Spiller has been at this business his whole life."

"I'm no shylock," Rock said, "but it didn't seem too hard to me—a smack in the mouth. I reached in his pocket and there it was."

Casings let go of a breath and considered the matter. Ahead of them Spiller swayed in his saddle. His left arm, which had been holding a wadded bandanna against his bloody forehead, fell limp to his side.

"Uh-oh, there he goes," said Casings, seeing the half-conscious gunman topple over out of his saddle and land in the cold, rocky dirt.

Rochenbach rode up slowly, grabbed the loose reins to Spiller's horse and drew it to his side. He watched Casings help Spiller onto his knees and steady him.

"Here's your horse, *Dent*," Rock said quietly, pitching the reins down to the bloody, addled gunman. "Try to stay on it."

"You've broken something . . . inside my head," Spiller gasped, struggling to stand with Casings' help.

"Wonder what that could be," Rock said in a dry, calloused tone.

"We're going to have to stop for a while," Casings said to Rochenbach, "let him get his senses back." He looked around in the pale moonlit night. "To tell the truth, my horse could use a little rest. I could use some hot coffee myself."

Without a word, Rochenbach stepped down from his saddle and walked his horse off the trail into the scrub. He found a knee-high rock and sat down on it, holding his rifle across his lap.

Casings helped Spiller to his feet and walked him off the trail with his arm looped across his shoulders. He led both horses behind him. When he'd helped the wobbling outlaw seat himself in the dirt, he looked at the bloody, swollen side of his head.

"Man!" he remarked to Rochenbach. "I've never seen a man struck this hard by a pistol barrel before."

Rochenbach looked out across the purple night and relaxed.

"How's that coffee coming?" he asked.

Casings stopped looking at Spiller's injured head and turned to Rochenbach.

"Who the hell put you in charge?" he asked. "I'm not the damned cook."

Rochenbach shrugged and said, "No offense. You said you wanted to rest your horse and have a hot cup of coffee. I figured you wanted to talk some more about how you're going to explain all this to Grolin."

"Talk *some more*?" Casings said. "I didn't say anything about explaining all this to Grolin."

"No, but you were leading up to it when your pal here fell from his saddle," said Rock. "I thought you might want to pursue the matter further before we get back to the Lucky Nut."

Spiller and Casings stared at each other.

After a tense pause, Casings turned to his horse,

flipped open his saddlebags, took out a small cloth bag of coffee beans and walked toward Rochenbach.

"You don't know what it's like sometimes, working for Andy Grolin," he said.

Looking past Casings, Rochenbach saw Spiller wobble to his feet and begin searching the ground for firewood.

Rock smiled to himself. "Oh?" he said. "Then maybe you should tell me."

Over a cup of coffee, Rochenbach listened as Casings spoke in a guarded voice, despite the fact that they were still seven miles out of Grolin's hearing range.

"See, we knew Edmund Bell was in bad shape the last time we were there," he said. "We had no doubt he'd be dead by the time we went back."

"But you didn't tell Grolin," Rock interjected.

"No, we didn't tell him," said Casings. "I know we should have." He hung his head for a moment. "Looking back, I wish we had."

Rochenbach studied him closely.

"How much did you collect?" he asked flatly.

"*Huh?*" Casings looked surprised; so did Spiller, who had recovered some over a cup of strong coffee.

"The last time you were there. How much did you two collect?" said Rock. "Don't take me for a fool, Pres," he cautioned the gunman. "We can talk it out here, or back at the Lucky Nut with Grolin, whichever suits you."

Casings rubbed his face and shook his head.

"Jesus . . . ," he said. "All right, we collected close to forty dollars last time."

"But you told Grolin you didn't collect anything," Rock said.

Casings just stared at him.

"Damn it, Casings, don't tell him," Spiller ordered, firelight flickering in his eyes.

"He's already figured it out," Casings said. "No, we didn't tell Grolin," he said to Rochenbach. "We figured ol' Edmund would be dead in a week, the kid and his woman would be cleared out and nobody would ever know." He gave a shrug. "Hell, Grolin is going to get the place for what's left owed against it anyway."

"Damn it to hell, Pres," said Spiller. "Shut up!"

Ignoring Spiller, Rochenbach said to Casings, "But Grolin wanted you two to check me out, so he sent you out earlier than anybody expected."

"Yeah," said Casings, also ignoring Spiller. "If he hears we held out on him, we're dead, Rock."

"I can see how he might want to kill you both," Rock said. "Especially when he figures it's not the first time you shorted him."

"No, it is the first time," said Casings. "I swear it is."

Rock smiled and looked back and forth between the two gunmen.

"See," he said, "I don't believe you myself, and it's not even my money we're talking about. Imagine what Grolin will think if he ever gets wind of it."

"Who's going to tell him?" Spiller asked menacingly, setting his tin cup down beside him and turning toward Rock from where he sat in the dirt. His hand rested on the butt of his holstered pistol.

Rochenbach slid his Remington from his belly holster and pointed its barrel straight up, gleaming in the flickering firelight.

"You don't want to be making threats," he said, "sitting there with your head split—didn't even check your gun to see if I unloaded it while you were knocked out." He held a piercing gaze on Spiller.

Without looking away from Rock, Spiller swallowed a knot in his throat.

"Did he fool around with my gun, Pres?" he asked, his head still pounding like a drum.

"How the hell do I know, Dent?" Casings said. "The man's kicked your nuts into your windpipe and cracked your head open. Why don't you quit acting tough and listen to what he's got to say?"

Spiller stared at Rochenbach with the same question burning in his red, pain-filled eyes.

"Nobody knows but me, Spiller," Rochenbach said in a dead-serious tone. His thumb cocked the big Remington standing beside his face. "You've got two choices. Either take your hand away from your Colt or bring it up—show us how much faith you have in yourself."

A tense moment passed until Spiller growled a curse under his breath and his hand slipped away from the Colt, eased back to the tin coffee cup and picked it up.

Rochenbach lowered the hammer on the big Remington and brought the gun down across his lap.

"Now back to who's going to tell Grolin," he said. "That would be me telling him, because I came out and collected the money. For all I know, Grolin could have told you to convince me you've been pocketing money, just to see whether or not he can trust me."

"It's not, Rock. I swear to God, it's not!" Pres Casings said. "We've had this little thing going on for a while, nothing big, just drinking money now and then."

"Damn it, Pres," said Spiller, "you're emptying your guts to him! He's got no reason to trust us. We've got even less reason to trust him."

"One of us has to bend a little," said Casings. He looked back at Rochenbach. So did Spiller.

Rochenbach sipped his coffee, considering it.

"All right," he said. "It looks like I'm the one who has to stick my neck out. The only way you two can trust me is to make me an accomplice." He patted the eighty dollars folded inside the lapel pocket of his wool coat. "If I don't turn this money in, and we all three tell Grolin that Edmund Bell is dead and his place was empty, I'm in with you up to my neck." He looked back and forth again. "If you're lying, we're all three dead."

They looked at each other, then back at Rochenbach.

"Because I'll kill you both while Grolin puts a bullet in my head," Rochenbach said.

"We're *not* lying, Rock," Pres Casings repeated, both outlaws looking relieved. "And you're in on our scheme from now on. Whatever we get, you get a third. Three-way partners. Right, Dent?" he said sidelong to Spiller.

But Spiller didn't reply. He continued to stare coldly at Rochenbach.

Rock still looked leery of them as he held his tin coffee cup in his gloved hand, ready to take another sip as if doing so would seal a pact among them. This was what he needed, a toehold into Grolin's operation.

"That's you talking," Rock said to Casings. "I haven't heard anything from your sporting friend here."

"What did you call me?" Spiller said in a dark tone.

Rochenbach just stared at him and finished his coffee.

"Dent, damn it, come on," said Casings. "I'm trying to work this thing out! Give me some help here."

Spiller simmered and settled, his head pounding, his crotch aching. He hadn't forgotten that Rochenbach was the source of his misery. But he let out a breath.

"Okay! From now on we're all three partners in our collecting scheme," he said.

"All right, then, we're all three agreed," Casings said. He also let out a breath and turned to Rochenbach. "Now that all that's settled, let's split the eighty dollars and get on back to town."

"I don't think so," Rochenbach said, standing up, the Remington still hanging in one hand. He slung the grounds from his coffee cup and rubbed out the fire with the side of his new boot.

"What do you mean?" Casings said in surprise. "I thought we just agreed we're partners."

"We did *just agree*," Rochenbach said. "But we hadn't agreed to it when I collected the money." Firelight flickered in his eyes. "Anyway, I'm the new man here. I've got some catching up to do."

Chapter 5

It was long after midnight when the three rode onto the street leading to the Great Westerner Hotel and the Lucky Nut Saloon. Spiller rode slumped in his saddle a few feet in front of Casings and Rochenbach. He looked up in time to see the weathered, one-horse buggy sitting out in front of the hotel; the edge of its usually tall canvas top was lined with dangling fringe-work. The sight of the buggy caused him to jerk his horse to a halt and turn toward Casings behind him.

"Look who's here, Pres," he said in a low voice.

"Yeah, I see it," Casings said, slowing his horse.

Rochenback looked at the buggy and slowed his big dun right along with Casings.

"Are you going to make me ask, *partner*?" he said to Casings.

"It's the Stillwater Giant," Casings whispered side-long.

"Garth Oliver . . . ," Rock said quietly, looking the buggy over good.

Casings looked at him, surprised.

"You know the Giant?" he said.

"Only by reputation," said Rochenbach. "I've seen his picture in Pinkerton's rogues gallery."

Casings gave him a curious, troubled look.

"You studied the rogues gallery a good deal, did you?" he asked.

"*Studied it?*" Rock said. "I helped construct most of it." He gave him a thin smile and nudged his dun forward toward an alley path leading to the livery barn.

"Jesus . . . ," said Casings, he and Spiller nudging their horses alongside him. "See, that's something I find unsettling about you, Rock. You spent lots of time working on ways to put ol' boys like the Giant . . . and Spiller and me behind bars."

"Luckily, I saw the error of my ways and became one of you," Rochenbach said wryly.

"Yeah, luckily," Casings said. As they reached the livery barn, he said, "What are you going to tell Grolin when he asks you what happened out there?"

"I'll tell him the truth," Rochenbach said, "that the house was standing empty and Edmund Bell is dead and in the ground."

Casings nodded and looked at Spiller, who'd been riding on in silence since they spotted the Giant's buggy.

"You got that, Dent?" Casings asked.

"Yeah, I've got it," Spiller said. "Don't worry about me. I'm not saying nothing that's going to get Grolin or the Stillwater Giant on me."

"Right," said Casings. Testing him, he asked, "And what happened to the side of your head?"

"I rode into a damned low-hanging tree limb along the trail," Spiller said grudgingly.

Casings chuckled to himself as the three of them brought their horses to a halt and stepped down from their saddles in front of the livery barn.

"Yep, that's what you did," Casings said, stifling a laugh, "and it seemed like it was no more than a minute after I'd cautioned you against doing that very thing."

"Don't mess with me, Pres," Spiller warned him. "I ain't in the mood for it."

They walked their horses inside the barn, lit a lantern and tended to the animals in the dim circle of light. Dropping their saddles onto saddle racks and hanging the bridles on wall pegs, they grained and watered the horses.

While the animals ate, the men wiped the lathered horses down, each with a handful of fresh straw. Once the animals were finished with their feed, the men led them into clean stalls for the night.

"All right," Rochenbach said, "it's time we take our story to Grolin, see how well we can sell it to him."

They walked back through the darkened alleyway, saddlebags over their shoulders, rifles in hand, down the street to the Lucky Nut. As they stepped inside the saloon doors, Grolin stood up from a corner table, lit dimly by a small oil lamp.

A squat, bald bartender stood behind the bar. Opposite him stood a miner who'd been drinking steadily since before dark. The rest of the dim saloon was empty, save for a large, hulking figure seated across the table from Andrew Grolin.

"Well, well," Grolin said, a cigar curling smoke from between his thick fingers. "Speak of the devil and who shall arrive?"

Rochenbach and the other two gunmen walked toward the table. But Grolin held a hand up toward Casings and Spiller, stopping them.

"You two take the night off," he said. "I'll let Rock here tell me how things went."

Casings and Spiller looked at each other. Neither of them liked the idea of Rochenbach speaking for them in their absence, but they both knew better than to say anything about it.

Grolin stood watching as the two turned and walked back out the door.

Once out on the empty street, Spiller glanced back over his shoulder to make certain they weren't being followed.

"Damn!" he said under his breath to Casings. "I never counted on that."

"Nor did I," Casings said, walking along rigidly, staring straight ahead. "But we'd have to trust him sometime. At least we'll find out tonight if he keeps his mouth shut or not." He paused, then added, "I say he will."

"If he don't, we're dead," Spiller said.

"Yep," Casings agreed, "deader than I ever want to be."

"Maybe I should get around to the window and put a bullet in his back before he gets started talking," Spiller said.

Casings looked sidelong at him and shook his head slowly.

"You got any better ideas?" Spiller asked, recognizing the way Casings looked at him.

"Don't talk crazy, Dent," Casings said.

They walked a block past the Great Westerner to a run-down house standing back from the street in a yard choked with dried weeds, wild grass and scrub. "All we can do for now is wait it out, see what the morning brings."

"Still," said Spiller, "I'm sleeping with my rifle tonight."

Casings gave him a tight, thin smile.

"Your private life is your own business," he said quietly.

Spiller cursed under his breath as he pulled the broken picket gate open and walked into the overgrown yard.

"I don't know how you can make jokes at a time like this," he said, walking along a weed-lined path, up onto a rickety front porch. "If this damned *ex-*Pinkerton law dog opens his mouth about how we've been collecting money, Grolin will have us skinned and—"

"Yeah, yeah, we've been through all that," Casings said, cutting him off. "Don't soil yourself." He walked along a step behind him, through the unlocked front door and into the dark, sparsely furnished house.

"What did you say to me?" Spiller growled. He watched Casings walk over to a table and pick up an oil lamp to light it.

"Forget it," said Casings. "You've just been getting on my nerves all day and night."

"Soil myself, you said?" Spiller persisted, his hand on the butt of his gun. "You've been making remarks all day. I won't tolerate sass from no—"

"*Shhh*," said Casings, cutting him off again.

Spiller saw Casings' face turn orange-blue and shadowy in the flare of a match as he lit the lamp. Their eyes cut searchingly away from the circle of lamplight as Casings trimmed down the lamp's wick and quickly set the lamp back on the table. They both heard the slight creaking sound of a floor plank in a dark, adjoining room.

Casings stepped away from the lamp table, his Colt streaking up from his holster, cocked and aimed blindly into the darkness.

"Whoever's there, *announce* yourself!" Casings said, ready to pull the trigger.

From the other room, a quiet voice resounded low and evenly through the darkness.

"What if I'm just a cat?" the voice said.

"Then you better start purring, you sumbitch!" Spiller called out, raising his Colt and taking aim in the direction of the voice.

Casings raised a hand toward Spiller. "Hold up, Dent," he said, letting out a tense breath. "It's Turley." He called out to the darkness, "Turley, don't be acting a fool with us. We're not up for it."

"You boys sound overwrought," said the voice with a chuckle. A gunman stepped out of the adjoining room into the circle of lamplight. "Tell ol' Turley all about it."

"Batts, you idiot," Spiller growled under his breath, letting the hammer down on his Colt and slipping the gun back into his holster.

"When did you get here?" Casings asked the gunman.

"I rode in with the Bonham and the Stillwater Giant about an hour ago," Turley Batts replied. He looked at Spiller's swollen forehead. "The hell happened to you?"

"Low-hanging limb . . . ," Spiller said in shame.

Batts laughed, making no attempt to hide his amusement from Spiller.

"What did you hear us saying when we walked in here?" asked Casings.

"Nothing worth saying again," Batts said, cutting his laughing short. "But I heard Low-Hanging Limb here mention *collecting money* when you came through the door."

"That figures," Casings said, glaring at Spiller.

"I hope nothing has happened to spoil our little sideline?" Batts said. "I can use some quick pocket money until Grolin gets this *big job* of his set up." He grinned and looked back and forth between the two gunmen. "We're still three-way partners on everything, right?"

"Jesus . . . ," said Casings, shaking his head. "Something's come up, Turley," he added. "We need to talk about our three-way-partners deal."

"Start talking, then," said Batts, looking at Spiller's swollen forehead again. "I'm nothing but *attentive*."

Inside the Lucky Nut, Andrew Grolin stood beside Rochenbach and gestured his cigar hand across the table toward a man who'd been hidden in the shadows of the dark saloon.

"Rock," Grolin said, "I want you to meet a *friend* and associate of mine. This is Mr. Garth Oliver." To the big man he said, "This is Mr. Rochenbach—*Rock* to his friends."

The Stillwater Giant . . . , Rochenbach said to himself. He touched his fingertips to his hat brim. "Mr. Oliver," he said aloud.

"Pardon me if I don't get up," said the Stillwater Giant, his voice deep and gruff. "It makes most folks nervous when I stand all the way up."

"I'm not the nervous type," said Rock, "but suit yourself."

"Word has it you worked for Pinkerton's boys," said the Stillwater Giant.

"Yes, I did," said Rochenbach, aware of Grolin watching, appraising his every word, every move.

The large figure leaned forward into the flicker of lamplight, staring straight at Rochenbach from across the table without having to lift his eyes.

"Good thing you're not tonight," he said with a cruel grin. "I'd be wearing you on my shoe soles."

"Maybe," said Rock, "or maybe you'd be leaving town over the back of a mule."

"Oh . . . ?" The Giant's gaze hardened, but turned curious.

Rochenbach studied his face, the broad, hooded

brow, the wide, thick chin, jawbones the size and shape of apples.

"There's five hundred dollars on your head in Texas," he said.

Recollection came to the Giant's face.

"I'd damned near forgot about that," he said. "How come you to know it?"

"Old habit," said Rochenbach. "I can't walk past a post office without looking at wanted posters, thinking how easy it would be."

"Easy . . . ?" said the Giant. He scooted his chair back and rose to his feet. Rochenbach looked up at him, judging him to be seven feet tall.

Grolin stepped in and said, "Unless you know how to open a Diebold safe, you best mind your manners here."

Mind his manners . . . Rochenbach kept himself from smiling. Until he swung the door of the Treasury car door open for Grolin, his safety here was guaranteed.

"In fact, go get yourself some rest," Grolin said to the Giant. "I want to talk to Rock here alone."

"Whatever you say, Andrew," said the Giant. He glowered down at Rochenbach. But he leveled his derby hat, turned and walked across the floor and out into the night air.

"Have a chair, Rock," Grolin said.

The two sat down across the table from each other. No sooner had they been seated than the bartender appeared at Rochenbach's elbow. He set a clean shot glass in front of him and filled it from a bottle of rye standing on the table.

"How'd the collection go?" Grolin asked as the bartender walked away.

"It *didn't*," Rock said, raising the shot glass and drinking half of it. "Edmund Bell is dead—so says his grave marker. The place has been standing empty awhile."

"Empty, huh?" said Grolin, studying his eyes closely. "What took you three so long?"

"We stopped for coffee," said Rochenbach.

Grolin considered the matter, then shrugged and said, "Well, it wasn't time wasted. I'll present my marker against the place to my attorney, have him take possession." He grinned.

Rochenbach finished his rye and slid his glass away. He saw no sign that Grolin had only been testing him. *Good enough,* he told himself. Now he needed to get away from Grolin and take care of an important piece of business before the night was over.

"Did Casings or Spiller talk about collecting my gambling debts on the way there?" Grolin asked.

"No," said Rock, "should they have?"

"Just curious," said Grolin. He leaned in a little and lowered his voice. "I think they cut a little off the top for themselves when they can get by with it."

"That's business between you and them," said Rochenbach. "When somebody else handles your money, it often sticks to their hands." He shrugged. "But you already know that."

"Yes, I do," said Grolin. "I was hoping if you saw anything out of the ordinary, you'd tell me," said Grolin.

"I've told you all I can tell you," said Rock.

Grolin studied his face for a moment, then said, "All right. Get some rest. I'm sending you out on a practice run tomorrow—see if you know the Diebold Bahmann safe as well as you say you do."

"You do realize I don't open safes for exercise and self-fulfillment," said Rock.

"You get a cut of everything you put your hand to for me," Grolin said.

"In that case, I bid you good night," Rock said, turning, walking out the door.

But instead of going into the hotel, he ducked into a darkened alleyway and hurried along in a crouch until he reached the rear door of the telegraph office. He produced a ring of lock-picking tools from inside his coat. Looking back and forth quickly in the darkness, he bowed over the door lock like some dark creature of night attending its prey.

Time to report in, he told himself as the lock clicked and the door opened an inch. He glanced both ways again, then opened the door far enough to slip inside as silent as a ghost.

Chapter 6

It the gray darkness of morning, Denton Spiller, Pres Casings, Turley Batts and the Stillwater Giant walked abreast along the empty street, making their way to the livery barn. As they arrived and started to go inside, a fifth man, an outlaw named Lonnie Bonham, came trotting along behind them on foot.

"Wait up!" Bonham called out, causing the four to stop at the barn door and look back at him. He trotted forward and stopped, his rifle hanging in his hand.

"Well . . . ?" said Spiller, looking the younger outlaw up and down.

"He's not there," said Bonham.

"You went on up to his room?" asked Turley Batts.

Bonham gave him a searing look.

"He's *not there*," he repeated. "I checked inside Turk's Restaurant on my way here. He's not there either."

"Now what?" said Spiller, looking all around. "I don't like being nursemaid to this bastard."

"Maybe he went to the Nut first thing," said the

Giant. His voice sounded like the rumble of low cannon fire deep inside a large cave.

"Maybe he fled away in the dark of night," said Batts. He grinned and said to the Giant, "You said him and you had some words . . . ?"

Giant gave him a wide, big-toothed grin.

"Yeah. It wouldn't be the first time I scared somebody off by just staring down at them," he said.

"He strikes me as a runner, this law dog," said Bonham.

The four looked at him curiously. Batts spit and shook his head.

Bonham shrugged slightly. "I mean . . . I've never met him," he said, "but from what I've heard yas say—"

His words shopped short as the barn door swung open, barely missing Spiller's shoulder on its way. In the open doorway, Rochenbach stood with his horse standing saddled and ready beside him, it reins in his gloved hand. He led his horse forward through the open door.

"Jesus!" said Spiller, surprised, his hand almost going to his holstered Colt.

"We were just talking about you, Rock," Casings said, also caught by surprise.

"Yeah, I heard," Rochenbach said flatly. He looked at the Giant. Then he looked Turley Batts and Lonnie Bonham up and down.

"We—we never met last night, Rochenbach," Bonham offered clumsily. "I rode in with Stillwater. I'm Lonnie Bonham. Most folks call me Lon. This is Turley Batts."

Rochenbach nodded at the two and touched his fingertips to the brim of his new slouch hat.

"Ready to ride, *Lon*?" he said quietly, walking past the five, stopping, turning to his horse.

"Hell no, he's not ready to ride!" Spiller cut in, sounding irritated. "None of us are. You can see we just now got here."

Rochenbach just looked at him. He swung up into his saddle and turned his horse toward the main street.

"Why don't I ride on ahead, make sure there's no low-hanging limbs?" he said.

Casings and Batts stifled a laugh; Spiller fumed, the side of his forehead still raw and swollen.

"Hey. You don't even know where we're headed, fellow," the Giant called out to Rochenbach in his big, booming voice.

"Central City," Rochenbach called back without turning in his saddle.

The Giant gave the others a bewildered look. They returned it.

"How'd you know that?" the Giant called out.

"I didn't," Rochenbach said, his horse moving on at a walk.

"This son of a bitch," the Stillwater Giant growled under his breath. "I wish Grolin would let me bounce his head around a little."

"Damn it to hell," said Spiller, "Grolin said not to let him out of our sight. Hold up, Rock! Give us a few minutes!" he shouted.

But Rock's horse turned the corner out of the alley and onto the main street.

"Damn it!" Spiller said, hurrying into the barn with the other four. "How are we supposed to deal with this man? It's like trying to corral a hardheaded tomcat!"

"Come on, Dent, hurry up," Casings said. "We let him get too far out of sight, Grolin will have our hides on a pole."

Spiller sidled in closer to Casings and whispered between them, "What's wrong with him? I thought we're partners, the three of us."

"I don't know," said Casings. "I'll talk to him first chance I get."

They quickly bridled and saddled their horses and led them out of the barn.

"Hell, he's halfway to Central City by now!" said Spiller. As he swung up into his saddle, he said to the Stillwater Giant, "Why the hell did you tell him where we're headed?"

"I didn't tell him!" said the Giant, but he didn't sound completely sure of himself. Turning to Casings, he asked, "Did I, Pres?"

In his saddle, Casings gathered his reins and tightened his hat down onto his forehead.

"Yes, you did," he said. "But it wasn't your fault. Not exactly anyway."

"He played you, Giant! Didn't you see it?" Spiller said harshly, jerking his horse around toward the main street. "Let's go, before we lose him altogether and have Grolin down our shirts!"

They booted their horses forward at a fast gallop along the alleyway and onto the street. A pedestrian had to leap out of their way as the five rounded the corner and raced away along the street out of town. A watchdog appeared out from under a boardwalk in front of a mercantile store, barking and jumping back and forth on the end of a chain as they galloped past.

At the corner of the next alleyway, Rochenbach sat just out of sight, his wrists crossed on his saddle horn. When the five had passed in a thunder of hooves, he tapped his dun forward and fell in twenty yards behind them at an easy gallop.

"Where the hell is he?" Spiller shouted at Casings, the two of them riding hard in front of the Giant.

Beside the Stillwater Giant rode Turley Batts, followed by Lonnie Bonham.

Bonham rode along as hard as the others. But when the younger outlaw happened to look back over his shoulder for no particular reason at all, he saw Rochenbach following them leisurely.

"Jesus! He's riding behind us!" he said, already reining his horse down as he shouted to the others.

The other four slid their horses to a halt and spun them in the middle of the street.

As he stared at Rochenbach, Spiller's hand went instinctively to his gun before he caught himself and turned it loose.

"Damn it, Pres," he growled to Casings, who sat his horse beside him. "See what I mean, this son of a bitch?"

Casings shook his head and kept himself from chuckling aloud.

"Come on, Dent. Can't you see he's just doing all this to get to you?" he said as Rochenbach rode closer and reined his dun down into an easy, sidelong gait.

"I'm just about there, Pres," Spiller said, barely under control. "I'm just about there. . . ."

Rochenbach stopped in the street ahead of them and looked back.

"Are we going or what?" he said quietly.

The Giant booted his horse forward.

"I'm about there with you, Dent," he said sidelong to Spiller.

Watching the men ride toward him, Rochenbach turned his horse back to the trail ahead. He knew he had them stirred up like a hornet's nest. That had been his intent. But now it was time to let them cool out a little, get himself on Casings' and Spiller's good side. That shouldn't be hard to do since he'd kept his mouth shout about them to Grolin.

It was nearing noon when the six riders moved off the trail and rested their horses in a dry wash under a tangle of brush and rock. The Stillwater Giant stepped down from his tired horse's back and turned to a shoulder-high cluster of rocks that stuck into the side of the wash.

"Look at this!" Batts said in amazement as the Giant yanked a small boulder out of the cluster, turned around with it against his wide chest and dropped it on the ground. It landed with a powerful thud.

"*Daaa-mn . . . !*" said Bonham, he and the others watching the Giant sit down on the rock and dust his big hands together.

The Giant grinned and flexed his powerful arms inside the sleeves of his coat.

"Anybody else need a rock to sit on?" he offered. As he asked, his eyes went to Rochenbach and stayed there. "If you do, I can pick one up and throw it on the ground for you easy enough."

Rochenbach ignored him. He had stepped down from his saddle a few feet away from the others, rifle in hand, and poured a small amount of water from his canteen into the crown of his slouch hat. He stooped onto his haunches and held the upturned hat to the dun's muzzle.

The horse drew the water in one breath and stood licking the inside of the hat when Casings walked up and kneeled down beside Rochenbach.

"Pay no mind to the Giant," he said quietly. "He's used to people naturally kowtowing to him because of his size."

"Size . . . ? I didn't notice," Rock said.

"Right." Casings grinned. "Fine dun you've got here, Rock," he said. He reached out and patted the dun's neck.

"Yep," Rochenbach said. He turned slightly toward him, knowing the outlaw hadn't walked over to talk about his horse or the Giant. He stared at him expectantly.

"Okay," said Casings, "the thing is, Spiller is asking me what's got into you since our talk on the trail back from Bell's place." He paused. "I told him it was because you overheard the group talking about you while you were in the barn."

Rock didn't answer. Instead, he shook his slouch hat off, placed it atop his head and stood up, his rifle in the crook of his arm.

"That *was* it, wasn't it?" said Casings, standing up beside him.

Before Rochenbach could answer, the Giant called out from where he sat watching the two.

"Hey, *Rock*, you need a *rock*. I can get you a *rock*, if you want a *rock*, Rock," he said, goading.

Rochenbach stood staring back at the Giant as he said sidelong to Casings, "Is something wrong with his mind?" As he spoke, he stared past the Giant at the big hole in the wall of the wash where the boulder had been.

Casings chuckled and replied, "No, he just don't always know what's going on around him. It makes him act peculiar."

Rochenbach's eyes narrowed, looking past the Giant and to the side of the wash. "Then he'd better start paying attention," he said.

The Giant stood up and called out to Rock in a surly tone, "Don't talk about me over there, law dog. I will jerk you up by the top of your head and stick my arm down your—"

His words stopped short; his eyes widened in terror as Rochenbach threw his rifle up to his shoulder, pointed straight at him.

"Wait, Rock!" Casings shouted.

But Rock paid him no attention as he took aim and squeezed the trigger. The other men scattered in every direction.

The Giant's mouth opened wide in fear as he saw the shot explode from Rock's Spencer rifle. He heard and felt the bullet whistle past his head. Behind him, crawling down the fresh-turned earth where the

Giant had unseated the boulder, a large bull rattler had raised its head, ready to make a strike at the back of the Giant's neck.

"Holy *God*!" shouted Casings, seeing Rochenbach's bullet snap the big rattler's head off in a bloody mist.

The snake's thick body flew up from the side of the wash, spun whipping in the air and landed limply over the Giant's right shoulder just as the Giant had started to draw his holstered Colt.

Seeing the snake suddenly dangling down his chest, the Giant screamed shrilly in spite of his usually deep, powerful voice. Instead of snatching the dead snake and tossing it away, the Giant lost all control of himself and jumped up and down on his tiptoes, screaming, his big hands flopping uselessly beside him.

"Jesus, *run, Giant*!" shouted Casings, seeing three more snakes spill down from their disturbed resting place among the cluster of rocks.

In his hysteria, the Giant caught a glimpse of one of the snakes slithering past his feet. He ran screaming in a wide circle, the dead snake flying from his shoulder as he plowed through the already spooked horses. The bloody bull rattler landed atop one horse, sending it into a wild kicking, whinnying fit.

"We need to stop him," Rock said quietly, watching in rapt fascination.

"Not me," said Casings, knowing what a job it would be wrestling the big man to the ground and holding him there.

The Giant, still screaming out of control, ran smack into another horse. His massive body knocked the animal to the ground as he bounced back from it, right into the kicking hooves of the horse with the dead snake flopping up and down in its saddle. A wild kick gave the Giant a glancing blow to his head and sent him staggering in a zigzagging line for a few feet while his thick legs seemed to slowly melt beneath him.

"Well, there's that," said Casings as the Giant slammed the ground with the same powerful thud as the boulder he'd thrown down in a show of strength.

Shots rang out as the other men hurried and killed the other awakened rattlers.

"Yes," said Rochenbach, "there's that."

He stepped forward and looked down at the Giant lying knocked cold in the dirt.

"He had to show off for everybody, lift that big rock," said Casings, stepping up beside him.

Rochenbach only nodded, wondering if this would soften the Giant's attitude toward him.

Chapter 7

A half hour later, the Giant sat on the same rock, this time facing a fire Bonham and Batts built so he could dry the crotch on his wet trousers. He sat in his long-john underwear and stockinged feet, his knees opened wide toward the fire, shivering even with a wool blanket clutched around him. His trousers hung on a stick stuck in the ground, and his enormous boots stood drying on the ground beside his trousers.

"God, I hate sna-snakes," he said, his deep, powerful voice broken and trembling. "Ever since I was a ki-kid," he added painfully. Blood ran down the side of his head.

"Lots of people hate snakes, Giant," said Casings, trying to help him calm down. "It's nothing to be ashamed of."

The Giant tried to settle down and breathe deep.

"Pres is right, Stillwater," said Bonham. "Jesus, a big ol' rattler like that. One bite and he would have filled you so full of poison—"

"Why don't you pour yourself a hot cup of coffee, Lon?" Casings said to cut him off.

The Giant started shaking all over again.

"I was just saying," explained Bonham, "a big bull like that. What if he'd fallen down your shirt before Rock got a shot at him?"

"Jesus, shut up!" Casings snapped. "The man hates snakes! Can you give it a rest?"

"He—he's right," the Giant said, shaking again. "The law dog sa-saved my life." He looked all around the dry wash. "Where is he anyway?"

"I'm right here, Giant," said Rochenbach. He stepped over from among the settled horses, a wet cloth in his hand. "But my name's not law dog," he corrected the Giant. He pressed the wet cloth to the Giant's hoof-grazed head and directed the Giant's large hand against it.

"Of course it's not, Rock," the Giant said. "No offense. I just ain't myself right this minute. Hell, you saved my life. I'll call you Mr. Rochenbach if you want. Man, if you hadn't been there—" He lowered his big head as his voice cracked with emotion.

Rochenbach and Casings gave each other a bemused look.

"It's *all right*, Giant," Rock said. "You need to put it out of your mind. It's over."

The Giant looked at his drying trousers, then at Rochenbach and Casings.

"I'd just as soon Grolin not hear about any of this," he said, shaking his swollen head slowly, the wet cloth pressed against it.

"I've faced a wild bear, once wrestled a Louisiana

alligator, killed men of every size, shape and color,"
he said. "I fear nothing—not the devil in hell. But a
damn snake gets near me, I fall plumb apart. That's
all there is to it."

"All right, we understand," said Spiller, sounding
a little tired of hearing it. He stepped in and put a cup
of steaming coffee in the Giant's free hand. "You need
to buck up and get control of yourself. Like Rock here
said, *it's over.*"

The Stillwater Giant lifted his eyes around to Spiller
and gave him a hard stare.

"Obliged for the coffee, Dent," he said, his deep,
intimidating voice starting to return. "But don't start
crowding me over this. I've also taken a hell of a lick
to the head. You ought to know how that feels after
what happened to you." He nodded toward the welt
on Spiller's head.

"Forget it," Spiller said. He backed off, not wanting hear any more remarks about low-hanging tree
limbs.

Rochenbach walked over to his dun and led it back
with him, his Spencer rifle in hand.

"What do you say, big fellow?" he asked the Giant.
"You feel up to riding yet?"

"I can ride," the Giant said. Then his deep, powerful voice turned childlike. "But can I—can I ride
alongside you?" he asked hesitantly.

Casings and Rockenbach shot each other a curious
look.

"Sure," said Rochenbach, "you're welcome to ride
right beside me."

The men looked at each other guardedly as the

Stillwater Giant stood up and stepped around the fire in his long johns and put on his trousers. As he dressed, his eyes kept looking warily all around on the ground.

"I've never seen a man fall apart so fast in my life," Spiller whispered to Bonham and Batts.

"It's plumb wrenching to watch," Batts whispered in reply, turning sadly away and looking out across the rock land.

But Spiller and Bonham continued staring at the Giant as he walked over to his horse, Rochenbach leading his dun alongside him.

Jesus. . . . Casings looked the two gunmen up and down with disdain.

"Think we can get going now?" he said wryly. "Or do you two need to be walked to your horses?"

"Hell no!" Spiller said. He and Bonham bristled at Casings' words. They both appeared to snap out of their transfixed state. "Come on, Lon, let's get the hell out of here."

Back in their saddles, they rode on at a strong, steady pace for the rest of the day until they'd made their way upward from the east to the foothills town of Central City. There, the six horsemen left the trail and rode along an abandoned miner's path into a string of gulches until the rocky land swallowed them.

When they were out of sight on a hillside below the booming mining town, they made camp around a small fire. They ate jerked elk and beans from airtights they'd brought along in their saddlebags.

As they finished their dinner, the Stillwater Giant looked back and forth from one face to the next.

"I want all of you to know that what happened to me back there today, it *never happened*," he said in his deep, strong voice. The threat was there and clearly understood. Yet he continued, saying, "If I hear anybody saying anything about it, I'll yank his tongue from his mouth and make a coin purse out of it."

The men only nodded and continued eating, afraid to even reply.

"That aside," the Giant said, turning to Rochenbach with a milder tone and expression, "I am obliged to you for what you did, Rock. I'm ashamed that I was goading you . . . yet you jumped in and saved my life all the same."

Rochenbach gave no response apart from a short, silent nod.

The Giant looked around at the others and said, "From now on, anybody says anything bad about this man—I *still* need a good coin purse." A wide, big-toothed grin spread across his face, making him appear all the more menacing in the flicker of firelight.

The men nodded as they ate.

After they'd finished the meal and washed it down with strong, hot coffee, they sat in silence around the fire and waited until darkness set in purple and deep around them.

Rochenbach noted that a calm air of confidence seemed to come over the five men riding with him. Without being prompted to do so, they each sat checking pistols, rifles, ammunition and equipment. When they'd finished, they sat quietly until each of them appeared ready for the trail.

With a sigh, Casings stood up and slung coffee grounds from his empty tin cup.

"It's time to do it," he said quietly.

In a ragged tent saloon on the lower, eastern outskirts of Central City, a former ore wagon guard named Macon Ray Silverette relieved himself over the edge of the rocky trail as the six horsemen passed behind him a few feet away. Recognizing Spiller, Batts and Casings all three, he quickly ducked his head, buttoned his fly and hurried back inside the tent before the six were out of sight, headed deeper into town.

At a rickety table in a darkened corner, a hard case named Dirty Dave Atlo sat with his hand up the dress of a young woman perched on his lap. She stared into his eyes with a frozen grin, wiry red hair and lips painted redder than rabbit blood. Across the tent, a drunken accordion player drooled with his mouth agape as his hands squeezed out a mournful rendition of "Sweet Betsy from Pike." Candle, lamp and lantern flickered around him like a broad circle of footlights.

"Damn it!" Dirty Dave growled, seeing Macon Ray weave toward him through a maze of tables, chairs and standing drinkers.

"You're not going to believe who I just saw riding in from Denver City!" Macon Ray said in an excited voice, stopping less three feet away.

"Christ Almighty, Ray!" said Dirty Dave. He looked embarrassed. "Don't you see what's going on here?"

Hurriedly, Macon Ray shot a glance at the accordion player, then back to Dirty Dave.

"Yep, it's fine music no doubt," he said. "But I just saw some of Grolin's men ride past the tent . . . headed into town . . . ?" He left his words hanging as a suggestion.

"Whoa!" said Dirty Dave. "Now, that *is* some good news." His hand came down from beneath the woman's gingham dress. "Hop on up, sweetheart," he said. "I'll be back soon."

He stood, forcing her to stand too or else fall to the dirt floor. To Macon Ray he said, "How long ago?" He fished a gold coin from his vest pocket with damp fingers and flipped it toward the table. The woman caught it before it landed.

"I just saw them and ran right in here. I knew you'd want to hear about it," said Ray, hurrying along behind him as Dirty Dave headed for the wide-open tent front.

"Where's Albert and Fackler, betting the birds?" He looked toward a far rear corner where a small group of miners were gathered around two battle-scarred roosters locked in mortal combat beneath a flurry of batting wings.

"Joe is. Albert's just watching. Want me to get them?" Macon Ray asked.

"Hell yes, get them!" shouted Dirty Dave. "Get them, get your horses—all of you bring shotguns, catch up to me on the trail. Once I hone in on these boys, I'm not letting them out of my sight."

As Macon Ray hurried, weaving through the crowd, Dirty Dave looked down at a table and saw a man sitting, staring engrossed at the drunken accordion player, a tall mug of beer standing in front of him. Dave stuck half his hand down into the mug, swished it around, raised it and slung beer foam from his fingers; he walked out of the tent, drying his hand on his trousers.

This was good, he told himself. He'd been wanting to get even with Andrew Grolin—kill his men, Spiller, Casings, the Stillwater Giant—any of his gunmen, ever since they had cheated him out of his cut in a robbery over a year ago.

Time to reap a little vengeance, he told himself.

He untied his horse from a crowded hitch rail, stepped into his saddle and turned the animal toward the trail leading farther into town. He rode hard along the rutted, treacherous trail until he caught sight of the six riders as they rounded a sharp turn in the trail.

All right, that had to be them, he decided, slowing his horse to keep from getting too close, lest the sound of his horse's hooves give him away. He watched them move out of sight in front of him, and looked over his shoulder toward the sound of hooves as Macon Ray led Albert Kinney and Joe Fackler along the trail.

When the three riders saw him sitting his horse in the middle of the trail, they slowed to a halt and gathered around him.

"Any sight of them yet?" asked Macon Ray, his rifle held up loosely in his left hand. His horse bounced back and forth on restless hooves, causing the tip of his rifle barrel to swing within inches of Dirty Dave's face. Dave had to jerk his head back from it.

"Settle your horse! Get that damn rifle out of my

face!" he growled in a low voice. "Unless you're meaning to blow my head off!"

Macon Ray jerked the feisty animal and lowered
his rifle barrel.

"Yes, I just spotted them," Dave replied now that
the rifle barrel wasn't threatening him. "If I hadn't
been here to slow you down, you'd've smacked right
into them."

"All right, then!" said Albert Kinney, sounding
excited. "How do you want to do this, Dave? Ride in
shooting? Chop them down before they know what
hit them?"

Dave gave him a flat stare.

"No," he said, then added with sarcasm, "As wise
and clever as that plan might be, I fail to see how it
would make us any money."

"Oh . . . ," said Kinney. He settled down. "I figured, these men screwed you out of money, you'd
want to kill them right off."

"I want to kill them," said Dave. "But if I have a
choice of killing them for free or getting my money
out of them first, guess which one I'd rather do."

"While you're thinking that over," Macon Ray said
to Kinney, "try to keep your mouth shut long enough
to hear what we're going to do."

Kinney nodded and listened, realizing he'd
already said too much.

"Can I ask a question?" said Joe Fackler, sounding a little surly, having been dragged away from the
cockfighting event.

"Sure thing, Joe, come right on out with it," said
Dave.

"What makes you so sure they've got any money?" Joe asked. "I happened to be winning at that cockfight."

"I never said they've got any money," said Dave Atlo, ignoring the cockfight remark. "At least not yet, they haven't—"

"But we know these thieving cutthroats," Macon Ray cut in before Dave could finish. "If they left Denver City, rode forty miles to be here, it's because they've got something in the works."

"Thank you, Macon Ray," Dave Atlo said a little brusquely. He paused long enough for his words to sink in. "They've come up here to rob something." He grinned. "As soon as they do, we'll be waiting to rob them."

PART 2

Chapter 8

———◆———

Rochenbach and the five other riders bypassed the main streets of Central City and rode upward on a steep trail overlooking the booming mining town. Keeping their horses at a walk, they moved along single file in the pale moonlight, past long rows of mining shacks and shaft entrances, where the sound of steel tools rang behind the curtains of night.

At an upward turn in the trail, two riders appeared from out of nowhere. Rochenbach's thumb slipped over his rifle hammer until he heard one of the riders call out to them from ten yards away.

"Dent, Pres, Giant," said the lowered voice, "is that you?"

"It's us, Frank," Casings replied, nudging his horee forward and stopping as the two men rode up to him.

Rochenbach and the others followed behind Casings. When they gathered in close to the two newcomers, Casings motioned a gloved hand between the two and Rochenbach.

"Frank Penta, Bryce Shaner, meet Rochenbach . . . You can call him Rock," he said.

Penta and Shaner touched their hat brims toward Rochenbach, who returned the gesture.

"So, you're the man who has us out working in the cover of night," Frank Penta said with a thin smile. As he spoke, he looked Rochenbach up and down appraisingly.

"I do my best work at night," Rock replied mildly.

"Yeah, well, we're just hoping you're worth the trouble, *Midnight Rider*," said Shaner.

"Enough talking. Why don't we go see?" Casings said quickly, knowing Rochenbach's low tolerance for surliness and badmouthing.

"That's what I say," said Penta, catching the apprehension in Casings' tone of voice. "Let's go do what we do best." He gave him another thin smile.

"Yeah," said Bryce Shaner, "let's go see what you've got." He gave an exaggerated sweep of his hand. "After you, Midnight Rider."

But Rochenbach only sat staring at him.

"Are you a gambling man, Shaner?" he asked in an even voice.

"I've been known to lay down a stack on the right play. Why? What's the wager?" Shaner asked.

"I'll bet you fifty dollars I can put a bullet in your right eye before you can call me Midnight Rider again," Rock said.

Uh-oh! Casings snapped his gaze to Rochenbach.

"Hang on, Rock—*Jesus!*" he said. "Bryce didn't mean nothing by that! He gives everybody a little nickname like that. Right, Bryce?"

Rochenbach saw Shaner's prickly attitude and demeanor change quickly.

"Yeah! Hey, amigo! I was just trying to get acquainted, more or less funning with you!" he said to Rochenbach, his pretense shattered.

"Is it a bet?" Rochenbach asked flatly, unmoved by Shaner's sudden change of heart.

Frank Penta sidestepped his horse away from Bryce Shaner; the other men backed their horses a step.

"Hey, come on, Mid—I mean *Mr.* Rochenbach!" Shaner said, talking fast, correcting himself. "I came out to do a piece of work tonight," he said soberly. "I didn't come out looking for a gunfight." He slid nervous glances back and forth from Casings to Penta, looking for any support he might find. "All I want to do is make some money," he said shakily. "That's all I'm here for."

"Me too," said Rochenbach, letting up a little now that he saw Shaner was only acting tough. "I heard you playing big dog, little dog. I thought I better make sure I showed up at the right party."

"He's right, Bryce," said Casings. "You come up acting like a turd—"

"I was joking, damn it," Shaner insisted, cutting him off.

"Good enough," said Casings, ready to turn his horse away and dismiss the matter. "Settle this to suit yourself. Rest of us have a job to do."

"Jesus, all right! Okay!" said Shaner. "I was being a little testy. I've had lots on my mind lately. Can any of yas understand that?" He looked at each stone face in turn, seeing nothing in their eyes in the shadowy purple moonlight.

"Does this mean the bet's off?" Rochenbach said coolly.

"Yes, it's off! Damn it, it's off—hell, it never was on!" said Shaner, sounding even more shaken than before. "I was only kidding. I want all of you to know that." He looked all around.

"Look at me, Shaner," Rock said quietly.

"Huh . . . ?" Shaner said, turning back to Rochenbach.

"So was I," Rochenbach said with a thin trace of a smile, turning the matter loose now that he'd established himself with another of Grolin's men.

A low ripple of laughter stirred among the other gunmen. Casings chuckled, but he let out a sigh of relief as he did so.

"He got you good, Shaner," he said.

Shaner was too baffled and browbeaten to do anything but let out a tense breath and try to collect himself. He shook his head.

"Damn it to hell . . . ," he growled, amid the chuffing and stifled laughter of the men. He knew he'd been made to look like a fool, but he was also aware he'd set it up himself, then walked into it blindly. He jerked his horse away from Rochenbach and stared upward along the windy mining trail. "Some folks you can't fun with," he mumbled, trying to save face at least with himself.

As Shaner rode a few yards away, Casings shook his head and adjusted his hat atop his head.

"Don't go scaring our dynamite man away," he said quietly to Rochenbach.

"Dynamite man?" said Rock, looking back and forth between Casings and Penta. "What are we doing with dynamite? I thought Grolin wanted to see you men waltz cheek to cheek with this safe."

"He does," Penta cut in. "But Shaner and I are going to blow it afterward, just to keep folks from knowing there's a big-time safe opener in these parts." He looked Rochenbach up and down. "Sound good to you?" he asked, appearing amiable enough.

"Sounds like good planning to me," Rochenbach replied. He turned his horse with Penta and Casings. The riders spread out single file and rode on, upward into the night.

Stay calm and collected, Rochenbach reminded himself, riding along the steep uphill trail. *It's all coming around.* He didn't like playing this tough, desperado role all the time. But it was what the job called for. It was what these men understood. Calling Shaner down in front of the others was risky, but it had to be done. He could never allow Grolin's men to talk down to him in any way. That wasn't the way to play this game—likely it would get him killed one day.

Had Bryce Shaner stood up to him and chosen to fight, Rochenbach knew without a doubt that he would have killed the man. But he had decided on the spot that Shaner was only trying to buffalo him— acting tough to impress both Rock and the others.

It was clear that Shaner was scared, Rochenbach had decided, basing his judgment on experience, having faced down the same kind of men under the same set of circumstances countless times before. It was risky doing it, he had to admit, but he knew of no other way to play this game of life and death except to play tough and play to win.

Luckily he'd been right—*again*, he reminded himself, riding along in the chilled night air. He took a deep breath and let it out slowly. Call it luck, call it skill, call it experience. Whatever it was, he thought, he wouldn't question it. He was still in the game. . . .

At midnight the men pulled their horses off the trail, to the rear entrance of Hercules Mining. Dismounting, they led their horses quietly through a cluttered alley strewn with ore buckets, iron storage bins and broken hand tools. Across the rear yard from a dim-lit shack, they tied their horses to an iron hitch. While Bonham stayed with the horses, the others crept nearer to the shack and stopped behind a broken-down freight wagon.

"Giant, get over there with your dirt sock and do your stuff," Casings whispered to the Stillwater Giant. Turning to Rochenbach he said, "You're going to like this, Rock."

The Giant walked boldly but quietly toward the rear door of the shack, a long sock filled with dirt and gravel hanging from his large right hand.

Without being told, Penta and Shaner slipped away across the yard in different directions. In a crouch they both circled wide of the shack and took positions, watching the trail from the edge of the dusty front yard. Spiller and Turley Batts stayed back, rifles in hand, while Casings moved forward and watched the Giant knock on the rear door.

"Sheriff's deputy," he called out in his powerful voice as he banged with urgency on the door. "Open up, we know you're in there!"

"Keep your shirt on, Deputy. I'm coming," a startled voice called from inside. "Is that you, Decker?"

The Giant stood sidelong to the door, the sock full of dirt drawn back and ready.

The iron bolt slid from its keeper with a squeaking sound and the big door swung open. The night guard stood in the open door, a lantern raised in one hand, a shotgun in the other.

"If I'd known you was coming by, Decker," he said, "I would've had you bring me something to eat—" His voice stopped short as the Giant swung the loaded sock into his face with enough force to send him crashing backward across the length of the shack and land upside down against the front door.

"I have to laugh every time I see this," Casings said, chuckling beside Rochenbach.

Rochenbach started to pull his bandanna up over his face.

"Come on," said Casings, an empty pair of saddlebags over his shoulder, "you won't need a mask. This fool will be knocked out cold the rest of the night."

Inside the shack, the Giant had slipped the sock into his coat pocket. He'd hurried over and picked the lantern the night guard had been holding up off the floor and righted it before it had time to go out. When Rock and Casings came through the rear door, the Giant peeled the unconscious guard down off the front door. They watched him scoop the guard into his arms, carry him over to the cot and drop him on it.

"Sweet dreams," the Giant said down to the man.

Rochenbach stepped quickly across the room into a large office where a huge, ornate Diebold Bahmann safe stood against the wall. Casings followed at his elbow.

Rochenbach pulled a leather case from his coat pocket and took three pieces of his Cammann stethoscope from it. Casings watched intently as Rock assembled the scope and hung it around his neck.

When Rochenbach stepped over to the big modern safe and rubbed a hand on it near the large combination dial, Casings stood even closer, watching every move he made. This wouldn't do, Rock told himself. He didn't come here to teach an outlaw how to open safes.

"I hear it won't be long before everybody will be using these dial safes," Casings said as if in awe of some large, iron monster.

Rock ignored him. Putting the earpieces into his ears, he raised the bell end of the listening device against the flat steel door of the safe. He listened for a moment as he turned the steel dial slowly, then frowned and tapped the bell against the palm of his hand.

"What's wrong?" Casings asked in a hushed tone.

"It's not going to work," Rock said. He tapped the bell against his palm again, placed it on the steel door. He turned the dial again. Then he frowned and shook his head. "It's no use; there's too much noise," he said. He took the earpieces out of his ears.

Casings looked all around the cluttered office, puzzled.

"Too much *noise*?" he said wrinkling his brow. "I don't hear anything."

"That's because you're not wearing this," Rock

said, gesturing at the stethoscope dangling down his chest.

"Damn it, what can we do?" said Casings. "I don't want to go back empty-handed, even if this is a practice run."

"There's a clock ticking somewhere," Rock said, looking through the open door into the rest of the shack. "Go find it and stop it. I'll be listening through this." He picked the earpieces up from his shoulders and put them back into his ears.

"A clock ticking?" Casings said. "I never heard of anything as—"

"Are we going to open this baby or not?" Rock asked, cutting him off. "If we are, I need you to stop that clock for me." He leaned close to the steel door and held the bell back against it.

"All right," Casings said, shaking his head. He left the office and walked through the shack, looking all around.

"What's going on?" the Giant asked, looking up from tying up the unconscious guard with a length of rope. He'd pulled a bandanna from his pocket and tied it around the guard's eyes.

"I'm looking for a clock," Casings said. "Help me find it."

"A *clock*?" said the Giant. "You wondering what time it is?"

"Help me find the clock," Casings said. "It's keeping Rock from hearing inside the safe door."

"Dang," the Giant said in his deep voice, greatly impressed, "this must be some awfully scientific stuff we're fooling with."

Chapter 9

Rochenbach had begun listening through the stethoscope as Casings turned to leave the office. Working as fast as possible, he managed to hear the fall of the first two numbers on the four-number safe by the time Casings and the Giant finished searching the shack and walked back into the office almost on tiptoes.

"Rock, we can't find a clock," Casings whispered, without daring to go any closer to the safe until Rochenbach turned and took the earpieces down from his ears with a frown.

"What?" Rock asked, turning from the safe, looking upset.

"I said, we didn't find a clock," Casings repeated, the Stillwater Giant standing behind him staring over his shoulder at the big safe.

Casings and the Giant started to walk closer, but Rochenbach raised a hand, stopping them. He had just found the third number. All that remained was to drift the large dial slowly to his right and listen, and feel the last tumbler fall into place.

"There it is again," Rock said, looking all around, then turning back to the safe. "I just about had the numbers in place, and then the clock ticking started again." Without turning to face Casings and the Still-water Giant, he asked, "Is one of you wearing a watch?"

"I am," Casings said. His hand went into his coat pocket and pulled out a gold pocket watch on the end of a horsehair watch fob.

"That explains it," said Rochenbach. "Get rid of the watch. Get it out of here! Hurry up, I need it to be quiet in here."

"*Jesus . . . !*" said Casings, turning, starting out of the room and toward the front door of the shack.

"Wait, hold it," said Rochenbach. "I've got it! Come on in." He looked over his shoulder, gestured them forward and stepped to the side as he pulled the heavy steel door open.

"Holy cats!" said the Giant.

Casings' jaw dropped open in delight and surprise as he stared at the stacks of money on a shelf inside the big safe.

"Yeah, *holy cats*," he said, echoing the Giant. He chuffed a laugh as he and the Giant looked at each other.

"Well, my part of the job is done," Rock said, plucking the earpieces out and taking the stethoscope down from his neck.

The Giant and Casings stepped across the office floor side by side. Casings took the saddlebags down from his shoulder and opened the flaps as he stared at the money inside the safe.

"I say there's ten thousand, maybe more here," he

said to no one in particular as he started taking hand-fuls of money and shoving it down into the saddle-bags.

What was so much cash doing on hand in an oper-ation like this? Rochenbach asked himself. It made no sense.

"You done real good, Rock," said the Giant with a grin. He clasped a big hand down on Rochenbach's shoulder. "Grolin is going to want to keep you around from now on, is my guess."

"That's great to hear, Giant," said Rochenbach, taking the stethoscope apart and putting the pieces away inside his coat. "But the fact is, I'm just doing this because I need a stake. I work better when I'm working for myself." He smiled. "After the big job, I'll be heading out on my own."

Casings looked around from stuffing money into the saddlebags. He looked Rochenbach up and down. Then he looked at the Stillwater Giant.

"Giant, go get Batts and Bonham. Tell them to get in here and take this money. We're ready to cut out of here."

"Whoa," said Rochenbach. "Why are Bonham and Batts taking the money?" Rochenbach knew that at some point it was his duty to see to it the money found its way back to its owners. He didn't want the saddlebags to get out of his sight.

The Giant hesitated. Casings gave him a nod to-ward the rear door.

"Go on, Giant," said Casings.

As the Giant turned and left, Casings turned to Rochenbach.

"It's the way the boss set it up," he said. "He said for us to split up afterwards. He wants you as far from this stolen money as you can get, in case the law happens onto us on our way home."

Good thinking . . . , Rock told himself. He seemed to consider it, then said, "Are you and the Giant riding back with me?"

"Yes," said Casings. "Bonham and Batts carry the money. We give them a head start. The three of us ride a safe ways back from them. Spiller, Penta and Shaner ride home together on a different trail." He looked Rochenbach up and down. "Does that sound about right to you?"

"Sure," Rochenbach said. He hiked his coat collar up and leveled his hat brim. "Let's get outside. I don't like talking about anything with the guard so close, even if he is unconscious."

They walked past the knocked-out guard. Looking down at him on their way to the open rear door, Casings chuckled again.

"Don't worry abut him," said Casings. "The poor bastard's got lots of explaining to do come morning." He stopped again outside the rear door and looked back at the guard. He said to Rochenbach in a lowered voice, "Did you mean what you said to the Giant in there?"

"What's that?" Rock asked.

"You said you were doing this big job to get a stake and go out on your own," Casings said.

"I've thought about it," Rock said. "Only thing keeps me from doing it is I don't have the connections that a man like Andrew Grolin has. It's one thing to know how to open a safe. It's another thing to know which one to open, and when. That's the kind of information a man like Grolin has. It doesn't come easy."

"What if I got you that kind of information?" Casings asked. "Would you go on your own, maybe take a partner or two with you?"

Rochenbach stared at him as they heard the Giant and Bonham and Batts hurrying back toward the shack.

"I would," Rock said. "Can you get us that kind of information?"

"I can," Casings said.

Rochenbach only nodded.

"Are these some of those partners you're talking about?" he asked, nodding at the men approaching.

"They just might be," Casings said, "once they see how well this went."

"It's worth talking about," Rock said. Then he shut up as the three men arrived.

"Man!" said Bonham, seeing Casings swing the stuffed saddlebags from his shoulder. "That wasn't just fast, that was lightning fast!"

"This man knows his business," Casings said, poking a thumb toward Rochenbach. "I saw it with my own eyes."

Batts stepped in, took the saddlebags and slung them over his shoulder. He looked at Rochenbach closely.

"Do you always work this smooth and quick?" he said.

"I try to," Rock said.

"Talk about it later, Batts," Casings said to them both. "You and Bonham get out of here."

"You heard him, Bonham," said Batts. "Let's ride."

As the two outlaws turned and walked away toward the horses, the Giant stepped over and looked inside the shack where the watchman had begun to come to.

"What about this one, Rock?" the Giant asked. "Want me to snap his neck before we go?"

"No, Giant," said Rochenbach, "I want you to carry him out of here and prop him against the wall before they blow the safe."

The Giant gave him a confused look.

"We came up here to make ourselves some money, Giant," said Rock, "not to get the law dogging us for murder."

The Giant shrugged and said, "I just thought I ought to ask. That's what Grolin would want me to do."

Casings and Rochenbach looked at each other. Then Casings turned to the Stillwater Giant.

"We might be doing things a little different from now on, Giant," he said.

A half hour later, from the bottom of the trail leading back into town, Lonnie Bonham and Turley Batts stopped and turned in their saddles. They stared up at the sudden clap of thunder that resounded from the hilltop behind them.

"It sounds like our boys just finished taking care of business," said Batts, talking about Spiller, Penta and Shaner, the ones left behind to blow open the door of the big safe.

"Yeah," said Lon Bonham, "and a damn good piece

of business it was." He rode with the saddlebags lying over his lap, prepared to quickly throw the money over the side of the trail and get rid of evidence should a party of lawmen come riding up the trail. But the probability of anyone investigating the blast was slim, especially with so many mines working throughout the night.

The two turned forward in their saddles and had started to nudge their horses when they saw four dark figures step into sight, forming a half circle around them on the trail.

Bonham raised the saddlebags and sat ready to hurl them away.

"Don't do something stupid," said a deep voice. The man moved closer, coming more clearing into sight in the pale light of the moon.

"Christ in a canoe!" said Turley Batts. "It's Dirty Dave Atlo."

Dirty Dave gave him a slim, evil grin, holding a double-barreled shotgun pointed and cocked up at him.

"See how smart you are, Batts, when you apply yourself?" he said. He looked past Batts at Bonham and said, "Lonnie, you stinking little bastard. I hope you do try to throw that money over the cliff, so I can air your guts out for you."

"Sit tight, Lon!" Batts ordered, knowing Bonham well enough to anticipate that he would drop the saddlebags and go for his gun. To Dave Atlo he said weakly, "What money are you talking about, Dave?"

"Jesus, I can't believe I let you Denver City idiots beat me out of money," said Dirty Dave. The shotgun bucked in his hand, lighting his face blue-orange in a blossom of firelight.

Batts flew from his saddle as the bulk of the scrap iron load sliced through his chest and face. His horse screamed loud and long. Catching some of the perimeter of the shot in its neck and withers, the animal reared high and fell away onto its side. But before it fell, as it stood on its hind hooves between Lonnie Bonham and Dirty Dave, Bonham made his move.

Slinging the bags over the edge of the trail, he jerked his Colt from its holster and fired furiously, one of his shots flinging Dirty Dave from his saddle. But the other three shotguns blossomed and exploded in the darkness, pounding Bonham mercilessly.

"That'll do!" shouted Macon Ray Silverette, rasping and choking in the looming broil of burnt powder. He called over to Dirty Dave, who stood bowed at the waist on the far side of the trail from him, "You hit, Dave?"

"Hell yes, I'm hit, you damn fool!" Dave growled as Macon Ray reached and gently took the shotgun from his hand. "I'm gut-shot . . . belly to backbone!" he gasped, and added, "I feel blood running down my ass."

"Now, there's a picture I would not pay to look at," said Ray, lifting Dave's Colt from its holster and shoving it down behind his belt.

"Wha-what are you doing?" Dirty Dave asked, in a distrusting voice.

"Lightening your load, Dirty Dave," said Macon Ray.

"I won't need no lightening, once I'm in the saddle,"

said Dave, pain coming to his voice. "And don't call me Dirty Dave. I've warned you enough!" he managed to growl.

"Dirty Dave, your warnings don't impress me the way they used to, say . . . an *hour* ago?" Ray grinned. He patted Dave on the back. "Anyway, I'm lightening your load so you don't have as much to carry, bringing the saddlebags up to us." He gestured a hand toward the edge of the trail, beyond the bodies of the two outlaws—beyond one dead, and one dying, thrashing horse.

"Are you—are you *kidding me*?" said Dave as Albert Kinney walked in closer from across the trail, his shotgun still smoking in his hands.

"Joe," said Macon Ray with a dark chuckle, "he wants to know if I'm kidding him."

Joe Fackler pitched a rope on the ground at Dave's feet.

Dave shook his bowed head and said, "You can't expect me to climb down that cliff. Look at me." He held a bloody hand up from his belly.

"I told you I was winning on that cockfight, Dirty Dave," Fackler said in a sullen tone.

"Well, there you have it," Macon Ray said, patting Dave's bowed back. "Tie that rope around your waist. We'll help you skin on down the cliff side. You just tie the saddlebags onto the rope and give it a yank, and we'll pull them up."

"I'm no fool," said Dave, his voice sounding more pained. "What about me? Are you pulling me back up too?"

"That's a tough one to call right now, Dave," said

Macon Ray. "I'd like to tell you we will, but knowing our outlaw nature . . ." He let his words trail.

"If you're not throwing the rope back down for me, I'm not going down," Dave said firmly.

"Suit yourself, Dirty Dave," said Ray. He looked at Joe Fackler. "We can't waste time here. You can bet Grolin's men are trailing the money." He looked back along the dark trail. "Air him out, Joe," he said.

"My pleasure," said Fackler, breaking open his shotgun, plucking out two spent shells and reaching into his pocket for fresh rounds.

"Please, Joe," said Dave Atlo.

But Fackler only stared coldly at him as he reloaded.

"I had just won twenty dollars on one fight," he said bitterly, snapping the shotgun shut.

"All right, wait! Hold it!" said Dave, forcing himself to straighten up. "I'll go down and send the money up. If you don't throw that rope back down for me, may you all rot in hell."

Fackler and Ray grinned.

Moments later, Ray stood watching, smoking a cigarette, rifle in hand, keeping an eye on the back trail as Albert Kinney and Joe Fackler lowered the wounded outlaw over the edge and down the steep rocky hillside.

"He's got it!" Kinney called back over his shoulder.

"Haul it up," said Macon Ray, walking over to the edge and staring down at Dave's shadowy, wounded figure standing on a ledge staring up at him.

"Here it comes!" said Kinney, pulling the rope up until the saddlebags flopped over on to the edge of the trail.

Ray chuckled and flipped his cigarette butt out over the edge. He stopped and untied the saddle-bags, opened them and looked inside with a widening smile, Fackler and Kinney crowding his elbow as he untied the rope.

"Boys, here's your cockfight," he said. Shaking the stacks of money in the bags, he closed the flaps, tied them and slung the bags over his shoulder.

"What about him?" Kinney asked, gesturing down into the darkness.

"Tie it off on a tree and throw the rope back down to him," said Ray, feeling generous. "He won't live the night either way."

On the ledge below, one hand holding his bleeding belly, Dave stared up toward the sound of their voices.

"What about . . . that rope?" he called up in a failing voice.

"Here it comes," said Macon Ray.

Dave saw and felt the rope lash down the steep hillside and dangle beside him. Grabbing it quickly, he tied it around his waist.

"All right, give me a pull," he said, holding on to the bite of the rope with both hands. "Ready when you are," he added, after a moment of silence from the edge above him.

"Ray . . . ? *Joe* . . . ?" He stood with blood running down him front and back. "Damn it to hell," he said finally, hearing the sound of horses' hooves move off quickly along the rocky trail.

Chapter 10

No sooner had Macon Ray and the other two ambushers fled out of sight down the mining trail into Central City than Rochenbach, the Stillwater Giant and Pres Casings rode around a turn in the trail and slid to a halt, seeing the bodies of Bonham and Batts and the dead horse lying in a heap. The wounded horse raised its head from the ground and whined pitifully.

"Who the hell could have done this?" Casings asked, turning his horse back and forth on the trail, the Giant doing the same right beside him.

"Nobody knew about this but us," said the Giant, swinging his rifle up as he scanned the steep, dark hillside.

Casings nudged his horse along the trail a few feet, then turned it and nudged it back. He looked all around, rifle in hand, cocked and ready.

Rochenbach drew his Remington and cocked it as he stepped his horse over to where the wounded horse lay suffering.

Both the Giant and Casings flinched as a shot from

the Remington exploded behind them and the horse fell silent.

"Somebody must've known something," Rock said, turning his dun, looking at the other two. His voice sounded suspicious.

"Don't go getting the wrong idea on us, Rock," said Casings. "We're as bewildered by this as you are."

Rochenbach looked at both of the dead horses and saw no sign of the saddlebags. This was bad. The safe money was gone—money that he personally took responsibility for.

"Rock! What's that?" Casings asked, interrupting Rochenbach's thoughts. He gestured toward the rope tied to a scrub pine and drawn tight over the rocky edge of the cliff.

"I'll check it out," said the Giant, nudging his horse closer to the edge, then stepping down from his saddle and testing the tension on the rope with the grip of his huge hand. "Somebody's down there," he said to the other two. Then he called down the steep darkened hillside, "Hey, who's there?"

"It's me, Giant . . . ," said Dirty Dave Atlo in a weakened and defeated voice.

"Give me a name before I start putting bullets in your shirt pockets!" the Giant warned, leveling his rifle down into the darkness.

"It's Dave Atlo, Giant," Dave called up to him. "I—I recognized . . . your voice."

"That doesn't make us pals, Dirty Dave," said the Giant. But he lowered his rifle now and looked to Rochenbach and Casings for direction.

"Ask him what he's doing down there on the end of a rope," said Casings.

Rochenbach sat watching, sliding his Remington back into its holster.

"What are you doing down there on the end of a rope?" the Giant called down, repeating Casings' question word for word.

"We robbed your boys and killed them," Dave said. "Bonham threw the money down here . . . put a bullet in my belly before he died. Macon Ray Silverette double-crossed me—sent me for the bags, left me down here to die."

"Ask him who put them on to us," Rock said to the Giant.

"Who put you on to us, Dirty Dave?" the Giant called down the hillside.

"Nobody," said Dave in a pained voice. "I—I saw you ride into Central City, knew somebody was about to get robbed." He paused, then said, "Suppose you could pull me up, Giant? I'm hurting something awful."

Rochenback and Casings looked at each other.

"Tell him we'll pull him up," said Rock, "but if he doesn't tell us where they're headed, we'll throw him right back down there."

Giant called out, "We'll pull you up, Dave, but if you—"

"I heard him, Giant," said Dave Atlo. "Pull me up. I got no reason to hold out on yas . . . not for Macon Ray's sake. Him and them other sons a' bitches left me here to die. I'd be a fool to stick with them."

The Stillwater Giant looked at Casings and Rochenbach.

"Pull him up, Giant," said Casings. "Let's hear what he's got to say."

Dave Atlo grunted and groaned in pain as the Giant pulled effortlessly, hand over hand, on the rope. When Dave's hands gripped the edge of the rocky trail, the Giant stood looking down at him.

"Hel-help me on up. Please?" Dave whined.

The Giant reached down with one large hand, grabbed him by the nape of his neck and raised him over the edge. He held him up at arm's length, dangling in the air, kicking his feet, screaming out in pain, both hands going to his bloody belly. Then he dropped him flat on the hard ground. Dave let out another pain-filled scream.

"Was this all because Andrew Grolin beat you out of your money last year?" Casings asked. He sat his horse sidelong to the downed outlaw leader, his rifle loosely pointed down at him.

"You bet it was," said Dave, pain-stricken, clutching both forearms across his bleeding stomach wound. "I—I expect it wasn't a wise thing, looking back on it."

"Damn Grolin," Casings whispered to Rock. "He caused this, cheating one of our own."

Rock only nodded, watching, listening.

"Where is our money headed?" Casings asked Dave Atlo.

But Dave continued reflecting. "I should . . . have forgotten what Grolin did to me, as it turns out."

"Get him on his feet, Giant," said Casings, seeing Dave was starting to drift and fade.

The Giant pulled the wounded outlaw up and steadied him for a second, then stepped back.

"Dirty Dave, look at me," said Casings, in a firmer voice. "Where is Macon Ray Silverette headed with *our money*?"

Dave sighed and shook his head, looking up at Casings.

"I was heading us up the gulch, north of Black Hawk," he said. "The Apostle Camp—been deserted for years, except for some old road agents who lie low there."

"The Apostle Camp, where the Toet brothers ate a squaw years back?" Casings asked.

"Yep," said Dave. "Regular folks shy clear of the place. But Macon Ray and I hide there all the time. We toss the old-timers some whiskey to keep them happy."

"Did you get a chance to count that money?" Casings asked. Rock sat listening in silence.

"No," said Dave, "didn't you?"

"I figured around nine or ten thousand," said Casings.

"Damn, that would have lasted me a long time," Dave said with regret.

"Any reason to take you into town?" Casings asked pointedly.

"No," Dave said grimly, "I'm done for. I just didn't want to die down there—not that it matters, I reckon."

"What do you want, Dirty Dave?" Casings asked, staring intently at him.

"Hell, you know what I want," said Dave. He shook his head and mused. "This was crazy of me. I was sitting in Central City, drinking, diddling a young whore. Now look at me."

Casings stared at him solemnly. "You should have kept on diddling," he said. His rifle bucked once across his lap. Dirty Dave flew backward off the edge as the bullet bored through his heart. The sound of the shot echoed off into the black distance.

"He's right back down there," Giant said, looking down the dark hillside.

"Yeah," said Casings, "but now we know what happened. We can tell Grolin where the money went." He started to turn his horse as the Giant climbed into his saddle.

"Wait a minute," Rochenbach said in surprise. "What about the money?"

"Forget it, Rock," said Casings. "Grolin said make the practice job, then ride straight back, get ready for the big job."

"*Forget* ten thousand dollars?" said Rochenbach.

"We don't know it was that much," said Casings.

"However much it was, I can't let it slide away from me," Rochenbach said. "This work is not my hobby. I'm in it for the money."

"I'm telling you what Grolin told me," Casings said. "Don't think I like riding away from this."

"Then don't," Rochenbach said flatly. He turned his dun and started to put it forward ahead of them.

"What are you saying?" said Casings.

"What I'm saying is, do what suits you best," said Rock. "I'm going after my money."

"All right, I'm in with you," said Casings, he and the Giant catching up to him. "But what about Spiller, Penta and Shaner? They won't know what happened to us."

"They'll have to figure it all out as they go," said Rochenbach, gigging his dun up into a gallop on the rocky hill trail.

Riding alongside Rochenbach, the Giant said in his deep voice, "Grolin is going to be madder than a hornet at us."

"If Grolin gets mad when we hand him a saddlebag full of money, we shouldn't be working for him anyway, Giant," said Rochenbach. He gave Casings a knowing look as he spoke.

"Yeah," said the Giant with a wide grin, "that's what I say."

Macon Ray Silverette and the other two ambushers swung wide around the main street of Central City, but they stopped long enough to load up on bottles of rye whiskey at a small trading post along the trail. While a bleary-eyed store owner concentrated on tallying the whiskey, Macon Ray wrapped a hand around a thick bundle of cigars and shoved them inside his coat.

"I saw that," the owner said, raising his eyes.

"No, you didn't," said Macon Ray, feeling full of himself after the night's robbery. "You just think you did." He drew his Colt and cocked it arm's length in the clerk's face before adding, "Otherwise you'd be calling me a thief and a liar right to my damn face."

"You're absolutely right, sir!" said the badly shaken

man as Kinney and Fackler both followed suit, raising their guns, cocked and pointed in the clerk's face. "I—I don't know what must have come over me!"

"That's what I thought," said Macon Ray. "You two grab that whiskey," he told Kinney and Fackler. "This man all but called me a thief; he's got to make recompense for it."

They gathered the bottles of whiskey and left without paying, while the owner stared helplessly at them, grateful to still be alive.

With their regular saddlebags stuffed with whiskey bottles, they rode on in the night through the mining town of Black Hawk and on through Gregory Gulch, a stretch of scrub, craggy cliff and ledges strewn with torchlit hard-rock mines. The odor of wood smoke and burnt sulfur loomed in the chilled air above glowing smelter mills.

When the last flicker of torchlight and furnace glow fell away behind them, the three riders turned onto a narrow path leading up to a long-abandoned mining camp perched on a sawtooth ridgeline. At the edge of a clearing hidden behind a stand of pine, Macon Ray brought Joe Fackler and Albert Kinney to a halt behind him, seeing a dark figure standing on the porch of a run-down mining shack.

"Who the hell goes there?" an unfriendly voice called out from the dark porch.

"Hobbs, it's us," Macon Ray called out across the small clearing. "Ray Silverette, Albert Kinney and *Cockfighting* Joe Fackler."

Fackler eyed Macon Ray in the dark.

"Nobody's ever called me that, Ray," he said.

"I just thought it fitting after what you did to Dirty Dave," Macon Ray said with a dark chuckle.

From the porch, Parnell Hobbs called out, "Where's Dave Atlo?

"In hell, I expect," said Ray. "But that's a long story, best told closer up."

"Come on up, then, Macon Ray. Let me get a look at you," said Hobbs.

As Macon Ray nudged his horse forward, Joe Fackler and Albert Kinney following right behind him, Fackler grumbled, "I don't like being called Cockfighting Joe. Don't get it started, Ray."

"Or *what*?" Macon Ray asked, feeling satisfied, the saddlebags full of money across his lap. "You going to shoot *me*?"

Joe started to cock the shotgun lying across his lap, but he thought about the money and eased his thumb off the gun hammers.

"I just don't *like it*, is all," he said, the three of them drawing closer to the porch.

"Who don't like what?" asked Hobbs as the three came to a halt and he stepped forward off the dark porch. He eyed the saddlebags across Macon Ray's lap, Ray's rifle lying atop them.

"Fackler here don't want to be called Cockfighting Joe," said Macon.

"Who's calling him that?" asked Hobbs.

"I am," said Macon Ray. He looked past Hobbs as the shack door opened and two more men stepped onto the rickety porch.

"Howdy, Raymond Silverette," said a lean old gunman named Latner Karr. He struck a match and lit a thin cigar. Then he stepped forward, eyeing the saddlebags. "Whatever's in the bag, I bet it recently belonged to somebody else."

"Howdy, Latner," said Macon Ray, recognizing the old man in the flicker of match light. "You'd win that bet," he added. "It's money, and some of it's yours for letting us hole up here."

On the porch, a sightless outlaw named Simon Goss stepped forward, testing his footing with each step. Following the sound of Karr's voice, he stopped and stood beside him. His right hand rested against a large Walker Colt hanging down his chest by a lanyard cord.

"What kind of money? How much is there?" he asked with great interest, his blind eyes searching aimlessly in the night. "Is some of it mine?"

"Howdy, Blind Simon," said Macon Ray. "It's money we *thieved* from Andrew Grolin's *thieves*." He grinned proudly. "And damned right, some of it's yours—all three of yas, like I said," he added.

Latner Karr stared knowingly at Macon Ray.

"Andy Grolin's men could be right on your ass, is that it, Raymond?"

"No, we got away clean as soap," said Macon Ray. "I'm just wanting to lie low awhile. Cockfighting Joe here threw Dirty Dave Alto over a cliff. I'm taking charge."

"Stop calling me that name," Joe said in an angry tone. "And I didn't throw Dirty Dave over a cliff. I forced him to climb down over it on his own."

"At the end of that goose gun he's packing," Macon Ray added, gesturing at the shotgun on Joe's lap.

"And he's dead now?" said Karr. "You're certain of it?"

"Yep, I'm certain of it," said Ray. He pulled Dirty Dave's pistol from his belt slowly and pitched it down to the lean old gunman. "You know how partial he was to this six-shooter."

"He wouldn't give it up without a fight," said Karr, inspecting the pistol in his hand.

"He got himself gut-shot by Lonnnie Bonham, so he was dying anyway," said Ray. "But that's the end of his string. Whatever he *was*, I now *am*." He smiled proudly and patted the saddlebags. "I'm hoping you three will celebrate with us."

Latner Karr looked off along the path they'd ridden in on. "I need to mull it over," he said.

"You do that, Lat. But believe me," said Macon Ray, "nobody knows we're here." He lifted the saddlebags and pitched them to the ground at Karr's feet. Blind Simon jumped a step at the sound of bags landing in the dirt. "So, mull it over while you help me count this money," he added with a sly grin.

"I smell whiskey," said Blind Simon, sniffing the air toward the three horsemen. "Cigars too."

"The *nose* on this man, I swear to God," said Macon Ray. He shook his head in amazement.

Chapter 11

Before daylight, Casings and the Stillwater Giant stood back holding the horses as Rochenbach rapped on the side door to the trading post where Macon Ray and his men had stopped for whiskey in the middle of the night. When the door opened a crack and the owner looked out and saw the three trail-weary gunmen, he almost gasped at the sight of the Stillwater Giant staring at him. He quickly began to slam the door shut, but Rochenbach's big boot jammed against the bottom of the door, stopping him.

"We mean you no harm," Rock said.

"That's what everybody says before they cut a man's throat or bludgeon him to death!" He struggled in vain to close the door.

"Not us," said Rochenbach, keeping his boot planted firmly. "We're tracking three men who robbed us on the trail down from the mines. I saw fresh tracks at your rail. Were they here in the night?"

"Will they come back and kill me if they find out I said they were?" the owner asked shakily.

"Point us right and they won't be coming back at all," Rock said firmly.

"Are you the law?" the man asked, still wary, seeing Rochenbach's big Remington belly gun, the rifles hanging in each man's hands.

Instead of answering, Rochenbach started to turn away from the cracked door. "I'll tell all their friends we came by here—how well you helped us find them," he said.

"Hold it! Wait a minute!" said the post owner, seeing the three men were ready to leave.

Rochenbach stopped and turned back to the door; it opened wider.

"They were here, sure enough!" said the owner. "They took whiskey and cigars, never paid a penny for either. Those kind of men never do." He looked Rock up and down and added quickly, "Not that I'm anybody's judge, you understand."

"I understand," Rochenbach said. "We'll be obliged if you'll sack us some food and boil us a canteen of hot coffee for the trail." Seeing the dubious look on the man's face, he fished a gold coin from his coat and flipped it to him. "For pay, of course," he added.

"Yes, sir, coming right up," said the trading post owner, catching the gold coin and hefting its weight on his palm. "I'll meet you at the front door and let you in."

The three walked around to the front of the log and stone building and waited for the man to unbolt the front door.

"How much farther is it to the Apostle Camp?" Rochenbach asked Casings.

"If we don't spend too much time here, we'll be there midmorning, maybe sooner. But don't expect to ride in and find these three alone. They're like us. They've got men everywhere. Some drift out, others drift in. There's an old blind road agent named Simon Goss who lives there most times."

"Blind, huh . . . ?" said Rochenbach. He thought it over. "We've got no fight with anybody except the ones who have our money," he said.

"That's good," said Casings, "because you never know when we might need to lie low there ourselves. Blind Simon's a good man to keep on our side."

The Stillwater Giant grinned and said guardedly, "Yeah, let's not forget we're some far-handed long riders ourselves, eh?"

When the door opened and the three stepped inside, the owner stared up at the Giant in awe. A canteen in the Giant's huge hand looked more the size of a tin of salve.

"I—I'm going to give you the pot of coffee I just boiled for myself a few minutes ago," he said. "No need in me holding you fellows up from your search."

"Obliged," came the Giant, handing him the empty canteen.

In moments, the canteen had been filled with hot coffee. The owner also packed a flour sack with fresh morning biscuits, tins of beans and a venison shank wrapped in brown paper and tied with a string.

"I'm going to make change for you," the owner said, sliding the flour sack across the worn-slick wooden countertop.

"Keep it for your trouble," said Rochenbach as

Casings picked up the sack and the Giant took the canteen of coffee in his bag hand. Leaving the store, the three unhitched their horses, stepped up into their saddles and turned the animals toward the trail.

"That's the biggest man I ever saw in my life," the trading post owner said aloud to himself, watching the riders fade back into the silver morning darkness from which they'd come.

Blind Simon Goss was the first of the outlaws to awake from a drunken sleep. He'd spent the rest of the night wrapped in a blanket, sitting in a wooden chair he'd dragged out onto the front porch and leaned against the front of the shack. A burnt-out cigar hung from his lips.

The warmth of morning sunlight creeping up his face had been the first thing to rouse him—but there had been something else pushing its way into his sleep. He'd begun to catch the faint scent of man and horse wafting up from the trail winding down the hillside.

Without opening his sightless eyes, Simon slid his hand over the stock of the shotgun lying on his lap. He put his thumb over both hammers and pulled them back.

Lying on the porch beside him, wrapped in a ragged blanket, Parnell Hobbs snapped his eyes open at the metal-on-metal sound. A cigar fell from his mouth.

"What is it, Simon?" he asked in a hushed tone, his fingers searching around for the burnt-out cigar. Under his blanket, his free hand went to the Colt holstered on his hip.

"Riders climbing the trail," said the blind outlaw, his sightless eyes roving aimlessly along the far side of the clearing. He spoke with a whiskey slur in his voice.

"Are you tracking their scent, or hearing them or both?" Hobbs asked, standing up stiffly, sticking the cigar back between his teeth. He let his blanket fall to the porch and picked up his repeating rifle, which was resting against a post. A half bottle of whiskey stood beside the rifle. He reached for it and pulled its cork.

"I'm smelling them," said the blind outlaw, "but I'll be hearing them when they make the last switchback." At the sound of the cork leaving the bottle with a soft *plop*, he reached a hand out in the direction of the whiskey.

Hobbs took a long swig and put the bottle into Goss' hand.

"I best wake everybody up," Hobbs said, turning to walk inside the shack.

"We're already awake," said Macon Ray, meeting Hobbs at the door, swinging his gun belt around his waist. He puffed on a freshly lit cigar. Behind him, Joe Fackler and Albert Kinney stood dressing in the light of a smoldering hearth fire, each with a cigar burning between his fingers.

Latner Karr stood by the hearth in his gray and frayed long-john underwear, sipping coffee from a thick mug. He clasped a bottle of whiskey in his other hand.

"You said nobody's dogging you, Raymond," he said in a prickly tone.

"I'm still saying there's not," said Macon Ray. "Far as I know, he could be smelling a mail buggy."

"He knows the smell of a mail buggy, drunk or sober," said Hobbs, standing in the open door.

From his porch chair, Blind Simon lowered the whiskey bottle from his lips and wiped his shirt cuff across them.

"They're at the switchback turn," he said. "Now I can hear them. Two of them," he added. "It *ain't* the U.S. Mail."

"The *ears* on this man!" Macon Ray marveled, shaking his head. As he spoke, he slung the saddlebags of money over his shoulder.

"Are you going to run or fight?" Karr asked, a long stub of a stolen cigar stuck behind his ear. He sipped from his bottle and chased it with a gulp of coffee. "There's two of them, six of us. We're beholding to siding with you, for the money and the whiskey."

Joe Fackler, Albert Kinney and Macon Ray looked at one another.

"Six to two . . . ," said Macon Ray. "What do you say? Do we make a stand, or make a run?"

"I'll get our horses," Joe Fackler volunteered. He turned and hurried out the rear door toward a small lean-to shed barn.

"Uh-oh," said Blind Simon, his right ear turned to the path leading into the stand of pine, "they've speeded up!"

"Can you three slow them down while we cut out of here?" said Macon Ray.

"*Slow them down?*" said Hobbs. "Hell, we can stop them cold, far as that goes."

"Kill the lot of them, is what we'll do," Blind Simon said drunkenly. He leaned his chair forward from the wall and stood up, letting his blanket fall. He held his cocked shotgun in one hand, his Walker Colt hanging down his chest by its lanyard cord.

"That's the spirit," said Macon Ray. He hurried off the front porch and grabbed his horse's reins as Fackler ran around the side of the shack leading the animals.

When the three outlaws had mounted and booted their horses off along a higher path behind the shack, Simon stood in front of the shack, a morning breeze blowing into his face.

"Come on, Simon," said Karr, his gun belt strapped around the waist of his long johns. "Let's get you inside the house. Me and Hobbs will flank the front yard." He turned the blind outlaw and led him onto the porch. Blind Simon followed stiffly.

"I don't want to hide and fight," he protested with a whiskey slur. "I want to fight straight up."

"You're drunk, Simon," said Karr, leading him through the front door into the shack. "Now settle down." He positioned the blind outlaw at an open front window and helped him level his cocked shotgun out across the window's ledge.

"They're coming through the pines!" Simon warned with a sniff of the air.

"You stay right here, Simon. Start shooting when we do," said Karr. "Don't shoot any ways except straight ahead."

"You got it, *mi amigo*," said the aged, drunken blind man.

Hobbs' eyes widened as he spotted the Giant's huge lurking figure among a stand of saplings. His cigar dropped from his mouth.

"There they are!" he shouted, opening fire into the pines with his repeating rifle.

A hundred feet from him, Karr also spotted the Giant and started firing. Then he saw Casings as the outlaw brought his rifle around the side of a larger tree to return fire and draw their rifles away from the Giant, who stood helplessly ducking bullets like a man being attacked by hornets.

From a cliff edge higher up the trail behind the shack, Macon Ray Silverette brought his horse to a halt, swung the animal around and looked down at the shack and the clearing below, seeing the gun battle rage.

"That's the way, old-timers," he said with a merciless grin. "Go down fighting." He looked at the other two and said, "Not a bad investment, eh? A little whiskey and a few dollars for all that protection?"

"They're going to get them-damn-selves killed down there," said Albert Kinney, sticking his cigar back into his mouth.

"Better them three than us three, right, Cockfighting Joe?" said Macon Ray.

Joe Fackler glared at Macon Ray.

"I've told you more than once now, I don't want to get that name started, Ray," he said.

Macon Ray only chuckled and said, "Relax, take it easy! I'm only funning you." He swept a hand toward the gunfight below them. "Think how good you've got it. We could be down there getting shot."

He turned his horse back to the trail and said, "Now come on, let's go spread our wealth around some."

The other two fell in behind him, but before they got their horses onto the trail, they stopped short and sat staring at Rochenbach, who sat staring back at them from atop his dun, the horse standing crosswise, blocking their path. His big Remington stood out at arm's length toward them, cocked and aimed.

"*Hello, now!*" Macon Ray said in surprise. "Who the hell are you?"

Even as Ray asked, his right hand went for the Colt holstered on his hip. The other two outlaws went for their rifles lying across their laps.

But Rochenbach's Remington wasted no time. The big pistol began bucking in his hand, firing with precision into the three gunmen he'd caught off guard.

His first shot hit Macon Ray squarely in the chest and sent him flying backward from his saddle, slamming him into Joe Fackler's horse behind him, causing it to spook and rear high. Fackler fired, but his shot went wild from atop the frightened animal. Rock's second shot hit Fackler in the head, the impact causing both man and reared horse to fall backward and slide over the edge of the cliff.

Albert Kinney's rifle bucked in his hands. His shot sliced through Rochenbach's coat sleeve, grazing his upper arm. But before Kinney could lever another round into the rifle chamber, Rock's third and fourth shots nailed him dead center and sent him flying sidelong to the ground.

Rochenbach cocked his forearm, raising the smoking Remington shoulder high as he looked back and forth, making sure the fight was over.

At the edge of the cliff, he heard the thrashing and scrambling of hooves and started to swing his Remington toward it. But then he stopped and watched as Fackler's horse climbed over the edge, shook itself off and stood on shaky legs staring at him, its saddle hanging halfway down its side.

In the clearing below, the gun battle continued. Rochenbach stepped down from his saddle, walked over and picked up the saddlebags of money that Macon Ray had been carrying across his lap. He opened the bags, looked the stacks of money over and was relieved to see the bulk of it was still there.

It won't be for long, he told himself.

Then he closed the bags and slung them over his shoulder. The question crossed his mind again, What was anybody doing with so much cash on hand? Even with a big steel safe to keep it in, a night watchman looking over it?

He turned at the sound of a weak choking cough and saw Macon Ray raise himself from the dirt on both palms and turn over on his elbows. Blood ran freely down his chest and from his lips.

"Did I ask . . . who are you?" Ray managed to say.

"Yes, you did," said Rochenbach, seeing the man was on his last few breaths. "I'm Avrial Rochenbach." He reached out, loosened the cinch on Fackler's horse and dropped its saddle to the ground.

"That Pinkerton detective . . . who came over?" said Ray.

"That's me," said Rock. He loosened the cinch on Macon Ray's horse's saddle and dropped it to the dirt.

Ray saw his horse standing bareback. He sighed, knowing what that meant.

"Of all the sumbitches I could have robbed . . . ," he said, and he lay back down on the ground and closed his eyes.

Hearing the firing stop in the clearing below, Rock loaded the bodies over their horses' backs and tied them wrists to boots under the horses' bellies with rope he'd taken from Fackler's saddle horn. He stepped back into his saddle with the three horses' reins in hand, turned them to the trail and led them down.

Chapter 12

In front of the shack, the Stillwater Giant stood drinking water from a canteen, watching as Rochenbach approached, leading the three horses and their grisly loads behind him. On the ground beside the Giant, Pres Casings sat stooped over Latner Karr, holding a bottle of whiskey to the wounded old outlaw's lips.

"Dang," said the Giant in his deep voice. "It looks like Rock kilt all three of them."

"I'm not surprised," said Casings. He looked out at Rochenbach for a moment, then back to Karr, who lay sprawled in the dirt in his long johns, leaning back against the porch, his chest covered with blood.

"Want me to take a look at it?" Casings asked, nodding at the blood-soaked, wadded bandanna Karr held against a gaping exit wound in his chest.

"You never . . . seen one?" Karr asked in a strained voice.

"I thought I might help you some way," Casings said.

"Just keep that whiskey bottle close . . . 'til I fade on out of here," said Karr. Still, he raised the bandanna for a second and let Casings get a look at the bleeding fist-sized hole in his chest.

Rochenbach stepped down from his saddle and stood over the downed outlaw. The Stillwater Giant took the reins to the three horses and tied them to a hitch rail. Rock caught a glimpse of the bullet hole in Karr's chest before Karr closed the bandanna down over it.

"He was shot by his own man, from behind," Casings said up to Rochenbach.

Rochenbach shook his head and looked all around the clearing. Ten yards away lay Parnell Hobbs, flat on his back, dead, his face missing, in its place an open bloody hull.

"That one shot himself somehow," said Pres. He turned back to Karr and gave him another drink from the whiskey bottle.

Karr swallowed the fiery rye and let out a whiskey hiss.

"He was running with a cocked shotgun . . . stumbled and blew his damned head off . . . ," he wheezed. "The poor bastard. . . ."

Rock let out a breath and looked at the third man lying a few yards away beneath a big pine tree.

"That one came running out of the shack shouting, shooting wild in every direction," said Casings. "He's the one who shot this one." He gestured a nod at Karr.

"You had to shoot him," Rock said.

"No, we didn't shoot him," said Casings. "He ran smack into that tree. Hasn't moved an inch since. Giant unarmed him and left him lying there for the time being."

"I take it that's Blind Simon Goss?" said Rochenbach, staring out at the downed man who looked to be peacefully sleeping.

"How'd . . . you guess?" said Karr in a weak but sarcastic voice.

"Want me to go tote him over here?" the Giant asked, holding the canteen out in his huge hand for Rochenbach to take.

"Yes, bring him on over," said Rock. Taking the canteen, he said, "Obliged," and sipped while the Giant trotted away to where Blind Simon lay knocked out cold.

"I . . . know you," Latner Karr said, squinting up at Rochenbach. He raised a weak bloody finger toward him.

"Do you, now?" Rock said flatly.

"You're that . . . detective who turned outlaw."

"That's me all right," Rochenbach said, knowing the old man wasn't going to be talking much longer.

"Some say . . . that's a lie," said Karr. "Some say you're . . . still a lawman . . . working among us ol' boys. Doing all . . . the damage you can."

"Do they, now?" said Rock, sounding disinterested. He noted the questioning look Casings gave him.

"If you are . . . you should rot in hell," Karr said, sounding weaker as he spoke. "Admit it. . . ."

Rochenbach and Casings looked at each other, then back to the dying outlaw.

"Go on . . . admit it," Karr persisted, coughing, wheezing.

"Yeah, you're right," said Rochenbach. "Looks like you've found me out, old-timer."

"I knew it," said Karr. He settled back and closed his eyes.

After a moment, Casings stood up, holding the whiskey bottle in his hand.

"He's gone," he said. He looked at Rochenbach and said, "He was talking out of his head, what he said about you."

"I saw no point in arguing with him," said Rock. "He's probably not the first man to ever suggest I'm still a lawman."

"If you were, you sure fooled the hell out of all of us," Casings said, seeing the Stillwater Giant walking up, carry the knocked-out blind man effortlessly in his arms.

Dismissing the matter, Rochenbach said, "We've got a problem."

"What's that?" Casings asked.

"I checked the bags," said Rochenbach. "There's nowhere near ten thousand dollars in them."

"There was that much," Casings said. "We both saw it. They didn't spend nothing for the whiskey and cigars."

"I know," said Rochenbach. He turned to his dun, pulled the saddlebags from across his saddle and pitched them to the Casings. "But it's gone. See for yourself."

Casings caught the saddlebags, opened them and looked inside, shaking three stacks of money around.

"Jesus, you're right," he said. He reached down into the bags and pulled up a handful of loose dirt and gravel. He let the dirt pour from his hand. "Whoever was carrying the bags was out to skin the others out of their share."

"That's how I figured it," said Rock. "But who did it? Was it Dirty Dave Atlo skinning Macon Ray and the others, or Ray doing the skinning after he got his hands on the money?"

"Looks like we'll never know," said Casings. He pulled up the three stacks of money, looked at them in disgust, then dropped them back in the bag. "We're down to three thousand, more or less. Grolin will throw a fit."

"How will he know it was ten or three?" Rochenbach asked, leading him toward something.

"Spiller, Shaner and Penta will all three say it was ten thousand when they get back," said Casings.

"I see what you mean," said Rochenbach, and he let it sit for a moment as the Giant walked up and settled the half-conscious Blind Simon in the chair on the porch.

"Maybe we just tell Grolin what happened: We followed Macon Ray here, but the money was gone."

"Take a thousand each and keep our mouths shut about it?" asked Rochenbach.

The Stillwater Giant stepped back off the porch and looked at them curiously.

"We're just talking about this money, Giant," said Casings. "Ray Silverette has shorted it down to three thousand dollars. We're saying split it three ways, to keep from having to explain things that wasn't our fault. What do you say?"

"I'm with you, Rock," said the Giant. "What do you say we do?"

"I'm with Pres," said Rochenbach.

"And I say we keep it," Casings cut in. "Besides, if Grolin hadn't cheated Dirty Dave out of his money last year, this wouldn't have happened."

"I get a thousand dollars, here and now?" asked the Giant.

"Yep, here and now," said Casings.

A broad grin came across the Giant's face.

"Give it to me, fellows," he said with no further hesitation.

"Rock, check your arm," said Casings, seeing the blood on Rochenbach's sleeve for the first time.

"I've got it," said Rock, loosening a bandanna from around his neck to shove down his coat sleeve onto his upper arm. "I took a graze a while ago," he said.

"Welcome to the fold," Casings said wryly. "Now you've shed your blood for Andrew Grolin, like the rest of us."

"That's right," said Rock. "Now I want to ride back to the Lucky Nut, see how much he appreciates it."

By the time Blind Simon Goss awoke, the Giant and Pres Casings had dropped the bodies of the three outlaws into an iron ore bucket tied off atop a steep set of rails that ran deep down into the hillside. The other two bodies they'd sent speeding down the rails in a flat cart that sat in front of the ore bucket.

"Adios, sons a' bitches," said the Giant, releasing the bucket's hand brake. Casings reached out with a knife and cut the short safety rope.

"It's better than any of you deserve," Casings said

to the rumbling iron bucket. He dusted his hands together.

The two watched the big ore bucket roll down the rails until it disappeared into the blackness. The rumble of the bucket on the rails still resounded as the two turned and walked away.

At the porch of the shack, they stood back watching Rochenbach press a wet cloth to Blind Simon's swollen face. Simon raised a hand and held the cloth in place.

"You upwinded me, didn't you?" Simon said to Rochenbach, who stooped beside the chair where the Giant had seated him.

"Yes, I did," said Rochenbach.

"What made you think to do that?" Simon asked.

"As soon as I heard that you're blind, I knew I couldn't slip up on you."

Simon chuffed and shook his head.

"You sound more like a damned lawman than most road agents I've known," Simon said.

"I used to be a lawman," said Rochenbach.

"What? *No*, don't tell me that!" Blind Simon said, sounding both amazed and disappointed. "I've been outthunk by a lousy lawman?"

"*Ex*-lawman," Casings said in a raised voice.

"Who's talking there? And why are you talking so damn loud?" Simon asked, turning his sightless eyes toward the sound of Casings' voice.

"It's Pres Casings. I work for Grolin," Casings said, still in a raised voice, stepping closer as if to make his presence more intimidating. "I was by here a long time ago. Remember?"

"Yeah, I remember," said Simon with a wince,

holding the wet cloth to his face. "My brain works fine. "Who's the stinking bastard beside you?" he asked. "The way he's breathing, he's taking up the air of three normal-sized men—sounds like a damn blacksmith's bellows."

The Stillwater Giant and Casings looked at each other.

"I'm Garth Oliver," said the Giant, the sound of his deep, strong voice causing Simon to jerk back in a start. "Most folks call me the—"

"The *Stillwater Giant*," said Simon, cutting him off, finishing his words for him. "I've heard of you. You are one big sumbitch, aren't you?"

"Bigger than most," said the Giant. "I can ride two horses side by side," he added.

"I bet either horse appreciates the other," Simon said with a chuckle.

The Giant looked puzzled for a second until he understood. He grinned.

"Yeah, I suspect they do," he said.

Rochenbach watched and listened.

"What do we need to do with you, Simon?" he asked.

"Put a bullet in my head," Simon said bluntly. "We lost here, fair and square. I beg no man's mercy."

"But you weren't with Macon Ray and his men when they robbed us," Casings cut in, still in a raised voice.

Blind Simon winced and lowered the wet cloth from his face.

"Will you tell this loudmouthed son of a bitch that I'm blind, not *deaf*?" he said to Rochenbach.

"He hears you," said Rochenbach. "But Pres is

right—you weren't with Macon Ray. We don't want to kill you." He paused and looked at Casings and the Giant. "We might need to hide out here ourselves sometime. You never know."

"You killed my pals, Hobbs and Karr," said Blind Simon. "They didn't rob you either."

"They were shooting at us," said Casings, his voice down to a normal volume.

Rochenbach noted that Casings didn't want to tell the man he'd killed one of his own pals.

"So was I," Blind Simon replied.

Rochenbach cut in, saying, "One of your pals shot himself. He was running with a cocked shotgun."

"That would be Hobbs," said Simon. As he spoke, he'd fished a pair of dark-lens wire-rim spectacles from his shirt pocket and put them on. "He was prone to that—a terrible practice." He shook his head in regret. "Who shot Karr?" He fished one of the cigars Macon Ray had given him from his shirt pocket and stuck it in his mouth.

Instead of answering, Rochenbach looked at Casings, judging how he would treat the matter.

"That's hard to call," said Casings, "everybody shooting the way we were."

Simon read the tone and pitch of his words.

"I hear you," he said. "You're telling me I killed him."

The three stood in silence while Simon sorted through it in his mind.

"Well," he said finally, taking a match from his shirt pocket, "if you're not going to shoot me, get the hell on out of here. I'm going to search around, find any whiskey left inside. Get myself drunk enough to monkey-pound a she polecat if I feel like it."

"You can ride into Central City with us," said Casings, "or on to Denver City, as far as that goes."

"Denver City, *ha!*" said Simon. "You know where they stick a blind man if they find one? The *crazy house*, is where." He struck the match and ran a finger out the length of the cigar. Finding the end of the cigar, he stuck the flame to it and puffed.

"We wouldn't let them," said Casings.

"*Huh . . . ,*" Simon chuffed dubiously. "I've heard that before." He blew out a stream of smoke.

"I'd give you my word," said Casings.

"Obliged," said Simon, "but I'll stick here. I'm alone here most times anyway. You just came by when Karr and Hobbs happened to be lying low with me. You want to do something kind for a *poor old blind man,* help me sort this shack into shape before you leave."

"We can do that," said Casings, "but you ought to think about our offer."

"I ever want to mosey down to Denver City, I know my way," said Simon. He gave a crooked smile, the cigar planted firmly between his teeth.

Casings and the Stillwater Giant looked at Rochenbach, as if asking if they should persist on the matter. But Rochenbach shook his head and nodded toward the shack.

"Come on, then, Simon, show us inside," he said. "We'll set this place up, but only if you'll allow us to stay here, we ever need to lie low."

"You've got a deal, *ex*-lawman," said Simon, leaning his chair forward and rising to his feet.

Chapter 13

On their way back to Denver City, the three avoided the trail they'd taken through Central City, lest someone recognize them and associate them with the bodies of Lonnie Bonham and Turley Batts left lying in the trail up at Apostle Camp. Instead, they rode wide of Central City and made camp outside the town of Idaho Springs.

The following morning, they rose early and rode east. Without pushing their horses, they saw the outskirts of Denver City rise in the long shadows of evening.

"Are we of one accord on everything, Giant?" Casings asked as the three rode abreast, watching the town grow up taller and wider atop the roll of the earth.

"Yeah, we're good," came the Giant's deep voice. "I'm not going to say anything I shouldn't, if that's something you're worried about."

"I'm not *worried*," Casings said. "But I am concerned."

"Ain't that about the same thing, Rock?" the Giant asked.

"It's close," Rochenbach said. "Pay attention, Giant. Hear him out."

"You got it," said the Giant. "I'm with you fellows. Whatever you tell me to say is how I'll tell it." He gave his wide, toothy grin. "Being big doesn't make me stupid."

Casings looked at Rochenbach, then back at the Giant.

"I know that, Giant," said Casings. "But we've got to go over this thing again—make sure we're all three telling Grolin the same thing. You've seen what he'll do to a man to get the truth out of him."

"Yeah, I know," said the Giant, his grin vanishing, replaced by a dead-serious expression.

"So," Casings continued, "we tell everything just like it happened, except we never knew exactly how much money was there . . . and it was on the trail behind Apostle Camp where we found the saddlebags. We all three found them with the money missing, instead of Rock finding them alone and taking all the suspicion on himself."

"I've been thinking about it, Casings," Rock said. "I don't mind telling Grolin that I found the bags on my own. He's not going to do anything to me, leastwise not until I've opened the safe for him."

"No dice," Casings said, shaking his head. "We all three took a cut, we all three put our necks on the same block. Right, Giant?"

"Right," Giant said. "Only, don't use a chopping block as an example." He gave a grin as he rubbed his thick neck.

"Sorry," Casings said with a short laugh.

Rochenbach looked at the two of them, almost feeling guilty that they were willing to lie for him.

"Obliged," he said quietly, not wanting to push the matter any further.

It was his job to gain their confidence. Still, deceiving men who had trusted him always left a bad feeling in his gut. He had to remind himself that in this case, it was not these two men he was after. In a sense, it wasn't even Andrew Grolin he was out to get.

He wanted to bring down the man who fed Grolin the information from inside the mint. That helped, he told himself. If there was any way for him to let these two off the hook when the time came, he would do so.

"This pretty much cinches things," he said. "It looks like we're going off on our own now for certain."

"Suits me," said Casings. "What about you, Giant?"

"Whatever Rock wants to do, I'll back him. You too," said the Giant.

"Too bad we can't pull Grolin's big job out from under him," Rock tossed in. "That would be a good one to start on." He looked at Casings. "You said you can get us information?"

"I can," said Casings.

"Find out who Grolin's man is inside the mint," he said. "If we can take this job over, we will. If we can't, we'll know who to contact next time."

Casings thought about it and said, "It'll be tough, but I'll get it. If not from Grolin, maybe from Penta or Shaner. He tells them things he wouldn't tell the rest of us. Grolin would never stand still for us using one of his contacts, now or ever."

"I wasn't planning on asking him," Rock said.

"How soon do we need to know?" Casings asked.

"The sooner, the better," said Rochenbach. "Once Grolin's *mint man* sees how easy it is to clean out the Treasury car, maybe he'll want to move on to some other big job. We bypass Grolin and that man will be all ours." Rock rubbed his thumb and fingertips together above his cutoff gloves. "When he knows I've got a knack for opening safes, he'll want to be as close to us as first cousins."

"That's to you, Rock," said Casings. "What's going to draw Giant and me as close as kin to this *mint man*?"

Rock looked them up and down. "There's nothing to keep you both from learning what I know about opening safes. I'm willing to teach you what somebody taught me. Is that what you want to hear me say?"

Both Casings and the Stillwater Giant smiled.

"I can't deny it," Casings said, "it's music to my ears."

They rode on toward Denver City at an easy gait, their horses' breath steaming in the chilled morning air. The last three miles, before they reached the trail leading to the Lucky Nut, they spotted Frank Penta, Bryce Shaner and Denton Spiller thundering toward them across a stretch of flatlands.

"Here comes our first test," Rock said to the other two. They stopped their horses on the trail and waited until the three outlaws rode up and slid their horses to a halt.

"Blast it, Casings," said Frank Penta, "where the

hell have you been? Grolin is walking up and down the walls! He told us to ride all night until we found you, dead or alive."

"We ran into trouble," Casings said.

Rochenbach sat watching, listening. His Spencer rifle lay across his lap. His hand rested on the small of the stock, his thumb near the hammer.

"Yeah? What kind of trouble?" Denton Spiller asked, eyeing Rochenbach sourly.

"We found Bonham and Batts lying dead on the trail down from Apostle Camp," he said.

Rochenbach saw the three outlaws give one another a guarded look. Giant and Casings saw it too.

"Hey! It's the damn truth," the Giant's big voice boomed out. He stepped his horse forward menacingly.

The three almost stepped their horses back. But they managed to hold ground long enough for Penta to raise a hand toward the Giant.

"Take it easy, big fellow!" he said. "We saw them lying there ourselves."

The Giant eased down and sat staring. Rochenbach stared with his hand still on his rifle.

"You did?" asked Casings.

"That's right, we saw them lying there," said Spiller. "Only difference is we rode on home like we was told to."

"We heard all the shooting coming down another trail," said Shaner. "It took us a while, but we crossed trails, rode over to see what it was about." He shook his head. "We figured you'd been there and was gone already. We kept expecting to catch up to yas along the trail back here."

Casings took an easier breath. Rochenbach let his thumb move an inch farther away from his rifle hammer.

"We went after the money," Casings said. "Couldn't see letting them get away with it."

"It was Dirty Dave Alto," said the Giant.

"I know," said Penta. "Dent here climbed down the rope hanging there and struck a match."

"Yeah," said Spiller, "Dirty Dave was hanging over a rock edge—deader than hell."

"Speaking of the money, where is it?" Shaner asked, looking their horses over for the saddlebags.

"It's gone," said Casings.

"Gone?" said Penta.

"You heard me," said Casings. He nudged his horse forward, through explaining himself. The others turned their horses and rode alongside him. Rochenbach and the Giant stuck close.

"We caught up to Macon Ray and two other bummers at Apostle Camp," he said. "They're dead. But we never found the money on them."

"Did you search around the old mines—?"

"We searched, Frank," Casings said flatly, cutting him off. "And that's all the talking we're doing for now. We've got to tell the whole story all over again to Grolin when we get there." He looked Penta up and down and said, "So, he's fit to be tied over us not riding straight back?"

Penta shrugged and said, "He knows what happened to Bonham and Batts. He was boiling mad because you didn't do like he told you. I expect he's settled some by now."

"He said, 'Escort you home,'" Spiller threw in to Casings, looking Rochenbach up and down. "He said bring you and Giant straight to him."

"What about Rock?" the Giant asked.

"I expect Rochenbach will have to see him when it's his turn," Spiller said scornfully. His face still carried the bruises Rochenbach had given him.

Rochenbach stared at him, making sure Spiller saw him looking at the long purple welt on the side of his head. Then he gave him a short, thin smile and turned his gaze back toward Denver City standing in the distance before them.

They rode on.

From his office on the second floor atop the Lucky Nut Saloon, Andrew Grolin looked out through a wavy windowpane and saw the riders approaching on the trail running west of town. Rochenbach, Casings and the Stillwater Giant rode at the head of the men. The others were gathered up loosely behind them.

"Well, well, Mr. Walker," Grolin said over his shoulder. "Speak of the devil, and who shall arrive . . . ?"

Behind him, the secretary to the director of the Denver Mint and Essay Office, Inman S. Walker, stood up from beside Grolin's desk and walked over beside him. Walker wore a fake goatee and mustache, a theatrical prop held in place by soft makeup wax. The unstableness of the mustache kept him pressing his fingertips to his mouth to keep it from dangling from his lip.

"So that is our burglar," he said, leaning forward and looking out the window. "And you have no doubt now that he is up to doing this job?"

"My men tell me he walked through Hercules Mining's safe like it was a lace curtain." He smiled proudly.

"Then I see no reason to put this off any longer, do you?" Walker asked.

"No," said Grolin, "we proceed now as planned. The next time you see me, I will have turned your share of the gold ingots into cash." He smiled and stuck his cigar into his mouth. "Unless you'd prefer to carry your loot around in a freight wagon instead of a leather satchel."

"A leather satchel will suit me fine," said Walker, stepping back from the dust-streaked window. "I have to admit, I'm still a little unsettled by this fellow being a former Pinkerton detective."

"Don't let it bother you," said Grolin. "I've had him checked head to toe. Everybody says the same thing. He's a straight-up *rogue*." Staring out the window at Rochenbach, he smiled and added, "I wish I had a dozen like him."

Walker gave him an apprehensive look, touching his fingertips nervously to his fake mustache.

"But you said after this is over . . ." He let his words trail.

"I know what I said, Walker," Grolin replied, taking his cigar from his mouth and holding it in the scissors of his thick fingers. "Don't worry about how I handle my employees. Don't worry about *anything*, except how you're going to spend all this big money."

He looked Walker up and down, then added, "Of course, I suppose the bulk of your loot will have to go to the Golden Circle Ring, eh?"

"How greatly I support the Golden Circle is entirely my own concern, Grolin," Walker said, jutting his chin.

"No offense," Grolin said with a slight chuckle. "We all have our vices."

"I hardly call supporting the Golden Circle a *vice*," said Walker. "We are the ideology that will lead this nation to its rightful place in history. Someday you will thank us for what we've done for this country."

"Yeah, yeah, whatever your world deserves," Grolin said dismissingly. He smiled and puffed on his cigar. "You best get out of here before these men arrive. They see the fake facial hair, they'll think you've gotten too personal with a groundhog."

"I don't find that sort of coarse frontier banter at all amusing," said Walker, again pressing his fingertips to his fake mustache. "But all the same, you're right, I should be going." He turned and picked up his coat and black derby hat from a chair.

"I'll see you again when we're both rich," Grolin said as Walker put on his coat and hat and headed out the door.

Once Grolin was alone, he looked back out the window, down at Rochenbach and his men as they rode up to the iron hitch rail out front and stepped down from their saddles.

Chapter 14

Out in front of the Lucky Nut, Rochenbach, Casings and the Giant tied their horses' reins and walked inside, following Spiller and Frank Penta.

As they crossed the floor toward the bar, Penta and Bryce Shaner directed Casings and the Giant toward the stairs up to Grolin's office. Spiller and the others veered over to the bar, keeping Rochenbach in their midst.

"What about Rock?" the Stillwater Giant asked, stopping at the foot of the stairs as if taking firm position on an issue. He looked at Penta standing before him and Casings, and at Shaner standing behind them. Both carried rifles in their hands.

"Let Spiller and the boys buy your pal a drink," Shaner said. His right hand held his Winchester in such a way that offered a quick rise to the Giant's chest if he wanted. Watching, Rochenbach saw his thumb slide over the rifle's hammer.

"Rock and I stick together," the Giant said in his

deep, strong voice. "If he stays down here and drinks, so do I."

"It that a fact?" said Shaner, raising his rifle an inch, threateningly. He gave the Giant a dark stare. "I didn't know you two were so sweet on each other."

The Giant returned Shaner's gaze. "I bet you didn't know I can turn a rifle barrel into a necktie either." He took a step toward Shaner, his big hands spread.

Casings saw fear sweep over Shaner's face, standing under the Giant's looming shadow. But fear or no fear, he knew Shaner wouldn't hesitate a second at pulling the Winchester's trigger.

"Hey, come on, big fellow!" said Casings, stepping in between the two, putting a flat hand on the Giant's stomach, as if to hold back a leaning boulder. "This isn't the time or place to go ruining a man's repeating rifle."

"Let him go," Penta said to Casings, in a calm but sinister tone, a sly half smile on his face. "Shaner and I can handle ourselves."

"So can I," Casings said, returning Penta's threat. His right hand wrapped around his gun butt. But he kept leaning, holding the Giant back, knowing if the big man wanted to, he could brush him aside.

Rochenbach shot a glance around at the other gunmen, aware they would side with Penta and Shaner when the shooting started.

"Hey, *Giant*," he called out from his spot at the bar, "can't I get myself a drink without you two hanging at my elbow?"

The gunmen around Rochenbach chuckled; Giant

heard them and gave Rochenbach a strange, hurt look.

Casings also shot him a look. But he quickly saw what Rochenbach was doing and he homed right in on it.

"Yeah, Giant," he said, "come on. Grolin wants to talk to us first, not him."

The Giant settled, stunned and red-faced at Rochenbach's words, and at the ripple of laughter from the other gunmen.

"You—you mean that, Rock?" he asked.

"Jesus! *Yes*, he means it, Giant," said Casings. He gave the Giant a friendly punch on his hard stomach. "What's he got to do to make you understand?"

"Is that right, Rock?" the Giant said, staring at Rochenbach with a hurt look.

Rochenbach didn't answer. He picked up a shot of whiskey Grolin's bartender poured for him and tossed it back. *Man, this hurts . . .* , he told himself. Seeing the look on the Giant's big, childlike face, he nodded toward the upper landing, where Grolin waited in his office.

"Get on up the stairs, Giant," he said. "We work for the same man, don't we?"

Watching through a peep-slot in his office wall overlooking the saloon, Andrew Grolin smiled to himself as he saw Rochenbach turn to face the bar for a refill. He stood watching a moment longer as the Giant and Casings walked up the stairs, Penta and Shaner front and rear of them. Then he slid the peep-slot shut and walked behind his desk as the sound of their boots wound the hallway and stopped at his door.

"Come in," he replied gruffly to the knock on his office door.

Frank Penta swung the door open and walked in, followed by Casings, the Giant, then Shaner, who closed the door and started over toward the desk with the others.

"That's all for you two," Grolin said to Penta and Shaner. "How far out did you run into my *missing* gunmen?" he asked as the riflemen started to turn and leave.

"Three miles, four maybe." Penta shrugged. He looked at Casings and added, "They were coming from the direction they should've been."

"Well . . . that's good to hear," said Grolin. He grinned, took a cigar from his coat pocket, sniffed it lengthwise and nodded Shaner and Penta on toward the door. "Take care of things, get ready to ride."

"Sure thing," said Penta, reaching for the door knob.

Ready to ride . . . ? Casings repeated to himself, curiously.

When the door shut behind them, Grolin noted the questioning look on Casings' face.

"Yeah, ready to ride. You heard me right," he said as if answering Casings' thoughts. "We're still doing business here. Did you think the world would stop because you two and Avrial Rochenbach weren't around to keep it rolling?"

"No," said Casings, "I was just curious, thinking you were talking about the big job."

"No, I wasn't," Grolin said in a short tone. He bit the end off the cigar and stuck it into his mouth. "Now, what the hell happened up there at Hercules?"

"It sounds like you already heard everything that happened," Casings answered, "except that Rock, the Giant and I went off after Macon Ray and his gunmen."

"Against my orders, you forgot to mention," Grolin added for him. "But I suppose that was all Rochenbach's fault?"

He pulled a match from inside his coat, struck it along the edge of his desk and lit his cigar. Casings watched, gauging Grolin's voice and demeanor, deciding he wasn't in any dark, terrible rage over what had happened. This was anger for the show of anger.

"No, it was *my* idea to go after them," Casings said.

"Yeah, mine too," said the Giant, "not Rock's."

"I saw how much money was in that safe, boss," said Casings. "I figured there was no way you'd want that much money to get away from you."

"So everything you two did, it was all for my sake, huh?" Grolin said dubiously.

"Not just for your sake," Casings said. "It was for all of us. Rock did say he couldn't let that much money slip through his hands—I couldn't blame him."

"Me neither," said the Giant.

"Sounds like you two are really sold on Avrial Rochenbach."

"We call him Rock," said the Giant.

"So I hear," said Grolin, still puffing.

Casings gave a shrug.

"You told us to keep an eye on him and tell you what we think," he said. "I figure you want the truth."

"I do," said Grolin, "so give it to me."

"The man is *damn good* at what he does," said Casings. "He opened that safe like it was never locked. When we found Bonham and Batts murdered and robbed, he threw right into the chase with us. When we caught up to Macon Ray and his men, Rock took them down while Giant and I kept the other three busy."

"I see," said Grolin, listening intently. "Let me ask you this. If he's so good, where the hell's the money?"

Casings and the Giant looked at each other.

"When we found them, the money was gone," said Casings. "That's all we can tell you about it."

"And you'd both tell me the same thing, if I had Penta and a couple of the boys work on your fingers and toes with a ball-peen hammer?" Grolin asked.

Casings withstood the harshness of the threat, feeling no real rage behind the gang leader's words.

"There's no other way we can say it, boss," Casings said. "It's all the sweet gospel truth."

Grolin stared them down and puffed on his cigar. He wasn't about to get any stronger with the Giant in his office, nobody covering him with a rifle or shotgun. If they were lying to him, he'd find it out in due time.

"It's near suppertime. Both of you get chowed down and tend to your horses," he said. "Get yourselves some rest and be ready to ride out tonight."

"Yeah, the big job . . . ," Casings said, smiling.

"Every job we do is a big job," said Grolin dismissingly. "You'll know where you're going once you get there."

Outside his office, Grolin stood on the landing at the handrail as the two men walked down the stairs toward the bar. He looked at the bar and gave a nod to Denton Spiller and a young gunman named Doyle Hughes, who stood flanking Rochenbach, rifles loosely in hand.

"Your turn, Rochenbach. Let's go," Spiller said, stepping back from the bar and gesturing Rock and Hughes to the stairs.

Rochenbach took his time, downing his shot glass of rye, timing it so he would cross paths with Casings and the Giant as they came across the floor.

"I said, let's go, *damn it!*" said Spiller. He started to grab Rochenbach by his arm, but the look Rochenbach gave him stopped him cold.

Above them, Grolin watched with a slight grin, seeing how expertly Rochenbach managed to take Spiller's temper to the boiling point, then defuse it as he saw fit.

You're good, Rock. That's for sure, Grolin told himself, watching Rochenbach turn from the bar and walk over to the staircase.

Rochenbach and the two riflemen stopped until Casings and the Giant stepped off the bottom stair and walked toward the bar. In passing, Rochenbach's eyes met Casings' for only a second. But in that second he saw Casings reassuring him that everything was all right. Grolin had no problem with them trying to retrieve the money—he had bigger plans in the making, Rochenbach decided.

Climbing the stairs behind Spiller, Rochenbach stared up at Grolin. When the three men topped the stairs and Spiller started toward the office door, Rochenbach stopped cold and looked at Grolin.

"Tell me, Grolin," he said, as Spiller turned around facing him, "am I working for you, or am I a prisoner here?"

"What a thing to ask, Rock," Grolin said cagily. "Of course you're working for me."

"Then why am I walking between these idiots?" Rock asked. "I know my way around."

Spiller and Hughes started to flare up, but Grolin stopped them both with a raised hand.

"All right, Dent, you and Hughes go back to the bar. We're good here."

Spiller stared coldly at Rochenbach, but he turned and gave Hughes a nod. Rochenbach and Grolin watched the two walk back down the stairs.

Grolin chuckled and said, "One word from me, Rock, Spiller would love to gut you." He turned, stepped over and opened his office door. "Why do you keep him so stoked up?"

"I don't know," said Rock. "I suppose because it's so easy to do."

Rochenbach followed Grolin inside the office. He took off his hat and stood at the front of his desk as Grolin walked around behind it. Grolin gestured toward a chair. Rochenbach seated himself as the outlaw leader sat down behind his wide oak desk.

"I've got no questions for you about the Hercules Mining money," Grolin said. "I figure anything Casings and the Giant didn't tell me, you won't tell me either. Anyway, it was a fluke, that much money being in the safe."

"Fluke money still spends," Rock said.

"Forget it," said Grolin. "The job was a practice run to see if you could open a Diebold safe."

Rochenbach only stared at him, confident.

"From what everybody tells me, you're the best," Grolin said.

"Obliged," said Rock. "But practice run or not, I hate losing that much money."

"So do I," said Grolin, "but it's over and done. I can't let it distract me from something bigger." He stuck his cigar in his mouth and stared knowingly at Rochenbach.

"So we're all set?" Rochenbach asked.

"Yep, Thursday night—four days from now, we ride," said Grolin. "There's a big shipment coming out. We're going to be waiting for it."

"All right," said Rochenbach, perking up in the chair. "Tell me all about it."

"Nothing to tell," Grolin said. He grinned and puffed on his cigar. "I've got everything covered. Now get out of here. Take a few days, rest, relax, enjoy everything the Lucky Nut has to offer. Come Thursday, be ready to ride out and make us both rich."

"It will be my pleasure," Rochenbach said, standing, putting his hat on and turning toward the door.

On the landing, Rock looked down at the bar but saw that all of Grolin's men were gone. *All right . . . ,* he told himself, heading down the stairs. He would find Casings and the Giant later. Right now he needed to report to his field superior, let him know that Thursday was set for the robbery. Other details he'd have to pass along as they came to him—*if* they came to him, he thought. If not, he was on his own. But that was all right. He was used to working alone.

Chapter 15

Leaving the Lucky Nut, Rochenbach walked his dun
to the livery barn. He slung the horse's saddle over
a rack and hung its bridle on a wall peg. He grained
and watered the hungry animal and wiped it down
with a handful of clean straw. He walked the dun
into a clean stall and pitched a fresh pile of hay at
its hooves. Patting its muzzle, he turned and left, his
Spencer rifle in hand.

After a meal of elk steak, beans and biscuits at
Turk's Restaurant, he drank a cup of hot coffee, paid
for his meal and left. As he walked along the dark
street back to his room at to the Great Westerner, he
thought about how he hadn't run into any of Grolin's
men—which was good, he reminded himself, enter-
ing the hotel lobby. Next door at the Lucky Nut, banjo
and twangy piano music spilled out into the chilled
night air as he closed the hotel door behind him.

Instead of going up the stairs to his room, Rochenbach slipped quietly through the hotel's main hallway and out the back door into a long alleyway that

would take him to the rear of the telegraph office unseen.

At the back door of the darkened building, Rochenbach looked all around, covered in the darker shadow of the doorway. Seeing nothing in the empty alleyway, he turned and deftly picked the door lock.

When he'd slipped inside and closed the door behind him, he looked around at the empty office and walked straight to the operator's desk. *Thursday . . . ,* he told himself, wishing he had more information to pass along. All right, it wasn't much. *But it's a start,* he reminded himself again. He leaned his rifle against the wall.

Instead of sitting down, he bowed over the telegraph operator's desk and clicked on the switch standing atop a brass-trimmed, oak battery case. He made three quick taps on the operator's key to ensure that both the key and the sounder were working properly. Then he clicked in the private identification code of his field supervisor.

Satisfied that the identification code was on its way, he quickly followed up, tapping out a six-word message in Morse code: *Train ride . . . Thursday night . . . all aboard.* He waited in the silence of the dark office for five minutes, then retapped the message. He stared intently at the sounder, waiting for a reply of any sort.

When no reply came, he tapped out the same message for a third time, hearing nothing in the silent office but the click of the telegraph key and the steady tick of a large clock hanging on the far wall.

Now what? he asked himself. Had the message gone through, gotten relayed on to its proper receiver? If so, why had his field office or even the supervisor himself not acknowledged him by now?

All right, send it again.

He began tapping out the message again—the same six words, once, twice, threes times. Then he straightened up from the desk and stared at the sounder, waiting. Still nothing. Too bad, he told himself. It was time to go.

He picked up his Spencer rifle from against the wall and started to reach out and tap in his own identification code, signaling that he had ended his message. But just as his fingers started to touch the key, the sounder suddenly came to life, tapping out a short unidentified message, meaning it could have come from anyone anywhere within range on the open wires.

Leaning back over the desk, Rochenbach listened closely, so as not to miss the message when it repeated itself. As soon as the tapping started again, he began translating the Morse code into words. But before he could get the first word spelled out, he heard something close behind him and he swung around, his rifle in hand.

"Quick, but not quick enough!" said Doyle Hughes, watching as Denton Spiller slammed the butt of his rifle full force into the side of Rochenbach's head.

Staring down at Rochenbach as he lay sprawled and unconscious across the operator's desk, Spiller grinned and lowered his rifle to his side. Next to Rochenbach, the telegraph key sat in silence, tipped over on its side, a wire having been pulled loose from the sounder.

"You can't believe how good that felt," he said to Hughes over his shoulder.

"You seemed to enjoy it *really* well," Hughes replied in the darkness, stooping down, picking up Rochenbach's rifle from the floor. He chuckled. "I don't ever want you carrying a mad-on like that at me."

"This bastard had it coming," said Spiller. He reached out and turned off the battery switch. "The only reason he's alive is that Grolin needs him. Soon as he's finished with him, he's all mine."

Hughes stepped in closer and looked at a trickle of blood running down the side of Rochenbach's face.

"Let's hope you haven't knocked his brain plumb out of his ears," he said.

"He's all right," said Spiller. "What did you hear him saying on this thing?" He nodded down at the telegraph key.

"He was spreading the word to somebody," said Hughes, "telling them our big job is all set for Thursday, the way I figure."

"Are you sure?" Spiller said.

"*Train ride, Thursday night, all aboard,*" Hughes said, repeating Rock's message. "What does that sound like to you?"

"Tickles the hell out of me," Spiller said, glaring down at Rochenbach. "Let's get this bastard up between us, drag him out of here. See what Grolin wants to do with him now."

"Man!" said Hughes. "I hope this ain't going to change our plans any."

"I can just about promise you it won't," said Spiller, reaching down, grabbing Rochenbach by the shoulder of his wool coat. "Grolin might walk away from that Hercules money, but he's not going to pass up a chance at the kind of money we're fixing to make."

"That's good to hear," said Hughes. Seeing Rochenbach's hat lying on the floor, he started to bend down and pick it up. But Spiller stopped him.

"Leave it," he said. "He's not going to need a hat, not for long anyways." He reached his boot out and kicked Rochenbach's slouch hat away.

Rochenbach awoke flat on his face in the dark, the sound of a large parade drum pounding inside his swollen head with each beat of his heart. He felt the vibration, the rumble and clack of steel rails racing along beneath him. Turning his face enough to look up, he saw the flare of a match followed by a glow of circling lantern light.

"Well, now, looks like our *tough guy* is finally waking up," said Spiller, seated on an empty nail keg near Rochenbach's throbbing head. "Can I get you something for the pain, *hoss*?" he asked, feigning concern. "I know how it feels getting smacked with a rifle butt, remember?" He patted the Winchester rifle lying across his lap.

The circle of lantern light clearly revealed Spiller's cruel grin. The shadowy faces of the other men stood in a half circle behind him. At the far end of the car, he saw the black shadowy outline of horses.

"Water—" Rochenbach said in a broken voice.

"What's that? You want some water?" said Spiller. He said to the others around him, "Hear that, fellows?

Any of yas got some water for an ol' ex-Pinkerton man? A dirty, rotten rat?"

Silence loomed for a moment beneath the rumble of the train. At floor level, Rochenbach saw stars and hill lines streak past the open doors on a blanket of purple darkness.

"Sorry, *Rock*, ol' hoss," said Spiller in a mocking tone. "Looks like no takers on your water request."

Rochenbach tried to push himself up off the floor on both palms.

"Obliged, all the same . . . ," he said in a pained voice.

"*Huh-uh*," said Spiller, slamming him back down beneath his boot. "You lie right there. The floor looks good on you."

Rochenbach groaned and rolled half over onto his side.

"Christ. I've got some water in my canteen he can have," said Doyle Hughes.

"He gets *no* water, Hughes," Spiller said firmly.

"It's not right, a man needing water and being denied it—"

"Hey, I've got an idea," Spiller said, cutting him off. He laid his rifle on the floor, stood up and said to Rochenbach, "You want water, I'll water you." He started unbuttoning the fly of his trousers.

"Cut it out, Dent," said Frank Penta, sitting back in the darkness against the wall of the rail car, staring out across the passing night. "I was told to deliver him in good condition, with a clear mind."

"Come on, Frank," said Spiller, a little upset. "I'm having some fun here. To hell with his clear mind and condition. You saw what this sumbitch done to me. I deserve my pound of flesh."

"He did nothing compared to what I'm going to do if you don't sit down and shut up."

The sound of a rifle cocking came out of the darkness from Penta's direction. The men all stepped back, making a wider circle.

"Whoa, now!" said Hughes, stepping quickly out of the way.

Spiller raised his hands chest high, his trousers halfway unbuttoned.

"All right, Frank, I'm down," he said, dropping onto his nail keg, his hands still up. "See? I'm seated here, just looking after the prisoner like I was told."

"Get your fly buttoned and see to it you keep it that way," Penta said. Under his breath, he said to Shaner, who sat silent in the dark beside him, "This crude, ignorant son of a bitch. . . ."

Spiller half stood and buttoned his fly. As he sat back down, he dealt Rochenbach a hard kick in his side.

Penta heard the kick, and the sound of Rochenbach's breath exploding from his chest.

"Damn it to hell," Penta said, rising, stepping forward into the circle of lantern light, Shaner right beside him.

"That was an accident!" said Spiller, looking up at Penta and Shaner. "They all saw it!" He gestured a hand toward the rest of the men gathered around the outside circle of light.

"Do we have to treat you like a damn kid, Spiller?"

Penta said. "Move away . . . go sit at the other end of the car."

Spiller saw the look in both Shaner's and Penta's eyes and realized he was in no position to argue.

"Okay, all right!" he said, standing, his hands raised chest high. He backed away and started to turn. But then he stopped suddenly, turned back around and took a step toward them. Both of their rifles swung up pointed at him and cocked.

"My gun?" he asked, a hand already out, reaching down for his Winchester lying where he'd left it on the floor.

Penta's boot clamped the rifle to the floor while Spiller stood frozen.

"Have you ever had smallpox, Spiller?" Penta said in a low, menacing tone.

"Smallpox? No," Spiller said, looking confused by the question.

"Then *right now* must be the closest you've ever been to dying," Penta said quietly.

Beneath their feet, the rumbling of the railcar only intensified the tense silence that fell over the men.

Finally, Doyle Hughes ventured into the silence in a hushed tone.

"Get it later, Dent," he said. "Now's a bad time to reach for it."

Spiller wiped his cold, sweaty palms on his trousers and backed away slowly.

"All right, Frank," he said warily. "Grolin put you in charge of him. I respect that."

Penta and Shaner stood in silence until Spiller backed out of the light and sank into the darkness.

On the floor, Rochenbach coughed and groaned.

Looking down at him, Penta said to Hughes, "Doyle, give Rock some water."

As Hughes stooped down and held a canteen to Rochenbach's parched lips, Penta uncocked his rifle and sat down on the nail keg. He laid his rifle across his lap. Shaner stood beside him, swaying slightly with the rhythm of the rolling train.

When Hughes had finished giving Rochenbach a long drink, he watched as Rock wiped a coat sleeve across his lips.

"Obliged," Rochenbach said in a raspy voice.

Hughes only nodded; he stood up and stepped back, capping his canteen.

Penta and Shaner observed Rochenbach closely. As Hughes backed away, Penta raised an ill-rolled cigarette to his lips, struck a match, lit it and shook out the match.

"I don't get you, Rochenbach," he said, dropping the burnt match and crushing it beneath his boot. "You come up here with skill that most long riders would sell their mother for. Grolin puts you into a job that'll pay more than most thieves make in their life. . . ."

He let the conversation hang while he took a long draw on the cigarette and blew it out.

"Instead of coming in and being one of us, what do you do? You start right off agitating, getting men like Spiller and Shaner here wanting to kill you."

"You're wanting . . . to kill me, Shaner?" Rochenbach said, turning his swollen head, looking up at Shaner through a purple half-closed eye.

"I wouldn't mind," Shaner said matter-of-factly.

"You need to do it now," Rochenbach said. "This is the only way . . . you'd ever be able to get—"

"See? There you go again," Penta said with a chuff, cutting him off. He held Shaner back with the side of his arm. "I'm starting to think you're one of them hardheaded sumbitches can't leave well enough alone. Got to always pick at somebody."

"That's me all over," Rock said. He noted the rifle on the floor, but knew it would do him no good, not now, not against this many guns. Besides, this game wasn't over. He needed to find out what these men knew, so he could plan his next move.

"We all know how good you are at what you do," Penta said. "Why couldn't you just take your cut like everybody else? Why'd you tip off your pards, try to bring them in and steal this job from Grolin?"

"Is that what you think I was doing?" Rock asked, feeling better.

"Hughes knows Morse code," said Penta. "He heard your message."

Rochenbach looked at Hughes.

"Train ride . . . Thursday night . . . all aboard?" said Hughes. "Sorry, Rock, I heard what I heard."

Rock looked at Penta and said, "What if I said he was mistaken?"

Penta blew out a stream of smoke.

"You'd be lying," he said flatly, "and Doyle here would get his feelings hurt."

Rock settled back on the floor of the railcar and closed his eyes.

"Where are we going, Penta?" he asked civilly.

"We're going to meet Grolin," said Penta. "You're still going to open that safe."

"Tonight?" said Rochenbach, opening his eyes. "He told me Thursday."

"He lied." Penta gave him a short grin.

"Whose train is this one?" Rock asked, gesturing a hand around the swaying railcar.

"It's *ours* now," Penta said. "So is the engineer, until we let him go."

"I see . . . ," Rochenbach said. He closed his eyes again and relaxed as the train rumbled on through the night.

PART 3

Chapter 16

The Stillwater Giant stepped down from the seat of a buckboard wagon on the edge of a cutbank cliff, peering at the long uphill rail grade in the pale moonlight. Beside the wagon, Casings sat atop his horse, holding the reins to a large Belgium draft breed beside him.

He handed the Giant the big Belgium's reins as the wagon turned a wide circle and rolled away along the trail bordering the cliff.

"Try not to wear him out first thing," Casings said to the Giant.

"I won't," the Giant said. He took the powerful horse's reins, but did not step up into the saddle. He had ridden there in the wagon to save the horse's strength, knowing the toll his enormous size and weight could take on an animal in a short period of time.

After a moment of silence, Casings turned in his saddle and looked at him beside him, almost at eye level, even with the Giant standing on the ground.

"You're worried, ain't you?" Casings said.

"Not about this job," the Giant said. "But yeah, I'm worried some."

They both looked off up the grade toward a thick stand of trees, where they knew Grolin and his men were waiting in the darkness.

"He's all right," Casings reassured him. "You know Grolin's not about to harm him so long as he needs him to open the safe."

"I know," said the Giant, "but that time is running out. What'll happen after he opens it?" He let out a tense breath. "Anyway, where is he? I don't like the way things are going."

"Neither do I," said Casings, "but I'm betting Rock has things under control. Let's not forget who we're talking about here." He grinned and added, "Rock is no shrinking violet."

The Giant spread his wide, big-toothed grin in response.

"I haven't forgot," he said fondly. "I know he kept me from getting bit by rattlesnakes."

"I was there," Casings reminded him. He stared both ways along the uphill grade, feeling the excitement of the job closing in around him.

The Giant stood in silence for a moment until apprehension slipped back into his mind.

"But damn it, where is he?" his deep voice burst out as if he were no longer able to contain it.

"Shhh, take it easy," said Casings. "Rock is all right. If I had to guess, I'd say he's on the train, coming this way right now." He nodded toward the black-purple distance.

"So, you think Grolin believes us about the Hercules Mine money?" the Giant asked.

"About halfway," Casings said. "Grolin's no fool. But he saw that this was a case where he couldn't accuse us of something without blaming Rock. He couldn't afford to do that—not now anyway."

"I hope you're right," the Giant said.

After a moment of silence, Casings said, "Yeah, so do I."

"There's the signal!" the Giant said suddenly, pointing farther up the grade where Grolin and his men were able to see out over the treetops and catch the first glimpse of a train rounding into sight from the west.

"It's about damn time," said Casings, reaching up and pulling his faded bandanna over the bridge of his nose. "Get your mask on," he said to the Giant, as if the big man's size alone wasn't enough to identify him.

Giant pulled his mask up. He'd had to tie two bandannas together end-to-end to comfortably encircle his big head. He wore the knot across the bridge of his nose, a point of each bandanna hanging down covering either cheek, still exposing his big, grim mouth.

"Ready to ride," he said, swinging up atop the big Belgium draft horse. Casings struck a match, cupped his hand behind it and waved it slowly above his head. Then he blew it out, dropped it and looked the Giant up and down. Noting the two bandannas, he chuffed and shook his head a little as they turned the horses toward a thin, winding path leading down to the rails.

———

At the high end of the long incline, Grolin saw the flare of the match and lowered the lantern he'd used to signal Casings and the Giant. He killed the lantern light and handed it over to Lambert Kane, one of the two Kane brothers seated in the wagon beside him. Lambert took the lantern and stood it on the floor of the buckboard between his boots.

"Take it on down, Bobby," Grolin said to the younger of the brothers.

"You heard him, little brother, let's roll," said Lambert, a long shotgun standing from his thigh.

The younger man slapped the reins to the wagon horses' backs and sent them bolting forward.

"*Yeehiii!* Yes, sir, brother Lamb!" he called out above the pound of hoof and the creak of wagon. "Let's go make ourselves rich!"

"Make our mama *proud*!" said Lambert, grinning, bouncing and swaying on the hard wagon seat.

"Make our pa smile down upon us, *rest his soul*!" said Bobby, the buckboard sliding a little sidelong on the steep treacherous path.

"Or *up* at us," said Lambert.

"Whichever the case may be!" said Bobby, the wagon rumbling on.

Stupid rube bastards . . . , Grolin told himself as the wagon disappeared down the dark hillside. He'd already made a mental note—he needed to thin out his crew once this job was finished. *Wait!* What the hell was he thinking? he corrected himself. After this job, he was out of this frontier squalor for good.

Damn right. . . . He bit the tip off a cigar, stuck it in

his mouth and turned his horse to the same trail, now that those inbred Kane idiots were far enough down to not run over him.

In the glow of firelight from the open grate on the engine's big iron boiler door, the train engineer looked over his shoulder at the fireman, Tom Bratcher. As the train slowed down with a lurch and started up the long uphill grade, Bratcher stood with a shovel in his hands, wearing a pair of elbow-length leather stoker gloves.

"I'll fill her some more, you want me to," Bratcher said.

Neither man heard Pres Casings and the Stillwater Giant ride up alongside the slowing train and scramble from their saddles onto the front platform of the disguised U.S. Treasury transport car.

"She's as good as you can make her for now," said the engineer, Odell Cheney, above the roar of the rails and the billowing fire in the boiler furnace.

"All right, then," said the fireman. He shoved the iron door closed with the toe of his boot and stuck his shovel in its slot on the wall.

"You best go wake the captain," Cheney said over his shoulder. "He said we should wake him at Signal Hill."

"I'll do it," said Bratcher, taking off the long, thick gloves and hanging them beside his shovel. "I don't know what he's doing here, to be honest with you," he said. "I don't even know if he's a real army captain, him and his boys not wearing uniforms. It don't seem right."

"Just wake him up," said Cheney. "I'm learning that what's *right* at breakfast is *wrong* by suppertime these days."

Shaking his head, the fireman stepped out of the engine, walked around the walkway and into a mail car.

"Ain't nothing like it's supposed to be no more," he grumbled under his breath.

He walked through the middle aisle of the loaded mail car and out onto its rear platform. On either side of the train, he saw the night moving slower and slower past him. The train shuddered beneath his feet.

When he'd walked past a freight car to a passenger car, Pres Casings and the Giant slipped from the shadows and went to work. Casings tied a safety rope around the Giant's waist and tied the other end of it to the handrail. The Giant stepped down between the two cars holding a can of oil and stood over the iron link pin connector that held the cars together. He stooped and poured the oil down into the connector while Casings watched from the swaying platform. Then he grinned, raised an arm and made a muscle.

"Don't fool around, Giant!" Casings said in a hushed tone, unheard by the rumble of the train.

The Giant stooped down over the iron pin holding the two cars together and wrapped his huge fingers around a steel ring that ran through the round head of the pin. Then he took a deep breath and pulled up on the pin with all of his enormous strength.

"*My God!*" Casings whispered to himself in awe,

seeing the iron pin rise upward slowly in spite of the weight of the two rail cars pulling against it. The Giant stood up with his wide grin and stepped quickly onto the platform, iron pin in hand, as the iron oblong link holding the cars together slid open and the cars separated slowly.

"I done good for us, huh?" said the Giant.

"Yeah, Giant, *real* good," said Casings.

Closing the mail car door behind himself, the fireman stepped inside a passenger car. His entrance wasn't quick enough to keep the sound of the rails from reaching inside and waking up a tough-looking young army captain lying sprawled in a seat, his army carbine across his knee. His head had lolled with the rhythm of the train until he jerked up with a start. The carbine swung up, pointed at the fireman.

"Don't shoot, Captain Boone!" the fireman cried out. "You said to wake you and your men when we reached Signal Hill."

"Right you are," said the captain, springing up from his seat. In the seat behind him, a man a few years his senior awoke and stepped out into the aisle, also carrying a carbine. He shook the shoulder of one of the two men in the seat behind him. In all, Captain Boone and five riflemen arose from their seats and took quick stock of themselves.

The fireman stared at them from the car door. The men all wore riding dusters and slouch hats. They busily gathered carbines, saddlebags and checked their big Colt sidearms.

"Not a uniform amongst 'em." He shook his head and grumbled under his breath. "There's nothing right about it."

Turning to the fireman, Captain Boone looked him up and down and said, "That will be all, sir."

As the fireman turned and left, Captain Boone called out to the five men as they finished preparing themselves for the trail.

"All right, troopers," he said. "This be just a trial run, but let's treat it like it's the real thing, because Thursday night it will be." He looked around over his shoulder as if to make certain no one was listening. Then he turned to the sergeant beside him and said, "Sergeant Goodrich, proceed with the exercise."

"All right, men," said the sergeant, "we're going up Signal Hill—the most likely place for a robbery. You heard my captain, tonight is a trial. When the time comes, three of you will be positioned on and around the Treasury car. But rather than reveal ourselves tonight, we'll proceed to our horses, ready them for the trail and stand by." He looked back and forth. "Are you men ready to chase outlaws?"

"Yes, Sergeant," the four men replied as one.

Beside the sergeant, a young corporal named Thomas Rourke stood awaiting an order.

"Corporal Rourke," said the sergeant.

"Yes, Sergeant." The corporal snapped to attention, standing in his long trail duster and slouch hat. He stood with the bearing of a military man in spite of his civilian trail clothes.

"Lead these men to the Treasury car as if we were

under attack. Proceed to the freight car, check your mounts and stand by."

"Yes, Sergeant," said the corporal. He turned quickly to the three riflemen.

Standing beside the captain, the sergeant said sidelong under his breath, "Captain, if I may speak?"

Captain Boone only nodded.

"This is a load of bull, Captain," said Goodrich. "These men need no *practice* exercise. These are crack troops."

"I am aware of that, Sergeant," said Boone. "But these are the orders. Tonight through Wednesday night, we will go through our exercises—prepare to expect the unexpected, as General Edwards always says."

"Yes, sir, of course, sir," the sergeant said. He looked himself up and down, his riding duster, his slouch hat in his right hand.

"Sergeant Goodrich, come quick! Our horses are gone!" Corporal Rourke called out from the rear platform through the open door.

"What the—" The sergeant rushed through the open car door, Captain Boone right behind him. Shoving their way past the three riflemen, both men stood beside the corporal, staring down the dark, empty tracks behind them. "The whole blasted train *is gone!*" the sergeant said.

"Son of a bitch," said Captain Boone in a low, even tone. "This is no longer a *training exercise*. Rourke, go tell the engineer to stop this train." He looked around at the other men while the corporal hurried back through the long, empty car. "Sergeant Goodrich, you and your men follow me." Before the sergeant could say a word, the captain jumped down from the platform onto the tracks and faded into the darkness behind the train.

"All right, you heard him, troopers," the sergeant bellowed to the men. "Does my captain have to do this job alone? Follow me!" He leaped out onto the tracks, his long duster tail flaring out behind him like wings. The other three men held their carbines high and followed close behind him.

Chapter 17

As the four severed rail cars slowed to a halt and began rolling backward down the long grade, the Stillwater Giant and Pres Casings hurried into the freight car that housed the soldiers' horses. The animals were rested, saddled and ready to ride.

"Holy Moses," said the Giant, "there's a posse on the train. They were aiming to ambush us! How'd they know about this job?"

The two stood staring, stunned for a moment at their discovery. Finally Casings pushed his hat brim up and grinned at the Giant, looking relieved.

"I don't know," he said, "but let them wait." He nodded toward the far end of the car.

Leaving the freight car, the two hurried down the aisle of the loaded mail car and out the rear door. They stood for a moment looking at the big Treasury car swaying along behind them.

"You can bet there's guards waiting for us in there," Casings said in a whisper.

"You suppose Grolin figured on it?" the Giant asked.

"If he didn't, he'd better," said Casings. "Come on. Watch your step."

The two crossed onto the Treasury car platform and climbed the iron brakeman ladder to a catwalk running the length of its roof. They hurried in a crouch along the swaying walkway and climbed down at the other end as the separated cars continued gaining speed, rolling backward.

Nearing the bottom of the grade, the two saw a lantern wave back and forth slowly in the air, where another set of iron rails intersected with the track. The intersecting rails ran seventeen miles north to a siding depot at an abandoned trade settlement.

"Looks like Grolin's right on time," Casings said to the Giant. Then he glanced at the rear of the Treasury car and said, "Keep your gun on that door, in case anybody inside wants to give us some guff."

The Giant drew a big Army Colt from under his coat and turned facing the back door of the car. The large Colt looked like a child's toy in the Giant's enormous hand.

"Anybody *inside* there better stay *inside*, until we tell them otherwise," the Giant said, loud enough to be heard by anyone listening on the other side of the thick railcar door.

As the cars coasted into a wide swing onto the siding tracks, a young thief named Lionel Sharp ran forward with the switchman's lantern and rifle in hand.

"Going my way?" he said, joking as he swung himself onto the platform beside Casings and the

Giant. The Giant grabbed the young man's shoulder and steadied him until he secured his footing.

"Depends on where you're going," Casings replied, recognizing the man.

The Giant gave his big grin and said, "And what you're going to do when you get there."

Casings looked him up and down, took the lantern he was holding and hung it on an iron hook beside the rear car door.

"Well, Sharp," he said, "it looks like you finally landed yourself work with some real long riders."

"Yeah, and I can tell you, I'm damned grateful for it," said the young outlaw. "I'm so sick of working with rubes and pumpkin busters. . . ." He leaned forward and looked around Casings at the Giant. "You must be the Stillwater Giant. I've heard so much about you," he said.

"What tipped you off?" the Giant asked with a flat, harsh expression.

Sharp stared up at the huge man, not knowing what to say.

Finally he managed "I—I didn't mean nothing—"

"He's funning with you, Sharp," Casings said, cutting the young outlaw off before he embarrassed himself.

Sharp looked relieved. "I'm mighty glad of that," he said.

"Tell me, Sharp," Casings said, "how many of you Denver City boys did Grolin bring in on this?"

"I don't know. Seven, eight maybe?" said Sharp, estimating. He shrugged. "I see some faces here that I've never seen before."

"Jesus . . . ," said Casings, shaking his head, staring ahead into the darkness as the loose cars slowed to a crawl along the iron rails.

As the train rounded a long turn in the darkness, the Giant nodded toward a glaring headlight shining through a stand of pine.

"Here comes our ride now," he said to the other two, even as they themselves spotted the huge outline of a train engine pushing a single freight car back toward them. Smoke billowed up from the engine's stack.

"Watch the bump," Casings cautioned the younger outlaw standing beside him.

"You don't have to worry," Sharp rattled on nervously. "I learned the hard way about holding on back last year when I was working with some of the—"

"Shut up," Casings said, cutting him off. "Pay attention here." He turned and took the lantern down from the hook and held it ready.

The three watched as an engineer backed the engine and its one car closer to the severed cars, slowing, judging as the three cars rolled forward at a snail's crawl. By the time the sets of link pins met and touched against each other, the engine had actually braked and started forward just enough to make a smooth, easy connection.

"Way to go, hoss," the Giant said to the engineer under his breath. He jumped down from the platform on the ground beside the railcars and stepped between them close enough to line up the link and stick the pin down to hold the cars together.

"All right!" Casings said with a gleam in his eyes.

"Let's get out of here and start robbing." He held the lantern out sidelong and waved it up and down. From a rear door on the freight car, Grolin stepped out into the night, carrying a lantern of his own. In seconds the engine started pulling faster on the level terrain.

"Where's Rock?" the Giant asked Grolin as he swung up from the ground and joined the others on the rear of the freight car.

"He's close by, waiting safe and sound—itching to get to work as soon as we bring him this nice big Treasury car," Grolin replied. Holding the lantern up and looking at Lionel Sharp, he said, "You're Sharp, right?"

"Yes, sir, Mr. Grolin, I'm Lionel Sharp," the young gunman said proudly. He started to say more, but Grolin cut him off.

Behind Grolin two riflemen rushed out of the freight car and stepped over onto the Treasury car platform.

"Go with these men," he said to Sharp. "The three of yas guard the rear door."

"Come on, hurry up," said one of the riflemen, already headed up the iron rungs toward the catwalk on top of the car.

Sharp hurriedly followed the riflemen.

As the three moved out of sight, Grolin gave a shrug and smiled in the glow of lantern light.

"These farm boys and guttersnipes are showing up younger all the time," he said. "Crime is about the only thing that pays these days." He looked at Casings and the Giant and said, "Did everything go as expected?"

"Yes, it did," Casings said. "But I need to tell you, there were guards or lawmen of some kind waiting to ambush us. We've got their horses in a freight car behind us."

"Well," Grolin chuckled, "if we've got their horses, I fail to see them as a problem."

"Just thought you'd want to know," said Casings.

"You're right. Good work," said Grolin. "We'll chase the horses away when we stop and unload the gold."

Behind Grolin, Frank Penta and Bryce Shaner appeared out of the freight car, their rifles at port arms. They followed Grolin over to the rear door of the Treasury car. Grolin looked around at Casings, the Giant and the other two gunmen. He smiled as he took a piece of paper from inside his coat and unfolded it in the light of the lantern.

"I love this part," he said, holding the paper up toward the car door.

"Hello, you two guards *inside the car*," he called out loudly enough to be heard through the thick closed door. "Hello? *Hello*?"

When no one answered, he called out, "Don't be bashful, now. Just answer right up when I call out your names." He consulted the piece of paper, then called out confidently, "Peter Joseph Campbell. Husband of Barbara Mae Campbell, father of two sons and one daughter, whose names I can also give you . . ."

Inside the car, the gunmen heard a rustle and the frightened whisper of lowered voices.

Grolin grinned and continued, "Alvin Carter, husband of Lynn Ann Carter. Father of a—"

"Hold on, mister!" a voice said through the door, cutting him off. "We're coming out!"

"Leave your guns on the floor," Grolin called out. He pulled his bandanna up over his nose and stepped back, watching Penta's and Shaner's rifles cover the door as it opened slowly and two men stepped up, their hands raised in the air.

"Here's where you get off, fellows," Grolin said, shoving them toward the iron step on the side of the platform. "Hurry up now, jump, before we gain any more speed."

The two men made their way down onto the step and leaped out, away from the moving train. They landed rolling alongside the track and came to their feet just before vanishing into the darkness.

"That's how easy it is," Grolin said, "when you have the right information at your fingertips." He laughed aloud and said joyously, "*Bless you*, Inman Walker!"

"Who?" said Casings.

Grolin had made a slip of the tongue; he caught his mistake quickly and said, "Nothing, forget it!" He turned and called out toward the woods at the two fleeing men, "If we see you come out of there, you're both dead!"

But the Giant and Casings had clearly heard the name, and they weren't about to forget it. They looked at each other guardedly, on into a dark stand of timber and through the purple darkness as the train continued on.

Rochenbach sat with the other men inside the dusty, abandoned depot. They had arrived in the night after forcing the engineer to drop the rest of his train mid-run and bring them and their freight car to the old trade settlement. On their train ride across a stretch of rolling plains, Penta and Shaner had kept watch on him, seeing to it that Dent Spiller left him alone.

But when they'd meet Grolin at the depot, and Penta and Shaner had both left with him on the engine to go meet the stolen Treasury car, Rock saw the gunman stand and start walking toward him with a dark look on his face.

But before he'd taken three steps, Doyle Hughes and another man stood up facing Spiller, their rifles at port arms.

"Put it out of your mind, Spiller," Hughes said firmly.

"To hell with it," Spiller said, turning away from Rochenbach, going instead to the depot door and looking out through the dirty broken glass. "I'm just restless, tired of waiting. I need something to do."

"You can go sit in the woods with the Kane brothers, help them tend to the wagon," Hughes said.

"Yeah, and you can go to hell," Spiller said over his shoulder. "I steer clear of the Kanes." He looked back out the dirty glass window.

Hughes lowered his rifle and leaned back against the wall.

"Here they come!" Spiller said, seeing the first glimmer of headlight show brokenly through the trees.

The men stood up, moved to the depot door, opened it and filed out.

"Everybody get their horses and get ready," Hughes said. "I'll signal the Kanes to bring the wagon up to the loading platform." He looked at Rochenbach and said quietly, "Rock, you come with me."

"Best watch him close, Doyle, in case he tries anything," Spiller warned.

"Jesus . . ." Hughes shook his head. "He's not going to *try anything*." He looked at Rochenbach and gestured him toward the open door. "He wants to get paid just like the rest of us, right, Rock?" As he spoke, he picked up a glowing lantern sitting on the dusty floor.

"You know it," Rochenbach said, walking out into the chilled night air.

Hughes raised the lantern and swung it back and forth toward the pines. In a moment, the Kane brothers rolled out of the woods in the freight wagon and came rolling up onto the loading platforms.

The four other men who'd waited inside the depot gathered around the empty wagon and stared toward the headlight breaking through the dark woodlands toward them.

The engineer slowed the engine and led the four-car train—the Treasury car, the car carrying the soldiers' horses, the mail car and an empty caboose—to a soft stop, sidling along the freight platform.

Grolin stepped down from the engine with his bandanna still hiding his face, his right hand clasped on the engineer's shoulder. He gave the engineer a shove.

"You did good. Now get out of here," he said. "You can tell your grandkids you were robbed by the James Gang."

"I—I can go?" the engineer asked in disbelief.

"That's right," said Grolin, "but if I look up and see you again before you get to those pines, I'll put a rifle slug through your backbone."

Without another word, the man turned and ran. Leaping down off the loading platform, he raced wildly toward the woods until the darkness engulfed him.

Grolin turned to Hughes and Rochenbach. Casings and the Stillwater Giant stepped down from the short train and walked toward them.

"Get started, *Rock*," Grolin demanded, waving Rochenbach toward the Treasury car with his rifle barrel. "It looks like whoever you tried to tip off didn't get your message."

"I wasn't tipping anybody off, Grolin," Rochenbach lied. "The message I sent had nothing to do with this job. If I tipped somebody off, where are they?" He gestured all around.

Grolin chuckled and said, "It doesn't matter now. If they *do* show up, it will be Thursday night. We'll be long gone away from here."

Casings and the Giant walked up in time to hear the end of the conversation.

"What's he talking about, Rock?" the Giant asked.

"Your pal, *Rock* here, got caught trying to tell some friends of his about this job, Giant," Grolin said. "Tell him, Hughes."

"It's true," said Hughes. "Spiller and me caught him sending a message. I know Morse code."

"I don't give *a damn* if you know the emperor of China," said the Giant. "I'll rip your head off and roll it like a—"

"Hold it, Giant," said Rock, looking around and seeing the men level their rifles toward the Giant as if Grolin had given them direction to do so. "This is no place for us to start fighting among ourselves. I came here to open a safe." He turned quickly to Grolin. "Am I going to do it, or not?"

"You can *bet* you are," Grolin said, lowering his rifle. He jerked a nod toward the Treasury car. "Go on, we're right behind you."

Chapter 18

Inside the Treasury car, in a glow of lantern light, Grolin and the men stood back and watched in awe as Rochenbach held the end of his stethoscope to the steel safe door. Grolin held a rifle in his left hand; in his right, he held Rock's big black-handled Remington.

Rochenbach knew he'd gone past the point of turning back on this job. He had no idea what the reply to his telegraph message had been. Spiller's rifle butt had cut his communication short. But at least he'd heard enough to know that his message had gotten through. Everything beyond that was pure speculation. Since he didn't close the message with his identification code, he wasn't sure what action would be taken.

At this point, he supposed it didn't mater. He couldn't put off opening the safe. The best outcome would be to find the big safe empty, meaning someone had stopped the shipping of any more bullion until the risk of robbery had been removed. Was that too much to hope for? he asked himself, adjusting the earpieces of the stethoscope in his ears.

Only one way to find out. . . .

He turned the dial slowly, listening intently through the stethoscope to the sameness of metal tapping metal until he heard a gap, followed by a slightly harder bump as one piece of the polished steel puzzle fell into place. *All right. . . .*

He stopped suddenly, let out a breath and took a short pencil from inside his coat pocket. He wrote down the number on the dial of the safe door, then started turning the dial backward to the left, listening again.

Outside the car on the loading platform, the Kane brothers sat waiting in the empty freight wagon.

"What the hell is taking so long in there?" Lambert shouted toward the open car door.

Inside the car, Rochenbach turned a disturbed look to Grolin as he scribbled the second number on the door of the safe.

Grolin shot the same expression to Spiller, standing beside him.

"Go shut that damned lunatic up!" he said in a hushed growl.

Spiller slipped quietly out of the car. Rochenbach turned back to the safe, pencil stub and stethoscope in hand, and turned the dial slowly to his right.

Grolin grinned and let out a breath of relief when he watched Rock write a third number on the door near the dial and straighten up and pull the stethoscope from his ears.

"Is that it?" he said in a hushed tone, stepping forward.

"Yep," said Rochenbach. "It's all yours. He took the big iron handle with both hands and swung the big steel door open.

"*Holy Moses!*" Grolin shouted. He turnèd to Lionel Sharp, who stood holding the lantern, and said, "Here, give me that!"

In his excitement, he shoved Rochenbach's big Remington down into Sharp's coat pocket and snatched the lantern from his hand. "Everybody stay behind me!" he said, hurrying forward, seeing the light of the lantern spill into the dark safe, revealing shelf upon shelf of small wooden crates.

Looking back at the men crowded behind him, Grolin spotted the Stillwater Giant and waved him forward.

"Open one of these, Giant. Let's take a look," he said in an excited voice.

The Giant stepped inside the huge safe, picked up the nearest ingot crate and slammed it to the floor. The lid of the crate split and came ajar. The Giant stooped down, ripped the lid the rest of the way off and threw it aside.

"My God! No, Giant, don't!" Grolin yelled. But he was too late to stop the Giant, who stood up and turned the crate upside down at chest level. The men stared wide-eyed as sawdust packing spilled out of the crate, followed by a downpour of gold ingots that clunked and rang and bounced and slid away all over the floor of the safe.

"Put it all back in the crate!" yelled Grolin to the

men as they feverishly scrambled and snatched up the spilled ingots. "We don't split it up until we're away from here!"

"Want me to open some more?" the Giant asked.

Grolin just gave him a burning stare.

Rock slid one of the ingots to the side and stood with his boot covering it until the men moved forward to put the ingots back into the crate. Then he stooped down, picked up the ingot, dropped it down his boot well and stood up quickly.

As the men gathered close together, dropping ingots back into the crate, Rock reached out unseen, lifted his Remington from Sharp's coat pocket and slid it into the belly holster beneath his coat. In the young man's excitement over the gold, the missing weight of the big gun went unnoticed.

"Everybody back away!" Grolin shouted, waving his rifle across the front of the men, forcing them out of the huge safe. "We're going to get these crates out of here and loaded on the wagon! Everybody's going to get what's coming to them! But not until we've cleared the hell out of here."

Rochenbach sat back out of the way atop a stack of empty cooperage barrels. In the glow of a lantern, he watched the men hurry back and forth across the loading platform carrying the small but heavy crates of gold ingots. On one trip back from the wagon, Casings swung over to him in spite of Grolin, Spiller and Frank Penta standing watching near the Treasury car door.

"Are you going to be all right once we're done here, Rock?" Casings asked.

"I'll make out," Rock replied.

"There's a posse riding the train we stole the car from," he said. "So watch your step."

"A posse?" said Rock. "How do you know that?"

"They had six horses saddled and ready in the freight car," he said, nodding toward the car sitting behind the Treasury car. "They're still there. Grolin told a new man to scatter them before we leave here with the gold."

Rochenbach stared toward the freight car and ran the information through his mind. Was this something the Denver field office might have done, sent extra guards out with the shipments, even before the Thursday date he'd given them?

"I still meant what I said, about us working together, the three of us," said Casings, cutting into his thoughts. "Don't think this big job changes anything between us."

"Don't worry about it," said Rock. "Make sure you and the Giant both get through this thing. We'll get back together down the trail."

"Good," said Casings. His voice lowered a notch. "I got the name of Grolin's contact at the mint." He passed a guarded glance over his shoulder toward Grolin and the others.

"You did?" Rochenbach was surprised. "How'd you get it?"

"Grolin let it slip," Casings said. "But it makes sense that he's the man who gives Grolin his information. It's Inman Walker. He's secretary to the mint superintendent. He knows everything that's about to happen there."

Rock made a mental note of the name. *Information received . . .*, he told himself. Not enough to act on, but a start. Now he needed to verify it.

"After I thought about it, I remembered seeing Walker's picture in the *Denver News*," Casings said. "I recalled seeing a man with a beard leaving Grolin's office one night. Without the beard, it was Secretary Walker. I'm certain. Come to think of it, his beard didn't look completely natural. It could have been a disguise of some sort."

"Good work, Pres," Rock said. "Now get going. Grolin's looking over here, about to bust a gut."

Casings only nodded, turned and went back to the Treasury car.

Rochenbach leaned back on the cooperage barrels and stared across the platform at Grolin and the others.

As the men finished stacking the gold crates onto the wagon and tying the load down, Shaner stood beside Grolin, cradling his rifle, the hammer cocked, his finger over the trigger.

"I'm thinking this brazen bastard won't try to make a run for it, boss," he said to Grolin. "Do you think he figures he's still got something coming, after Hughes catching him tipping somebody off?"

"I don't know," said Grolin, staring across the platform at Rochenbach. "If I was him, I'd be cutting out of here something fast."

"Yeah," said Spiller, "he has to know that one of us is going to kill him, now that he's done what we needed him to do."

"So you would think," said Grolin, his brow narrowed in contemplation. "This man has troubled me ever since I first laid eyes on him. I can't figure his angle in all this."

Frank Penta chuffed, also staring over at Rochenbach.

"Maybe he just figures he's done his job. Now he wants what was promised to him for doing it," he said to Grolin.

"Frank, are you worried about getting your cut of the gold?" Grolin asked Penta without taking his eyes off Rochenbach.

"No, I'm not," Penta said.

"Then don't worry about his cut either," Grolin snapped. He turned from Rochenbach and looked at the wagon, the load tied down, ready to go. The men walked over to their horses a few yards away.

"You asked," said Penta, "so I told you."

"To hell with this," said Grolin. "Shaner, tell him to go with you to turn those horses loose. Take him out of sight behind the freight car and shoot him in the head." He paused, then added, "Wait until we're all out of sight. If Giant sees what you're up to, he'll go crazy. He acts like *Rock* is his long-lost brother."

"I've got it covered," said Shaner. "I've wanted to shoot this bastard ever since I met him." He hiked up his coat collar and lowered the hammer on his rifle to keep from alerting Rochenbach of his intentions.

Across the platform, Rochenbach watched Shaner walk toward him. *Here we go . . .* , he told himself, standing up off the empty barrels, picking up the lantern.

"Rochenbach," Shaner said, "Grolin says to go help me unload the horses from the freight cars and turn them loose."

"When do I get my cut?" Rochenbach asked, walking along beside the rifleman toward the freight car. "I want to get away from this bunch quick as I can."

Shaner chuckled and said, "Yeah, we all love you too, Rochenbach. You'll get what's coming to you soon enough."

Rock looked over and saw Grolin and the other two walk to their horses as the wagon turned on the ramp. By the time Rock stepped forward and slid the freight car door open, both the freight wagon and the horsemen had faded out of sight into the darkness. A dead silence fell over the empty depot and the long moonlit loading platform.

Stepping inside the freight car, Rochenbach held the lantern up and looked at the saddled horses standing in a row gazing back at him.

Stopping at the sound of the rifle hammer cocking behind him, Rochenbach turned to face Shaner.

"Before you pull that trigger," he said calmly, his right hand on the butt of the Remington, "you've got to tell me something."

"No, I don't," said Shaner, taking aim on Rock's forehead from only a few feet away.

"Why do you suppose Inman Walker sent me here to check up on you guys?" Rock asked. Inside his unbuttoned coat, his thumb slid over the hammer of his Remington.

Shaner's rifle lowered an inch.

"What?" he asked, not trying to hide his surprise.

"You heard me," said Rock. "Are you stupid enough to believe I just dropped in out of the blue? Walker sent me." He stopped and said, "Or am I wasting my time? You don't even know who Walker is?"

"Oh, I know Secretary Walker is our setup man in the mint," said Shaner. "I've met him in person." His rifle lowered another inch.

Information verified . . . , Rochenbach told himself. Now to get out of here alive.

"Then you *know* why I'm here," he said. "I'm here to find out why Walker didn't get his cut from the Denver-Platte Canyon ore train robbery last month."

Shaner looked puzzled and lowered his rifle a little more.

"You're talking crazy," he said. "We didn't rob that train last month!"

"Maybe you and your pals here didn't," said Rochenbach. "But Grolin did the job. He had men from somewhere helping him. Maybe he held out on you and others. But it doesn't matter. Walker expects to get his cut—so do I."

"Damn!" said Shaner. "I don't know whether to believe you or not, Rochenbach." He lowered his rifle all the way to waist-high, the barrel pointing down at the floor.

Rochenbach stepped sideways to him. The Remington slid from his belly holster inside his coat, cocked at arm's length.

"It doesn't matter *now*," he said quietly. He squeezed the trigger; the hammer fell. A streak of blue-orange fire belched from the open car door. The explosion caused the six horses to jerk against their tied reins. They whined and snorted fearfully in protest.

"Settle down, fellows," Rock said to the skittish animals, walking toward them. "We've got a long ride ahead of us tonight."

Along the seasoned loading platform, the sound banged like a forging hammer on steel and echoed off through the woods.

Two hundred yards up the winding rocky trail, Grolin jerked his galloping horse to a halt and swung in around on the trail.

"That was a pistol shot," said Spiller, sliding to a halt, turning his horse beside him.

"Lionel Sharp?" Grolin called out to the new man.

"Right here, boss," Sharp said, proud to hear Grolin call his name.

Grolin budged his horse over to him and said, "Where is that pistol I gave you to hold for me?"

Sharp patted his pocket and realized the Remington was gone. *Uh-oh . . . !*

"I don't have it, boss!" he said, his voice already trembling.

Grolin stared back into the darkness.

"Want me to go back and see what . . . ?" Spiller said, his rifle in hand.

"I already know *what*," Grolin said. "Adios, Shaner," he said in the direction of the depot. He looked Sharp up and down, turned his horse and rode away.

Sharp started to turn his horse, but Spiller grabbed its reins.

"Not so fast, *fool*," he said. "This is as far as you make it."

Chapter 19

———

Rochenbach pulled the gold ingot bar from his boot well and looked at it in the glow of the lantern light. The two-inch-by-three-and-a-half-inch shipping ingot glittered in the flickering light. He knew that the only purpose of an unmarked shipping ingot was its ease of transport and handling until it reached its final destination. There it would be resmelted, weighed, marked and stamped respectively.

He hefted the ingot in the palm of his fingerless leather glove. It looked right; it felt right. *Yet . . .* He reached down, pulled a knife from a sheath on the dead outlaw's gun belt. He carved a corner of the soft metal, making the cut large enough to see into the core of its quarter-inch thickness.

He studied the ingot closely, noting to himself that for all its weight and glitter it was nothing more than a gold-plated utility slug—a bar useful for weight balancing and exhibition, nothing more.

Turning the plated ingot in his palm, he felt a sense of relief. It was good to learn that he hadn't opened the big safe door and allowed hundreds of thousands of dollars' worth of gold to fall into the hands of thieves.

This was the reply to his telegraph. Without receiving his identification code at the end of his message, the Denver field office chose the safest and most reasonable action. They had replaced the gold shipping ingots with gold-plated slugs. How had they done that without Inman Walker knowing?

Who knows? He shrugged. He wasn't the only Secret Service agent operating west of the Missouri.

But why tonight? he asked himself. Why not Thursday—the night he'd told them the robbery would happen?

That was something he would have to resolve later for himself, he thought, squeezing the sliced corner of the ingot back together and gripping it in his gloved hand. Right now, Grolin and his men still had to be stopped, real gold or not. They'd taken a train by force, held its engineer hostage and stolen a shipment of U.S. gold en route from one federal mint to another.

You've had a busy night, Grolin, he said to himself. Shoving the shipping ingot into his coat pocket, Bryce Shaner's rifle in hand, Rochenbach led the six horses out of the freight car onto the loading dock.

With a coiled rope he'd taken down from a wall peg in the freight car, he strung the horses into a line. He led the string single file across the platform to where Shaner's horse stood waiting at a hitch rail for its rider to return. The lone horse piqued its ears at him and the unfamiliar string.

Rock checked Shaner's rifle and shoved it down

into the empty saddle boot. Then he unhitched the horse and stepped up into the saddle.

Leading the horses down the wide ramp and off the loading platform, he turned onto a narrow path running parallel along the rails. He followed the trail through the grainy purple darkness onto a wider trail that wound through the pines and down over a long wooded hillside.

Once he'd cleared the pine woodlands, he rode at an easy gallop. He kept the long dark ribbon of rails in sight over his right shoulder; he searched and listened intently as five miles slipped beneath the horses' hooves.

Staying parallel to the winding black rail clearing, he rode a mile farther before he slowed his horse and the string to a halt and stared down onto the black rails snaking beneath him.

There they are. He watched as a row of dark figures on foot crossed along a rolling edge of land against a stretch of purple starlit sky.

The posse . . . ? Yes, he was sure of it, he told himself. Now the trick would be to get their horses to them without either blowing his cover or getting his head shot off. He'd spent too much time establishing himself as an outlaw, a long rider who would do most anything for money. He wasn't about to throw all that away— *ruin my bad reputation,* he thought with a wry smile.

Besides, he'd learned from experience that if he told them he was an agent for the U.S. government, they wouldn't believe him anyway.

But here's something they will believe . . . , he thought

to himself, nudging his horse, leading the string behind him.

On the rail tracks, Captain Boone halted his men with a raised hand in the darkness.

"I heard it too, Captain," Sergeant Goodrich whispered, a step behind him.

The six turned in the dark, their carbines in hand, and searched the treed hillside to their right as the sound of hooves moved closer.

"Take cover, men," Captain Boone said, crouching, moving from the rails into the trees, his thumb cocking his carbine as quietly as possible. "Corporal Rourke, advance, see what we have here."

Soundlessly, the corporal moved away deeper into the trees and took position above a thin trail that jarred softly with the beat of oncoming hooves. Captain Boone, his sergeant and the three other soldiers spread out, ten feet apart, and ducked down along the trail.

When Rochenbach caught sight of a shadowy figure taking position, he closed his horse to a walk and led the string forward. *Here goes . . .* , he thought, bracing himself for what came next.

Damn! the corporal thought, seeing the single rider and the six horses draw closer. Without waiting for an order from the captain, who, he was certain, didn't see the lone rider yet, Rourke stood up in the moonlight with his carbine cocked and aimed at Rochenbach.

"Halt, right there!" he called out, loud enough for both Rochenbach and the other soldiers to hear.

Seeing the rider caught by surprise and jerking his horse to a sudden halt, the corporal took a step forward as Rochenbach raised his hands in the air.

"Don't shoot!" Rochenbach said. "I'm just passing through. I mean you no harm."

He sat staring as five more dark figures stood up along the trail and hurried forward. They quickly formed a half circle around him and the horses. He saw the shorter barrels of carbines pointed up at him, already noting a military bearing to the men.

"We're lawmen. Dismount, keep both your hands in sight," Rock heard a voice demand. *Yep, very military sounding,* he told himself.

A rifleman hurried forward and grabbed Rochenbach's horse by its bridle, holding it in place as Rochenbach stepped down, careful not to let his hands get close to his Remington or the rifle in the saddle boot.

"*Lawmen?* Thank goodness, gentlemen," Rochenbach said amiably. "You've scared the bejesus out of me and my horses."

But the captain was having no small talk.

"State your name, sir," he said, "and your reason for being here *this night.*"

Rochenbach looked across the faces in the pale moonlight, the first sliver of sunlight wreathing the distant horizon.

"I'm . . . Smith," Rochenbach said in a deliberately halting voice, "John Smith. I'm a stock dealer from Central City, just passing through, coming back from a horse swap—"

"John Smith *indeed,*" said the captain, cutting him short. He stepped in, slid the big Remington from across Rochenbach's belly and looked at it in the moonlight.

Corporal Rourke had circled the six horses and looked them over closely.

"They're *ours*, Captain! No doubt about it, sir!" he said, casting Rochenbach a searing stare.

"You're mistaken, mister," said Rochenbach, needing to offer some sort of defense. He kept his hands raised, but turned half around toward him as Rourke loosened the lead rope from the last horse in line and led it forward for the captain to see.

"Mistaken? I don't think so," said Rourke. "I believe I know my own damn horse."

Rochenbach fell silent, as if he'd been caught redhanded.

"You appear to have run short on conversation, *Mr. Smith*," the captain said, "so I'll do the talking."

"I didn't steal your horses," Rochenbach said, sounding as guilty as any horse thief he'd ever heard. "There has to be some mis—"

"Shut up," Rourke snapped at him, poking the tip of his carbine into Rochenbach's side, just enough to send a sharp pain through his ribs.

"Enough of that for now, Corporal," said the captain. To Rochenbach he said, "I'm Captain Daniel Boone."

"Daniel Boone *indeed*," Rochenbach couldn't resist saying after the captain's earlier sarcasm.

"I'm warning you, *long rider*," said Rourke, gigging him again with the tip of the carbine barrel.

Captain Boone continued with a turn of his hand toward the sergeant and the corporal. "This is Sergeant

Goodrich. This is Corporal Thomas Rourke." As an afterthought, he nodded toward the other three. "These men are their troopers."

Rochenbach looked back and forth among them.

"Soldiers, huh?" he said. "What's soldiers doing out here?"

"We're rail transport guards tonight. We were guarding the rail shipment you and your consorts stole," said the captain. "You, Mr. *Smith*, are under arrest for train robbery and theft of a government gold shipment."

"I don't know what you're talking about," Rochenbach said.

Again the carbine barrel gigged his side, this time harder, more painful, with a dark promise of more pain to come. Rochenbach caught himself, kept himself from bowing forward and falling to the ground.

"Listen to me, Mr. *Smith*," said the captain, his voice turning grim, all business now. "Thanks to you showing up with our horses, we'll catch the rest of the thieves, with or without your help. For all I care, I can have Sergeant Goodrich and Corporal Rourke hammer your face until you beg me to put a bullet through your brain." He cocked Rochenbach's black-handled Remington in his other hand and stuck the barrel up tightly under Rochenbach's chin.

"Or . . . we can escort you back to Denver City in chains," he added. "Let you fight this thing out peacefully in a court of law for the next year." He leaned in close to Rochenbach's face. "Make your choice quickly . . . I'm through talking."

Rochenbach let out a sigh of submission. It had gone far enough. He'd made it look good.

"All right, you win, Captain. Ask me anything," he said. "Want to know who's leading the gang? I'll even lead you to where we left the Treasury car sitting empty."

The captain uncocked the big Remington and lowered it from under Rochenbach's chin. He hefted the gun on his palm, as if judging the weight and balance, liking the feel of it.

"You have shown good sense," he said, in an almost cordial tone. "We have it on good authority an Andrew Grolin is the gang leader." He gave Rock a knowing look, then turned and looked at the far horizon, judging the coming dawn. Finally he looked at the waiting sergeant and said, "Sergeant Goodrich, have the men sort out their horses and look them over good. We're going to ride hard until we've closed the gap between us and these thieving dogs."

"Can I lower my hands now, Captain?" Rochenbach asked as the men busied themselves sorting and checking their mounts.

"Yes," the captain said to Rock, "but I hope you have the same good sense to realize that I'll kill you at the slightest wrong move."

"I understand," Rochenbach said. He lowered his hands and stood watching, waiting until the soldiers were ready to ride.

So far, so good, he told himself. They had their horses back—hand-delivered, instead of him leaving the animals tied to a tree for them to happen onto. Now that he'd managed to insert himself into their ranks, he could lead them to the rail depot and point them in the right direction. From there he would leave them on their own—or so he hoped.

"Mount up, Mr. *Smith*," Sergeant Goodrich said to Rochenbach as the men swung into their saddles. "You're going to remain right by my side until we've caught up to the rest of your gang. Is that clear?"

One of the troopers rode forward and handed Rochenbach the reins to his horse, having taken the rifle from its boot.

"Clear as can be, Sergeant," Rochenbach said, taking the reins and swinging up into his saddle. As the sergeant mounted his horse beside him, Rock said to the captain, "The car is at an abandoned rail depot six miles up from here. We can follow the rails, but it's quicker taking the trail I was on."

The captain looked at the sergeant.

"It's true, Captain," Goodrich said. "The trail will cut over the hillsides instead of winding through the woodlands."

Captain Boone nodded and said, "Lead us on, then, Mr. *Smith*."

The sergeant and Rochenbach rode in silence, side by side across the rolling hillsides for the next half hour.

Finally, Rochenbach took a chance.

"Not offense intended, Sergeant," he said, "but if you're rail guards, how did the robbers steal that train out from under you?"

"You mean your accomplices?" The sergeant stared at him in the grainy moonlight. Rochenbach only gave a shrug.

The sergeant said, "We were unprepared."

"*Unprepared*?" Rochenbach let the word hang.

Goodrich let out a breath, as if confessing.

"We were expecting the robbery Thursday night, not tonight—" He stopped short, catching himself. "But I'll have no more talk of the robbery, not with one of the thieves who committed it."

Good enough. Rochenbach didn't reply. He only nodded and gazed ahead into the night. He had no more questions. The Secret Service had done its job. So had he. All he had to do now was get off the case without getting himself shot.

Chapter 20

Along the trail away from the abandoned rail depot, Grolin had the Kane brothers stop the wagon twice, ten miles apart. At each stop, he pulled out a wallet stuffed with bills, paid his extra men their night's pay and sent them away in different directions. After the second stop, when the last two new men had disappeared onto trails leading off toward different mining towns, he looked around at his regular men seated atop their horses around the loaded wagon.

Dent Spiller, Frank Penta, Pres Casings and the Stillwater Giant looked at him from their saddles. The Kane brothers half turned toward Grolin as he stepped from his saddle over into the wagon bed.

"Well, men," Grolin said with satisfaction, "this is what it always comes down to in the end." He picked up the opened crate of ingots and set it atop the rest of the load. "Just a few good men—close friends I can count on to get a job done." He looked at each man in turn as he took the loose lid off the crate.

"Speaking of good men," Casings said, "what's happened to Rock?"

"Yeah," said the Giant, "we heard the shot back there. What have you done to him?"

"The shot you heard was from a pistol," Grolin reminded the two. "Most likely it was Rochenbach's Remington. I left Shaner there to put a bullet in his head."

The Giant stiffened in rage and started to step his big Belgium horse forward, but Spiller and Penta both closed their horses in front of him. Casings held a hand up to stop the Giant.

"Easy, big fellow," he whispered.

Grolin continued. "But I'm guessing that as slick as Rochenbach is, he killed Shaner instead." He shook his head in regret. "Poor Bryce. He couldn't match wits with a man like Rochenbach—none of yas could. I saw it right off."

"Give me my share, Grolin," the Giant said, barely managing to control his rage. "I'm going back to see about him. I better not find him harmed."

Grolin took his cigar from his mouth and let out a breath of exasperation.

"Giant, Giant . . . ," he said, shaking his head. He looked at Casings. "What about you, Pres? Are you all broken up over me leaving Shaner behind to kill Avrial Rochenbach?"

"It was a dirty deal, Grolin," Casings said, "and you know it."

"Well, *hell yes*, it was a dirty deal, Pres," Grolin chuffed. "Do you think every deal is supposed to be straight up and honest? This is an outlaw gang, not a Christian choir! I saw there was no way to control a man like Rochenbach. He was too shifty, too hard to deal with. He stayed three moves ahead of the game! He'd've had us all killing one another if I let him keep at it. *He had to go!*" Grolin's words ended in an angry shout.

Silence fell over the men for a moment. Finally Casings broke it.

"Maybe you're right," he said, sizing the odds he saw standing against his and the Giant. "I don't want to argue about it. You're the boss."

"Yeah, so I am. . . ." Grolin looked surprised. "Does this mean no more foolishness about you and the Giant going into business with Rochenbach?"

Casings just stared at him; so did the Giant. There was no way Grolin could have heard anything about it, unless Spiller had told him. Still, Grolin wanted to hear Casings admit it. But Casings wasn't going to.

"If I wanted to go into business on my own, I would have done it long ago. And I wouldn't have done it with a man like Avrial Rochenbach—for all the reasons you just gave." He sat relaxed, in spite of the tension he felt in his spine, seeing that Frank Penta, Dent Spiller and the crazy Kane brothers were ready to kill him at the slightest signal from Grolin.

"Oh . . . ?" said Grolin in a more even tone. "Maybe I was misinformed." He slid a sidelong glance to Dent Spiller and blew out a stream of cigar smoke.

Now Casings knew Spiller had told him something, but how much?

"Yeah," said Casings, "maybe you were." He stared at Grolin, knowing the others had their eyes on him and the Giant.

Grolin laid a hand on the opened crate of ingots.

"Giant wants me to pay him off, let him go check on his pal, *Rock*," he said cynically. "What about you, Pres? You want to ride back with him?"

"If you stopped us here to split up our shares anyway," Casings said, "yeah, I'll take mine and ride with the Giant—like always."

Grolin looked at the Kane brothers, then at Penta, then Spiller and back to Casings. He took his hand off the crate and slipped it inside his coat to his lapel pocket.

"Sure thing," he said. He jerked the thick wallet from his coat, pulled out a handful of large bills and started riffling though them, counting to himself.

Casings and the Giant looked at each other, then at the stone faces on the other four.

"Come on, Grolin," Casings said quietly, almost sounding like his feelings were hurt. "This is *us*, the Giant and me. We're not some extra help pulled in to watch horses and load wagons. We take our cut in gold."

"Used to be, Pres," Grolin said sharply. "Not this time." He held a stack of money out in one hand. His other hand lay on the butt of a Colt holstered on his hip. "Take it and go. Split it up between the two of you."

"I don't like this," said Casings, turning leery of Grolin and the men around him. "Giant has always done right by you. So have I."

"Giant maybe," Grolin said, "but not you." He glanced at Spiller and said, "Tell him, Dent. Tell him what you told me."

Spiller said to Casings, "I told him everything, Pres—how you and your pal Rochenbach offered to cut me in as a partner when you start your own gang."

Casings sat staring at Spiller, feeling the world tighten in around him.

"Keep talking, Dent," Grolin said with a thin, cruel smile.

"I told him about the Hercules Mining money. When we saw how much was there, you and Rochenbach offered me a cut of it to keep my mouth shut, say it was only a couple thousand dollars. But I turned you both down."

"You *lying* son of a bitch!" shouted Casings, unable to take it any longer.

Seeing Casings swing his rifle up into play, the Giant did the same, just as Spiller, Frank Penta and the Kane brothers started firing.

A bullet from Lambert Kane sliced through Casings' side; another shot from Spiller grazed the side of his head. Seeing Casings in trouble, the Giant let out a loud bellow and slapped his rifle barrel to the rump of Casings' horse. The animal bolted sidelong and cried out just as a bullet from Penta's gun hit its neck. The wounded animal spun and raced back along the trail, Casings, badly wounded himself, barely hanging in his saddle.

The Giant charged forward into the gunmen, still bellowing, drawing a big saddle Colt and firing it as he kept swinging his rifle barrel like a club. Bullets struck his shoulder, his chest and sides like angry hornets. Grolin leaped from the wagon to keep from getting his head bashed in.

"Somebody kill him!" he shouted.

Another shot hit the Giant as he rolled from his saddle onto the wagon bed. His rifle flew from his hand. Bobby Kane reached out to shoot him, but a backhanded slap from the Giant's big, powerful hand sent him flying high into the air and left him lying limp in the trail.

Lambert Kane fired three wild shots at the Giant from less than ten feet, but none of the bullets hit him. From horseback, at close range, Spiller and Penta both fired repeatedly. But only one bullet hit the Giant; the rest sliced past his head and whistled away into the night.

Without Bobby Kane at the reins, the wagon started rolling forward, the spooked horses wanting out of there.

"Somebody, *please kill him*!" Grolin shouted, his voice turning shrill, seeing the wagon start to pick up speed.

Another hard, open-handed slap sent Lambert Kane flying from the wagon. He slammed backward against a large pine and hung there, ten feet off the ground. A stub from a broken branch stuck from the center of Lambert's bloody chest. He bucked and coughed and convulsed, then turned limp and silent.

"Damn it! Get the wagon!" shouted Grolin, seeing the load of gold start to bounce and fishtail on the rocky trail.

Spiller and Penta gave chase as the Giant lost his footing and fell from the back of the wagon. He tumbled along the trail, finally coming to a stop, and lay there limp and silent. Grolin ran to where his horse stood watching nervously. He swung up into his saddle and raced along the dark trail in the stir of dust and looming gun smoke.

Galloping ferociously, he heard the sound of horses crying out in terror as wagon, horses and all swung out over the trail and tumbled down the steep hillside. At a clearing along the edge of the trail, he saw the black silhouettes of Penta and Spiller and their horses against the purple sky.

"What a lousy *damn* mess," Spiller said as Grolin slid his horse to a halt and jumped down from his saddle beside him.

They watched as the two wagon horses came climbing up, broken rigging, wagon tongue and the front boards of the wagon hanging between them. They snorted and whinnied low, still shaken from their ordeal.

"Grab your saddlebags!" Grolin said to Penta and Spiller. "We're not leaving here without this damn gold!"

At the depot, Sergeant Goodrich and Rochenbach stepped down from their horses beside Captain Boone, Corporal Rourke and the other three soldiers.

The captain struck a match and checked the time on a gold pocket watch.

"I have to admit, we made much better time following this trail of yours than we would have following the rails," he said to Rochenbach. He looked Rock up and down curiously. Turning to Goodrich, he said, "Sergeant, take the men and reconnoiter these rail cars. I'll guard Mr. Smith."

"Yes, sir, Captain," said the sergeant. He turned to the corporal and the troopers and said, "You heard the captain. Secure your mounts and follow me."

When the soldiers were out of hearing range, Captain Boone turned back to Rock.

"I can't help wondering, what exactly is your game, Mr. *Smith*?"

"My *game*?" said Rochenbach. "My game was not wanting to get a bullet in my head, remember?"

The captain smiled and looked around at the Treasury car, the freight car and the mail car sitting behind the stolen engine. Goodrich and two soldiers stepped up into the engine. Corporal Rourke and the other two walked into the empty Treasury car.

"Yes, but I have a nagging feeling there is more to you than that," he said. "There's something out of the ordinary about you."

"I suppose I could say the same about you and your men, Captain," Rochenbach replied. "*Soldiers* out of uniform, guarding a rail shipment that ordinarily has two civilian guards, at the most?"

Boone ignored his words. "I find it entirely *too* fortuitous that you should come along at just the right moment, leading a string of horses that you obviously know are stolen." He studied Rock's eyes closely. "And you lead them right down off the safe trail you were on and onto the rails, knowing full well my men and I would be walking those rails in pursuit."

"So . . . what is it you're getting at, Captain?" Rochenbach asked, playing dumb.

The captain lowered his voice and said, "When I received a dispatch on this mission, I was told there may be a government operative secreted among these perpetrators. I believe you are that government operative, Mr. *Smith*."

Rochenbach stalled for a moment, knowing that once his cover was blown, it was blown forever. All the work and time he'd put into establishing himself in the world of the lawless would be washed away.

"And if I am that man?" he asked warily.

"If you were that man, then of course you would be free to go. I would thank you for your help in bringing us our horses and let you ride away."

Rochenbach weighed his answer. What outlaw would turn down an opportunity to walk away?

"All right," he said as if letting go of a tightly held secret, "you found me out, Captain. I am that man."

"I knew it," said Captain Boone.

"So," said Rochenbach, half turning toward his horse, "if we're all through here, I'll just get out of your way and—"

"Hold it, Mr. *Smith*!" said Boone. His right hand rested on the butt of a holstered Army Colt. "I was also told that this operative would give me a four-number identification code that only he would know."

Rochenbach stared at him, his hand on his saddle horn, ready to swing up onto his horse.

"I—I forgot the numbers," he said. "But I'll have them sent to you as soon as—"

"As you were!" said Boone, cutting him off. His

Colt streaked up from the holster behind his riding duster, pointed and cocked at Rochenbach. "Take your hand away from that saddle horn, *Smith*, before I put a bullet through it."

Rochenbach drew his hand away slowly and held both hands chest high.

"You made the offer, Captain," he said. "Can't blame a man for trying."

"Indeed . . . ," said the captain, still studying him, now with a curious and puzzled look on his face. "I'm not sure if what you just did was meant to persuade me that you *are that man*, or to convince me that *you're not*."

Rock stared at him.

"That's something you'll have to decide for yourself, Captain," he said. "Whoever you decide I am. For now it's safe to say we're both on the same trail."

Boone stared at him for a moment, then nodded his head as if in agreement. He holstered his Colt and let his riding duster fall closed.

"Do not try me again, *Smith*," he said with resolve.

Chapter 21

———

Dawn wreathed the eastern horizon as the Stillwater Giant awoke cheek-down in a wide pool of thickening blood. He pulled himself hand over hand from the blood and up the side of a large rock standing beside the trail—the rock he had landed against head-first when he fell from the runaway wagon. His huge head pounded like a bass drum.

Dang. . . .

He batted his eyes and cleared them enough to look down the front of himself. Dirt and dark blood had caked thick over the bullet holes in his chest, his shoulders, his leg. The thick black paste had slowed his loss of blood almost to a stop. He considered the fact that he was still alive in amazement, and scratched his bloody, swollen head.

Where's Pres . . . ? he asked himself dreamily. *Where's Rock . . . ?*

Ahead of him where the wagon had gone off the trail, he heard the sounds of Grolin, Spiller and Penta gathering gold ingots on the rocky hillside. Broken crates and pieces of busted wagon frame lay everywhere. At the edge of the trail above them, Bobby Kane leaned back against a rock, still looking dazed and half conscious from the hard backhanded slap the Giant had planted on the side of his head.

Steadying himself with both hands against the rock, the Giant collected his addled senses and staggered from rock to rock along the edge of the trail, back in the direction of the depot—the same direction Casings had ridden off in. Fifteen yards down the trail, he looked up and came to a sudden startled halt, seeing Lambert Kane hanging impaled on a thick branch of the tall pine.

The stub of the broken tree limb stuck from Lambert's chest covered with black blood and ripped pieces of the outlaw's heart. Lambert wore a wide-eyed look of shock on his pale blue face. His bloody mouth formed a large O.

"Sorry, Lamb . . . ," the Giant murmured to Kane's grisly corpse.

Summoning his waned strength, the Giant staggered on along the trail until the sound of the gold gatherers fell away behind him. As silver morning light rose slowly in his wake, he half walked, half stumbled his way for another two hundred yards, until he couldn't go on any longer. He stopped and leaned against another large rock to collect his strength.

Fresh blood had begun to trickle from his wounds. The Giant had no idea how much blood had been inside his monstrous body to begin with, but judging from the thick pool he'd awakened in, he was certain he'd lost a large portion of it. He bowed his head, feeling spent and weak, when he heard Casings' voice from a few feet farther along the trail.

"Giant . . . help me," Casings called out in a shallow voice.

"Huh . . . ?" The Giant snapped his head up and stared toward the sound of Casings' voice. "Pres . . . ? Is that you?"

"It's me . . . Pres," Casings managed to say. "Over here."

The Giant saw Casings lying across the trail, a leg pinned beneath his dead horse.

"Dang! Hang on, Pres . . . I'm coming," said the Giant, pushing himself upright. His strength began to surge as he saw Casings in need of help.

"Garth Oliver . . . Stillwater Giant . . . ," Casings murmured weakly. He managed a thin smile of relief and laid his face back on the cold, bloody ground.

"You're . . . damn right it's me," the Giant said, stooping down, lifting the dead horse up enough to free Casings' leg from beneath it. "You just take it easy now. Don't worry about nothing. I've got . . . you covered, Pres," he said. He did his best to hide his own pain and weakened condition.

Dragging Casings a few feet, he propped him up against a boulder and limped back to the dead horse, reached for a canteen and limped back with it. More fresh red blood seeped from beneath the layer of dirt and black blood covering him. He uncapped the canteen and shook the water around.

"Here . . . drink this," he said, collapsing beside Casings, sticking the canteen into his blood-caked hands.

Casings sipped water and looked up at the Giant sitting beside him in the dirt. His eye went from wound to wound as he saw the fresh blood trickle freely now.

"Jesus, Giant . . . ," he said, already sounding better. "You're shot all to pieces."

"This . . . ain't nothing," Giant said haltingly. "I'm not hurt . . . you're the one hurt." He looked at the bloody bullet hole in Casings' side, and the bloody graze along the side of his head. As he spoke, he jerked the bandannas from around his neck, wadded them and pressed them against Casings' wounded side. Then he placed Casings' hand on top. "Hold this here," he said.

Casings looked down at the bandannas and chuffed with a weak smile.

"Whoever heard of . . . a head so big . . . it takes two of these to go around it?"

The Giant grinned in spite of his wounds.

"Just me . . . the Stillwater Giant," he said. "Nobody else."

Casings handed the canteen back to him and collapsed back against the rock.

"Now . . . I'm going to go to sleep . . . for a while," he said dreamily.

"No, you're not!" the Giant growled. "I'm not . . . letting you die on me!" He reached a huge hand over and shook Casings roughly. "Wake the hell up! I'm taking you back to the depot."

"Why, Giant?" Casings asked. "There's . . . nothing back that way but the law by now," Casings said. "Let me sleep."

The Giant shook him again, roughly.

"I said . . . stay awake!" he growled, keeping his deep voice down in case Grolin and the others might hear him.

He struggled to his feet, stooped down and scooped Casings up in his huge arms like a rag doll. Then he staggered in place for a moment until he found his balance.

"See?" he said. "Nothing to it. . . ."

"Put me down, Giant," Casings said.

But the Giant would have none of it. He staggered off along the trail leading back to the abandoned rail depot.

"You'll be all right . . . you'll see," he said, sounding stronger. "Rock is back there. He'll know what to do."

The Giant struggled along the trail, Casings cradled in his huge arms, as morning rose around them. Two miles down the trail, just as the Giant felt his strength leaving him, he spotted the team of wagon horses, the broken wagon tongue, reins and rigging still on them. The horses stared at the Giant with apprehension, as if remembering him from the night before.

"Easy, horses . . . ," he purred in his deep but weakened voice. "How about giving the Giant . . . and his pal here a ride?"

The two horses chuffed and grumbled under their breath.

On the hillside, Grolin and the others had emptied everything from their saddlebags and stuffed them full of the gold ingots. They'd also stuffed ingots into their coats, their trouser pockets, boot wells and hats. When Bobby Kane's head had cleared enough for him to know what was going on around him, he located the big Belgium the Stillwater Giant had been riding and led it to the side of the trail.

With the help of the other three men, Bobby tied six undamaged gold crates over the big horse's back with lengths of rope from a coil Penta carried on his saddle horn. With their hats full of gold and tucked up under their arms, the gunmen struggled under their weight and climbed up into their saddles. What gold they couldn't carry, they had gathered and stuffed under rocks and beneath dried brush.

"I hate leaving this much gold behind," Grolin said, taking one last look down the hillside. "As soon as we meet Swank and his men, we'll get a wagon and return for it."

Spiller and Penta looked at each other from their saddles.

"That posse from the train is going to be coming down this trail with blood in their eyes," Penta said. "They didn't just give up and go home because we stole their horses with the freight car."

"Tough knuckles," said Grolin, red-faced. "We're not leaving that gold here any longer than it takes to get a wagon and haul it out."

"I understand," said Penta, backing off.

Bobby Kane sat weaving drunkenly in his saddle, the Giant's Belgium on a lead rope beside him.

"That damn Rochenbach," Grolin cursed. "He caused every bit of this, stirring everybody up—him and his damn cocky attitude. I feel like kicking myself in the ass, ever bringing him in."

Spiller and Penta gave each other another look.

"He was damn good at opening a safe," Penta conceded with a sigh. "Damn shame he was such a hard-headed, tricky sumbitch."

"He wasn't worth the damn trouble of keeping him around," Grolin said, turning his horse toward the trail.

"What about this one?" Spiller asked, nodding toward Bobby Kane. "Is he going to be all right?"

"Holy Joseph!" Grolin said in disgust. He stopped turning his horse and looked at Bobby Kane, who sat wobbling in his saddle, his eyelids drooping, almost closed. The side of Bobby's face was swollen and purple where the Giant had backhanded him the night before.

"Bobby! *Bobby!*" Grolin shouted, trying to catch the gunman's drifting attention. "Are you able to lead that horse, with all that gold?"

"I'm good," Bobby said. Yet, no sooner had he said it than he toppled sidelong from his saddle and landed facedown in the dirt.

"Jesus Christ!" Grolin said to the other two. "Get him up and throw him over his saddle. Give me the horse."

The two climbed down from their saddles and

handed Grolin the Belgium's lead rope. As they lifted the downed gunman between them, Bobby stared all around, blinking his bleary eyes.

"I—I think the Giant jarred something loose inside my brain," he said to Grolin.

Grolin just shook his head as the two lifted Bobby and dropped him over his saddle. At first Bobby resisted and tried to right himself. But as they finally turned to the trail, he gave in and collapsed, his arms dangling down his horse's sides.

"We lost the whole night fooling with this mess," Penta said as they nudged their horses on along the trail. "You think Swank and his pals will still be waiting for us?"

"I think they will if they want this gold," Grolin said. "How many deals this big do you think come their way?"

"I don't know," Penta said, "not many, I suppose."

"Damn right, not many," said Grolin. Then he cursed under his breath and shook his head. "I've never had anything get so damned fouled up in my life." He spit sourly and stuck a cigar into his mouth. "Lousy Rochenbach bastard!" he grumbled to himself.

The soldiers and their prisoner rode hard throughout the night, following the wagon tracks. Rochenbach, the sergeant and the captain rode abreast. The corporal and the three troopers rode behind them. At dawn, when they rounded a turn in the high trail, the three jerked their horses to a halt so quickly that the soldiers following had to jerk their animal sideways to keep from plowing into them.

"Good God in heaven! What *is this*?" shouted Goodrich at the sight of the wagon horses plodding toward them.

The bloody Stillwater Giant stood between the two horses on the broken tongue and front wagon boards, his huge head bowed onto his chest. His enormous size dwarfed the otherwise large wagon horses. He held one large arm looped over each horse's back. Pres Casings hung limp and bloody over his right shoulder.

The sergeant snatched a Colt from behind his riding duster and cocked it toward the unconscious Giant.

"Don't shoot, Sergeant," Rock said. "That's Garth Oliver."

The sergeant held his fire, but he looked to the captain for direction.

"Sir . . . ?" he asked the captain.

"Do hold your fire, Sergeant," Captain Boone said without taking his eyes off the approaching wagon horses and their bloody cargo. "You know these two, Mr. Smith?"

"Yes, sir," Rochenbach said. "Captain, may I go see about them? You have my word I won't make a run for it."

"We'll all go *see about them*," the captain said. He looked at Rochenbach. "You have *my word* we'll shoot you in the back if you try."

Rock and the sergeant dropped from their saddles and walked forward. The corporal and the other troopers followed close behind them. The Giant didn't even raise his head. The two horses tried to continue right past Rochenbach and Goodrich, but Rock grabbed one of the horses by its bridle. Goodrich grabbed the other in the same manner.

The Giant lifted his bowed head a little as the horses halted in the trail.

"Is that you, Rock?" he asked weakly.

"It's me, Garth," he said, not wanting to use the Giant's familiar name, lest the soldiers were aware the Stillwater Giant was a wanted man in Texas.

The Giant looked around at the soldiers, then back at Rochenbach, who hoped the big man had gotten the message.

"Pres . . . needs water," the Giant said, his head drooping slowly back down on his chest.

"Can we get some water?" Rochenbach asked, stepping in and pulling Casings' bloody body down from the Giant's shoulder. Casings groaned.

Rochenbach dragged him from between the horses and laid him on the ground. The soldiers stared, not knowing what to do about the Giant. Goodrich stooped down beside Casings with an uncapped canteen.

Captain Boone sat atop his horse and watched Rock lead the Giant from between the horses and sit him down in the dirt beside Casings.

"Did I hear him call you *Rock*?"

"Yes, you did," said Rochenbach. "It's a name some folks call me."

"I see," said the captain. He looked at the two bloody men on the ground. "And these fellows, are they part of your band of thieves?" He looked at the massive Giant sitting slumped on the ground. "I think I now understand how you were able to pull the coupling pin on a moving train." Even sitting, the Giant was nearly as tall and twice as broad as one of the soldiers standing beside him.

"These two are a couple of businessmen from Denver City, for all I know," Rock said, ignoring the captain's speculation. "My guess is they stumbled onto the thieves, and this is what happened to them."

The Giant raised his bloody head slightly and turned it enough to give Rochenbach a look. Then he lowered it again.

"Of course, I see," the captain said with a touch of sarcasm. To the sergeant he said, "Get these wounded men watered and take them to the side of the trail. We'll stop here long enough to rest our horses and dress their wounds."

Chapter 22

Captain Boone, Rochenbach and Sergeant Goodrich stood watching as two of the troopers and Corporal Rourke washed and dressed the Giant's and Casings' wounds as best they could with scraps of bandannas they tore into strips. As they finished cleaning the two up and both Casings and the Giant began to come to, the soldiers crossed Casings' wrists and snapped a pair of handcuffs on them.

They did the same with Rochenbach. Unable to get the cuffs around the Giant's thick wrists, the soldiers tied his hands together with rope.

"Now that we have three prisoners, Mr. Smith, we wouldn't want any of you wandering away from us," Boone said.

"I told you these men had nothing to do with the robbery, Captain," Rochenbach said for the Giant's and Casings' benefit. As he spoke, he looked down at the cuffs, realizing he had a key that would open them tucked inside the lining of his coat sleeve.

"You certainly did, Mr. Smith," said the captain. "But you also said the same thing about yourself." He offered a tight smile. "You can see how I might be a little skeptical."

"What are you going to do with us?" Rock asked. "These men need more than bandannas stuck against their wounds. They need a doctor, some proper bandaging, some serious treatment to keep these wounds from bleeding all over again."

He had taken this case as far as he could. It was time for him to bow out, let these soldiers do their job. In spite of their wounds, it looked as though Casings and the Giant were going to make it now that the bleeding had slowed.

"We're taking the three of you to the jail in Dunbar," said the captain. "There's a doctor there who'll properly attend to these two. I'll telegraph my superiors, tell them you're there. My men and I are going on after this Andrew Grolin and his gang."

Rochenbach had no doubt Boone and his men could chase Grolin down now that they were hot on their trail. Besides, he reminded himself, there was no real gold stolen—only decoys, gilded ingots. *Fool's gold*, he thought to himself. It was time to share that fact with the captain.

"If you'll permit me, Captain Boone," he said. He reached inside his coat with his cuffed hands.

"As you were, Smith!" the captain barked, jerking his Colt from its holster and aiming it toward Rock.

"Easy, Captain," Rochenbach said. "I only want to show you something." He pulled out the ingot slowly.

With his thumbs, he pressed open the corner slit that he had made with his knife. He handed it to the captain.

As Boone studied it closely, Rochenbach glanced over at Casings, who sat watching intently.

"I'm not an expert, Captain," Rochenbach said, "but this is the dullest gold I've ever seen."

Boone studied the ingot, then looked up at Rock.

"You're telling me this is from the stolen shipment?" he asked.

"Yes, it is," Rochenbach said, knowing better than to say any more on the matter, not with the captain already wondering who he really was, especially not with Casings and the Giant listening close at hand.

The captain took Rochenbach by his handcuffs and led him farther away from the others. Rochenbach looked over his shoulder and shrugged toward Casings and the Giant.

"This isn't *real* gold," the captain said. "Why did you show me this? What is your angle here?"

"No angle, Captain," Rochenbach said. "I figured I'd give it to you, let you decide if it's worth dying for." He shrugged. "I'd feel guilty otherwise, if something bad happened to you or your men."

"I bet you would," Boone said skeptically. He tightened his fist around the ingot. "Of course you might only be showing me this in hopes it would lighten my efforts of capturing your cohorts."

Rock stared at him.

"That would be one more possibility, Captain," he said. It wasn't a matter he could push any further without the risk of exposing who he was. But he wasn't overly concerned with them catching Grolin. If they didn't catch him now, they would catch him when he returned to his hotel and saloon in Denver City. Either way, it was over for Andrew Grolin. Rock was being honest about the cheap gilded ingots; they weren't worth dying for.

Boone studied Rochenbach's eyes, trying to decide whether or not to believe him.

"Sergeant," he called out finally, without taking his gaze off Rochenbach, "get those men ready to ride. We're following the wagon tracks until they lead us to the thieves."

"Yes, sir, Captain," said Sergeant Goodrich. "But what about this big fellow? He'd wear a poor horse down in no time."

"*Damn it all!*" Captain Boone hissed to himself in his frustration. He gave Rock a strange look. "How did I get stuck with a wounded giant?"

Rock just stared.

"Captain, sir," the sergeant called out, "might I suggest we assemble a travois and pull both these men on it until we get to Dunbar?"

"Yes, Sergeant, please see to that," the captain said. He hefted the gilded ingot on his palm in contemplation.

"Captain," Rochenbach said quietly, anticipating the question on Boone's mind, "since your *superiors* knew to expect a robbery Thursday night, do you suppose, as a precaution, they decided to ship these fake ingots all week long?"

Boone let out a breath, still hefting the ingot.

"As a precaution? Just in case of some last-minute

change, such as this?" the captain said, as if he'd forgotten he was talking to, *possibly*, one of the thieves.

"It's a thought, Captain," Rock said.

"*It's a thought . . . ,*" said Boone, bemused, as it suddenly dawned on him what he was doing. "Just who the hell are you, *Smith*? What the hell is it you're doing out here?"

Rochenbach gave him a cool, level stare, his hands cuffed in front of him.

"Aren't you supposed to know who a man *is*, and what he's doing *out here*, Captain, before you haul him off to jail?" Rochenbach said.

When Pres Casings and the Stillwater Giant were bandaged, watered and ready to ride, two soldiers helped Casings onto a hastily constructed travois made from four long pine saplings, the broken wagon tongue and front wagon boards. When the soldiers offered to help the Giant, he fanned them away with his tied hands. He allowed Rock to steady him and help him to his feet and lead him to the travois.

"I heard you, Rock," he whispered in his thick, deep voice. "You didn't tell these suckers nothing." He gave him his wide, toothy grin. "You're my pal. Soon as I get rested, I'll break these strings and—"

Strings . . . ?

"Don't do it, Giant," Rock said, cutting him off, looking down at the strong rope double-wrapped around the Giant's thick wrists. "You're my pal too. Don't make these soldiers kill you. Stick with Casings. Do what he tells you, all right?"

"All right, whatever you say, Rock," the Giant

whispered, lying back beside Casings. The two wagon horses stirred and collected themselves, feeling the weight of the Giant on the travois poles.

Rochenbach shot Pres Casings a look. Casings nodded, a blood-soaked bandanna tied around his head, wrapped around the bullet graze. He held a torn, bloody bandanna to the wound in his side. Whatever Rock was up to, Casings saw that he had his and the Giant's interests at heart.

"Obliged," he whispered.

Rock only nodded and turned away.

Captain Boone sat watching from his saddle, seeing the three whispering back and forth. He took note of it but decided to say nothing. These two wounded men were as guilty as sin; he knew it.

Garth Oliver indeed. . . . He'd heard of the Stillwater Giant. Who else could this monster of a man be? The captain smiled to himself as Rochenbach walked over and took the reins to his horse from him. As far as he was concerned, *Mr. Smith* was guilty too, until something proved him otherwise.

Undercover operative? Maybe, Boone thought. *But if he is an operative and not willing to say the four numbers that will get him off the hook, he must have a good reason for it.* Whatever that reason might be, Boone had probed the matter as far as he could. He would jail the three in Dunbar and let the law sort them out.

"Let's move out, Sergeant," he said.

Beside him, Goodrich raised a gloved hand and waved the men forward without a verbal command.

On the other side of the captain, Rochenbach nudged his horse forward at a walk.

The party rode along the trail in silence for the next hour until the sergeant threw up a hand and stopped suddenly at the sight of Lambert Kane's body stuck to the large pine, the frozen expression of surprise on his purple face.

"Holy *be-jesus*, Captain," Goodrich said.

"Yes, Sergeant, I see it," said Captain Boone, sounding as if it wasn't the first time he'd found a man spiked to the side of a tree by a limb stub, ten feet off the ground. "Have your men take him down."

"Two men forward," the sergeant called out, looking back at the mounted soldiers.

As two soldiers booted their horses forward to assist the sergeant, Boone gave Rochenbach a sidelong look, followed by a backward nod directed toward the travois.

"Something your friends had a hand in, no doubt?" he said.

"I wouldn't know, Captain," said Rochenbach. "I wasn't here."

"No, of course you weren't," said Captain Boone correcting himself. "You were busy leading our horses back to us."

"That's right, Captain," said Rochenbach. "That's what I was doing, any way you look at it."

Just to see if he could get by with it, Rock nudged his horse forward, watching the two soldiers stand atop their saddles and lift the body off the tree stub. Hearing the captain's Army Colt cock behind him, he stopped and gave him a faint, wry grin.

"What, Captain? No warning first?" he said without looking around. "You'll just shoot me?"

"You've been warned, *Smith*," Boone said in a somber tone. "No other warning is needed."

Without another word on the matter, Rochenbach turned his horse, rode it back slowly and turned it beside the captain. Boone uncocked the Colt, but kept it in hand. They watched the soldiers lower Lambert Kane's body to the sergeant, who in turned laid it out on the ground.

Boone looked over his shoulder at the three soldiers fixated on Lambert's body and the blood-streaked tree where it had hung.

"Corporal Rourke, scout ahead two hundred yards, then fall back and report," he said as Goodrich and the two soldiers dragged the body out onto the trail.

"Yes, sir," said the corporal. He swung his horse around Rochenbach and rode away at a gallop. One soldier remained, the lead rope to the travois in hand. He looked back nervously at the Giant and Pres Casings, but saw them both sleeping, their hats pulled over their eyes.

The captain and Rochenbach nudged their horses over and looked down at the body, able to see the ground through the wide, gaping wound.

After a moment, the captain straightened in his saddle and shook his head.

"Sergeant," he said, "search the body for identification, then drag him off the trail and pile rocks over him. We're not a burial detail," he added, as if to justify himself.

As the sergeant and the two soldiers followed the captain's orders, Rochenbach and Boone sat atop their horses in silence. A few moments later, they both turned toward the sound of the corporal's horse galloping back around the turn toward them.

"Captain Boone," he said, sliding his horse to a halt and sidling over to the captain. "I found this alongside the trail, less than two hundred yards from here, sir." He held out a closed hand and opened it in a way as to reveal its contents only to the captain.

"It's all right, Corporal," Boone said, taking the ingot from Rourke's hand and eyeing it in the mid-morning sunlight. Looking at Rochenbach, he said to Rourke, "Your knife, Corporal?"

Rourke reached into his boot well, came out with a bowie-style knife and handed it to him.

"Thank you, Corporal," said Boone.

He carved a deep cut across the corner of the ingot and examined it. Then he squeezed the cut closed and handed the big knife back to Rourke. He gave Rochenbach a look that said the ingot was the same as the one he'd taken from him.

"And this is the only one you found, Corporal?" he asked.

"Yes, sir," said Rourke. "I saw where the wagon went off the trail. It's broken up all over the hillside. There's busted crates everywhere."

"Empty, I presume?" said the captain.

"From what I could see, yes, sir," said Rourke. "I didn't climb down and check. I knew you would want to hear this straightaway. There must have been some shoot-out there. There's blood everywhere, sir."

"Good work, Corporal," said the captain. He turned to Sergeant Goodrich and said, "Sergeant, prepare your men to move out."

At the sergeant's command, the troopers abandoned Lambert Kane's body, leaving it only partially covered with rocks. In moments, they had mounted and assembled behind the travois. Leaving Goodrich and the three troopers to escort the slow-moving travois, the captain, Corporal Rourke and Rochenbach moved ahead along the winding trail at a gallop, until they reached the spot where the wagon tracks veered off the trail.

The three dismounted, Captain Boone and the corporal keeping the handcuffed Rochenbach between them. They stood looking down at the splintered wood and empty gold crates scattered on the rocky hillside.

"Corporal, bring Mr. Smith and follow me," Boone said.

The three climbed down to where three busted crates lay close together in front of a large stand of brush and rock. Seeing the scraping of boots in the dirt, Boone smiled to himself.

"Mr. Smith," he said, "how do you suppose these men transported all that gold down the trail after losing their wagon?"

"Only by horseback, Captain," said Rochenbach.

"Yes," said Boone, "meaning they could not have taken much of it."

"Meaning a lot of it is still here," Rochenbach said, picking up on what the captain was saying.

Boone nodded, stepping forward. Separating the

brush with his hands and looking down into it, he saw broken crates and piles of ingots lying on the ground.

"Here's some of it," he said, reaching down and picking up an ingot. Rochenbach stepped over for a closer look as Boone raised the ingot between his teeth and bit down on a corner of it.

The two studied the ingot in the sunlight.

"It's gilded," the captain said, "just like the other two."

"But if Grolin knows it's worthless, why would he even bother hiding it?" Rochenbach asked.

"Clearly he doesn't know it's not real, Smith," the captain said. "He thinks this is pure gold lying here. And if you left gold lying on this hillside, what's the first thing you would do once you left?"

"Get a wagon and get right back here with it," Rock said.

"Exactly," said Boone. "They think the gold is real. They *are* coming back for it, and we *will* be waiting."

Chapter 23

At midmorning, Heaton Swank, a broad-shouldered, tough-looking gunman with a bullet scar running from his right cheek to his ear, took out a gold watch from inside his black duster and checked it. He cursed under his breath, snapped the watch's lid shut and put it away. He turned to an equally fierce gunman named Silas Dooley, who sat atop his horse beside him.

"If this bastard doesn't show up, he'd better be dead, Dooley," he said.

Silas Dooley spit a stream of tobacco. He sat with wrists crossed on his saddle horn. Inside his gray wool coat, a big Dance Brothers revolver hung under his left arm in a tooled leather shoulder rig.

"If he's *not*, he will be," he said, "I get my hands on him."

"Stay back here," said Swank, nudging his horse forward for a better look at the trail winding upward before them.

Strewn out in a loose line beside Silas Dooley, three

other well-dressed men sat atop their horses. One of them, a hired killer named Lyle Myers, raised a silver flask of whiskey to his lips, took a drink and passed the flask along to an elderly gunman on his right.

"How long are we going to wait for this *bartender*, Grolin?" he said to everyone.

Dooley eyed him up and down and spit again.

"How long does anybody wait for a man bringing them a half million dollars in smelted gold?" he asked.

"Just about as long as we already *have*," Lyle Myers said.

To his right, Eli March, the elderly gunman who'd taken the flask, drank from it and passed it along to the next man.

"He's not just a bartender," March said in an irritated voice. "Sumbitch owns a saloon, a hotel and a whorehouse. Not to mention a string of houses and dirt holdings." He wiped a hand across his lips. "*Bartender*, your ass," he grumbled through a scraggly gray beard.

"Excuse the hell out of me, then," Meyers said, taking off his black high-crowned range hat in a sweeping gesture. "Andrew Grolin is not *just* a bartender. He's a bartender, a desk clerk and a *pimp*." He stared at March. "Does that suit you any better, old man?"

"I hate *unfactual* jawing, is all," Eli March said in the same abrasive tone. "You call a horse a chicken long enough, pretty soon folks think they heard him cluck."

"Unfactual jawing . . . ?" said Myers. His hand pushed his plaid wool great coat back enough to rest easily on the black handle of a Colt holstered on his hip.

March seemed unmoved by Myers' threat.

"You heard me right," he said. "The longer I wait here, the less I like hearing it." He nodded at Myers' gun hand. "If you think that move scared me any, you chose the wrong place to be this morning."

Meyers thought about it, but decided to let it go. He chuffed and shook his head and looked away. His hand moved away from his gun. "You can't put a bunch like us together for long, expect things to stay friendly—somebody not kill somebody."

"It's only natural," said a gunman named Lou "the Dog" Duggins. "Where I'm from, it's all but destroyed the whole notion of family reunions." He capped the silver flask and pitched it back to Meyers. "And I think it's a damn shame," he added.

"Riders coming," Heaton Swank called back to the others from where he'd sat his horse closer to the trail.

"It's about *damned* time," said Dooley, perking up in his saddle.

"No wagon, though," Swank called out.

"Damn!" said Dooley. He slumped, recrossed his wrists on his saddle horn.

"A horse packing wooden gold crates," Swank called back to them. "Get everybody up here, Dooley."

"Now you're talking, Swank," said Dooley, straightening himself again. He grinned. "Come on, fellows. Let's go *oversee* this gold transaction, like we're paid to do."

He booted his horse and galloped forward. The others rode along behind him. When they got to Heaton Swank, the big gunman fell in beside Dooley.

"Keep a close eye on Andrew Grolin and his men," Swank said as they galloped on along the trail. "He's been known to show up at a swap like this and leave with everything in his pocket."

"Not today, he won't," said Dooley, riding close beside him.

A hundred yards up the trail, Grolin slowed his horse and veered off the trail into the trees as he saw the riders come riding toward him and his men. When Swank and his men arrived and followed the same path, they found a dazed Bobby Kane in a small clearing holding the reins to the big Belgium. Grolin, Spiller and Penta had spread into a half circle around the edge on the clearing, rifles in hand. Grolin spoke from behind the cover of a thick pine.

"That's close enough, Swank," he called out. "Have you got our money?"

"I've got your money, Grolin," Swank said, his men also spreading out around the clearing, staying atop their horses. "Have you got the gold?" As he asked, he looked curiously at the Belgium carrying the six wooden crates. He noted the stuffed saddlebags behind Grolin and his two gunmen.

"I've got it," Grolin said. He gestured toward the big Belgium.

Swank and Dooley gave each other a look. Dooley shook his head slowly.

"I was told *twenty-four* crates of gold ingots, around

a half million in gold," Swank said across the small clearing. "Has my arithmetic taken a bad turn, or am I only counting six?"

"There's six crates here," Grolin said. "We've got another crate and a half in our saddlebags."

"There again," Swank pointed out, "seven and a half crates sounds a lot shorter than twenty-four."

"I had a couple of men try to double-cross me," Grolin said. "We lost a lot of the gold along the trail. But we've managed to get this much to you. I'll get you the rest in a day or two. You've got my word."

"Your word . . ." Swank shook his head and stepped his horse forward, looking the Belgium up and down, casting a glance at the bleary-eyed Bobby Kane, holding its reins.

"What happened to this one?" he asked, noting Kane's swollen face.

"The Giant backhanded him," Grolin said.

"Jesus," Swank mused. "No wonder he looks like he's forgot his way home."

"What do you say, Swank?" said Grolin. "You want us to drop these crates and start counting?"

"'This much' don't cut it, Grolin," Swank said, stopping his horse and staring down at where Grolin stood close to the big pine. "My investors can buy this much gold for seventy-five cents on the dollar any day of the week. It takes a half million or better to make it worth their time." He gave him a tight smile. "They're *big cats*, these fellows of mine."

Grolin let out a breath and gripped his rifle a little tighter.

"All right, let's hear it," he said.

Swank looked over the six crates again appraisingly.

"This much gold, we're talking thirty-five cents to the note," he said firmly.

"And when we bring you rest?" he asked.

"The rest means another trip for us. We're still talking thirty-five cents—"

"Forget it," said Grolin, cutting him off. "We'll split it among ourselves and cash it as we go. Right, fellows?" he called out to the others, as a reminder to Swank that there were rifles aimed at him and his men.

"Damned right," said Spiller. "We're not giving it away."

"Not without a fight," said Penta in a threatening tone.

After a tense pause Grolin said, "There you have it, Swank. We're all—"

"So *do I*," Bobby Kane cut in mindlessly, as if just catching up to the conversation.

Grolin and Swank looked at the witless gunman, then back at each other.

"Believe it or not, Grolin," Swank said, "we're not out to rob you. But I meant what I said. The people I'm turning this for would get real ugly if I came back to them with a small amount of gold for seventy-five cents on the dollar."

"Then you've made this trip for nothing," said Grolin, "and I'll bid you good day."

"Adios," said Swank, touching his hat brim and backing his horse to turn it.

Damn it. . . . Grolin watched as the horsemen

started backing away, behind Swank, their rifles still at the ready.

"*Wait*," he called out to Swank, "I've got a proposition for you."

Swank turned his horse back to Grolin; his men moved back into position.

"I've got to get a wagon to haul the rest of the gold in," Grolin said. "If you can give me a day, stall your men and still pay our original price, we'll cut you a share right off the top. Right, fellows?" he said to Spiller and Penta.

"It's right with me," said Penta.

"Me too," said Spiller.

Grolin and Swank both looked expectantly at Bobby Kane, who sat with his mouth slightly agape. Bobby made no reply.

Swank nodded and said, "We'll have a wagon here before you can say—"

"Keep up the good work," Kane blurted out in a slurred voice, cutting him off.

Grolin and Swank stared at Kane.

"Jesus," said Swank. Lowering his voice, he said just between him and Grolin, "You ought to put that one out of his misery."

"Don't worry about him," said Grolin. "Just get us a wagon and let's get this thing done, *partner*."

"One hour," said Swank. "Be ready to ride when we get here with it. We might have a teamster or two shooting at our tails."

When Swank and his men were well on their way back along the trail toward the town of Dunbar, Silas

Dooley rode up close beside Swank. The other three gunmen rode up on his other side. Swank looked back and forth at them. He grinned.

"If this is a robbery, you got here too early," he said. "You should have waited until I took possession of a wagon full of gold ingots."

"That's the very thing we wanted to talk about, Heaton," said Dooley. "We want to know how we fit in on this deal you're cooking with Grolin. We were hired on to guard a wagonload of gold for you and the people you work for."

"Nothing's changed," said Swank. "You'll all still get paid, just like we agreed to."

"Except, now we might have to ride right into a posse," said Dooley, "or end up fighting the Stillwater Giant and whoever is sided with him against Grolin."

"Dooley's right, Swank," said Eli March. "This job has taken on a whole new hazard."

"You wanting out, Eli?" He shrugged. "Okay, you're out," he said. He looked at the others. "Anybody else want out?"

"I'm not wanting out," said March. "I'm saying what we're all thinking. We want a better deal."

Swank jerked his horse to a halt and stared from one to the other.

"All right," he said, "how about this? You give up the pay you've got coming—take a share of the gold instead?"

The men fell silent in contemplation.

Dooley said, "You mean take a share of *your* share?" He shook his head. "That doesn't sound like much to me. We're better off with what we started out with—"

"Look at me, Dooley," he said. "All of you," he added, looking around at them. "Tell me if I look stupid enough to settle for a share of this deal, when it's clear that Grolin is too weak to defend himself."

The men looked at each other. A crafty smile crept onto Dooley's face.

"We're going to take it all, ain't we?" he said.

"Think about it," Swank said. "There's five of us. Grolin is down to three men and one of them has been knocked cock-simple. I'd hate for anybody I know to hear that I had a chance like this and didn't take it. Wouldn't you?"

"Well, yes, putting it the way you said," Dooley replied.

"So, what do you say, fellows?" Swank said in a chiding tone. "Want to get one of them freight wagons that run out of Dunbar every day, or what?" He didn't wait for an answer; he batted his boots to his horse's sides.

The five nodded and booted their horses into a gallop behind him.

Chapter 24

Hidden among large rocks and scrub pine above the trail, Corporal Rourke and one of the troopers, a young man named George Winslow, sat with their rifles ready as they kept watch in both directions. Overhead, the sun stood farther west. Winslow let out a breath.

"How long you figure the captain will wait here for these men, Corporal?"

"I don't know, Trooper," said Rourke. "We can't leave soon enough to suit me." He drew a watch from inside his duster pocket, flipped the lid open and checked the time.

"Me neither," said Winslow. "We've been perched up here like squirrels all day."

"Three hours," Rourke corrected him. He closed the watch and put it away.

"All right, three hours," said Winslow. "I can't believe we're here. Seems like the captain would want to get right on their trail and ride them down."

Rourke looked at him.

"I'm just saying it's quite a gamble the captain has taken," Winslow explained. "What if they don't come back for the gold at all? We'll look like fools when the general finds out."

"No," said Rourke, "Captain Boone will look like a fool. But I'm sure the captain thought all that out before he decided to stay here."

"I don't mean to be second-guessing the captain," Winslow said. "It just seems risky, is all." He shrugged. "Although there are always risks in this man's army, one could argue."

"Yes, life is risky. And now it's going to start getting even *riskier*, Trooper," Rourke said, staring off down the trail below.

Winslow looked down in the same direction and saw three riders moving into sight single file.

Rourke lifted a palm-sized signal mirror from the inside lapel pocket of his duster and wiped it on his sleeve. He gave Winslow a grin.

"It appears the captain just won his feathers for the day, eh?" he said.

"Yes, he has," said Winslow, looking almost relieved. "I'm happy to say I was wrong."

Rourke raised the signal mirror and cocked it to the afternoon sunlight. He moved it back and forth slowly.

Among the rocks on the steep hillside thirty yards back along the trail, Sergeant Goodrich saw the flash of piercing sunlight blink on and off. He turned to the trooper beside him, a young man named John Trent.

"All right, Trooper, be ready. Hold your fire until I give you the order," he said.

"Yes, Sergeant Goodrich," the young soldier replied somberly.

Goodrich turned and waved a hand back and forth toward Captain Boone, who sat in the cover of rock farther down the hillside.

"We have riders moving up the trail, sir," Goodrich called out, keeping his voice as quiet as he could.

Boone waved in acknowledgment, then backed away in a crouch and hurried down a few yards to a level spot where the third trooper stood watch over the three prisoners.

"Trooper Lukens, the thieves have arrived," he said, seeing Rochenbach seated against a slender pine, his arms behind him, cuffed around the tree's six-inch trunk. "Are you prepared for a fight?"

"Yes, sir, Captain," the trooper said, snapping to attention in spite of his civilian trail clothes. "Ready and willing, sir."

"Good man," said Boone. "See to it these prisoners are secured and come with me."

"Sir, should I gag them with a length of rope to keep them quiet?" Lukens asked as he stepped around the tree and checked Rochenbach's handcuffs.

"I think not, Trooper," said the captain. He stared down at Rochenbach, then at Casings, whose hands were also cuffed around a slender pine. "If I hear either of you try to call out and tip off your cohorts, I'll send someone down here to shoot the three of you. Is that clear enough?" he asked.

Rochenbach and Casings both nodded. At a much larger tree a few feet away, the Stillwater Giant sat sleeping soundly. His big hands, already tied at the wrists, were now held snuggly to his chest by a rope that wrapped around him five times, tying him to the tree.

"Back to our positions, then, Trooper," the captain said. "These men aren't going anywhere."

The two turned and hurried away through the brush and rocks. No sooner were they out of sight than Casings turned to Rochenbach.

"Got any ideas, Rock?" he asked. "This place could turn inhospitable in a hurry once the shooting starts."

Before Rock could answer, the Stillwater Giant said quietly, "I've got an idea."

The two looked at him in surprise.

"We thought you were asleep," said Casings as the Giant stared down at the thick rope on his wrists.

"I was a long time ago. But now I'm rested." He gave a grin. "I feel good enough to break this rope. Once I get my hands free, I can break the one holding me to this danged tree."

"Wait a minute, Giant!" Rochenbach said, seeing the big man begin to strain hard against the rope on his wrists. "You start that, you'll get your wounds opening up again. You'll bleed yourself to death." Behind him, he went to work getting the key from inside his sleeve lining.

"That's all right," the Giant said. "I'll get you both out of here before I do." He started to strain against the rope binding his wrists.

"No, Giant!" said Rock. "Look at me!" He quickly raised a freed hand from behind his back. "See, I'm loose. Don't get yourself bleeding again. I'll cut you both loose as soon as they get too busy to check on us."

Casings chuckled and shook his bandanna-wrapped head. He looked Rock up and down as Rochenbach wrapped his arm back around the tree, appearing to still be handcuffed.

"How'd you manage to get the key from the soldiers?" he asked.

Rochenbach relaxed against the tree. "Who said I got it from them?" he said. "Maybe I just a carry one in case I ever need it."

"I don't care how you got it," Casings said. "I'm just glad you've got it." He looked up toward the edge of the trail above them. "As soon as the shooting starts, we grab all the gold we can carry and get ourselves out of here."

"Huh-uh," Rock said, "No gold."

"What do you mean no gold?" said Casings. "This is our chance to turn this whole mess around—"

"The ingots are worthless," Rock said, cutting him off. "They're not real. Leave them lie."

"Rock, what are you talking about?" Casings asked.

"The ingots are nothing but gold-plated lead," Rock said. "That's what I'm talking about."

"How do you know that?" Casings asked, giving him a curious look.

"I checked a couple of them," said Rock. "Trust me, they're not real." He stared closely at Casings and past him toward the Giant. "When the time comes, get to the horses and get yourselves out of here. Don't stop for nothing and don't look back. I'll keep you covered in case—"

"Wait a minute," said Casings. Now he was cutting Rochenbach off. "You're coming with us."

"Yeah," the Giant cut in, "we're not leaving you behind."

"I'm only staying behind long enough to make sure you're both out of here without catching a bullet in your backs. Then I'll catch up to you."

"We don't need you covering our backs, Rock," said the Giant. "Come with us."

"You're both shot up," Rock said. "You both need a doctor."

"I can't argue with that," said Casings, looking down at his blood-crusted shirt.

"Then don't argue," Rochenbach said. "You're going to need cover to get out of here. Listen to me on this. I'll catch up to you."

The Giant started to say more on the matter, but Casings shook his head.

"Let it go, Giant," he said quietly. "Rock says we need cover. All right, then, *we do*. I would not want to turn him down—have him saying 'I told you so' to my dead body."

"All right," said the Giant, giving in. "Seems like when we do like Rock says, things have a way of going better for us."

"I've noticed that myself," Casings said, giving Rochenbach a look. "But I've got to say, I'd feel better if I saw one of these ingots, satisfy myself they're not real."

"I don't have one to show you right now," Rochenbach said. "You've got to take my word on this."

"I do take your word, Rock," Casings said. "The thought of that damned gold caused me to lose my head there for a second." He grinned. "But I'm all right now."

Rochenbach settled back against the tree and waited for the fight to begin on the trail above them.

The first two riders, Silas Dooley and Lou the Dog Duggins, eased their horses around a turn in the trail and rode forward at a walk. Grolin and Swank led the wagon warily, fifty yards behind them. Grolin kept Bobby Kane close to his side, keeping him from mindlessly wandering away. Eli March drove an empty freight wagon, his horse tagged along behind, its reins hitched to the wagon's tailgate.

"What do you say, Dog?" said Dooley, stopping on the trail and looking back for the others. "Think they backed off—these posse men, Pinkertons, railroad detectives, whatever the hell they were?"

"Nobody backs away when gold's in the mix," Lou the Dog said, his voice lowered. He sniffed the air as if scenting for trouble. "Leastwise, nobody I've ever seen." He kept his horse at a walk, his rifle propped up on his thigh, his shooting finger on the trigger.

"That's a fact," Dooley said. He stepped his horse away from Lou and rode along on the other side of the narrow trail.

When the two stopped again, they'd reached the point where the wagon tracks led off the side of the trail. They looked down at the pieces of broken wagon lying strewn down the hillside.

"Damn," said Dooley, "a wagonload of gold flying

out off this trail . . ." He shook his head at the wonderment of it for a moment. Then they both turned and looked back as the wagon and the other horsemen rounded the turn and rode forward. Dooley waved the men toward them.

"I'm all for getting this thing done and getting out of here," Dooley said. "A place this quiet always gives me the willies. . . ."

Atop the trail, spying down from the cover of rock, Corporal Rourke raised his thumb over his rifle hammer and cocked it back.

"Once we commence," he said sidelong to Trooper Winslow, "don't let them back around that turn. As long as we keep them down here, we've got them in a box. They get around the turn, they're gone."

"Six of them, and six of us. Sounds fair enough to me," Winslow said. He cocked his rifle and looked down the sights at Silas Dooley's back.

"Leave those two to Goodrich and the others, Trooper," said Rourke. "Work on the wagon, pin it down first thing."

Winslow moved his sights away from Dooley and back to the wagon, which was slowly rolling forward.

"Good move, Trooper," said Rourke. "Now let's wait for our sergeant to start this ball."

No sooner had the corporal said the words than rifle shots rang out from Goodrich and Trooper Trent's position farther along the edge of the trail.

"And there it is now, Trooper!" said Corporal Rourke. "Fire at will!"

Winslow and Rourke both opened fire on the wagon.

Trent's first shot startled Eli March, who let out a scream as a bullet thumped into the seat beside him.

Farther up the trail, Goodrich and Trent fired steadily on Dooley and the Dog. Dooley and the Dog both leaped from their saddles as the sergeant's first shot sliced through Dooley's shoulder. Making a mad scramble for cover, the two returned fire as their horses raced away along the trail, a gray rise of burnt powder already wafting on the chilled air.

"I've got the wagon driver this time!" Winslow said, rising from behind his rock as he took careful aim. He squeezed the trigger, felt the jolt of the rifle against his shoulder and saw the wagon driver fly from the seat in a spray of blood as he tried swinging the wagon around on the trail. His rifle flew from his hand over the edge of the trail.

The empty freight wagon skidded sideways and jammed its rear wheel down into a three-foot-deep washout rut on the inside edge of the trail. It stuck there, the team of horses bucking and rearing to no avail.

"See, Corporal Rourke! I got that sucker! Got him good!" Trooper Winslow shouted, still standing, gunshots resounding along the trail below.

"Get down, Trooper!" shouted Corporal Rourke. But his warning came too late for Trooper Winslow.

A shot from the rocks above them exploded, picked the young soldier up and hurled him off the cliff in a mist of blood. His body struck the steep, jagged hillside twice on its way down, then landed with a smack facedown on the hard, rocky trail.

"*Uh-oh!*" Rourke saw the shot had come from above

them and realized there were more men than the six on the trail below. He swung his rifle up and fired as he saw the glint of a rifle barrel in the afternoon sunlight. But as he fired, two other riflemen along the top of a high ridgeline sent shots ricocheting and screaming all around him. As he ducked down, one of the bullets hit him in the collarbone, snapping it like a seasoned twig.

"Damn it, Rourke!" he said, chastising himself. "Just look at you now." He squeezed the bloody, broken collarbone with his good hand.

On the edge of the trail below, Sergeant Goodrich saw the dead trooper facedown in the trail; he saw the riflemen firing heavily on Rourke's position—Rourke not firing back at them.

He called out to Trooper Trent, who sat firing from behind a rock ten feet away.

"I fear the corporal is wounded up there," he shouted. "Give him some help!"

As Silas Dooley and the Dog kept up a merciless barrage of rifle fire, the sergeant and Trent turned their fire up along the high ridge long enough for Rourke to get himself into deeper cover and return fire himself. Between shots, he pulled a dusty bandanna from around his neck, wadded it up and stuffed it inside his coat onto the bleeding collarbone wound.

Captain Boone and Trooper Lukens had moved along the hillside, traveling upward diagonally until they reached a thick stand of rocks at the edge of the trail. The driverless wagon sat a few yards away.

Crouched down behind the wagon, unable to turn the wagon horses or the wagon's single stuck wheel back onto the trail, Grolin and Swank returned fire relentlessly. But they found themselves pinned down by rifle fire coming from above them and down the edge of the trail. Beside Grolin, Bobby Kane sat leaning back against the wagon wheel without a care in the world. As shots pinged and thumped and whistled past the wagon, Bobby raised his rifle backward and gazed curiously down its dark barrel.

"God almighty!" Grolin cursed in disgust, seeing Bobby grin dreamily. He grabbed Bobby's loaded rifle and handed Bobby his empty, smoking Winchester.

"Here, load this, *idiot*!" he shouted. "You've got to be good for something."

"Will do," Bobby said calmly, the side of his face still purple and swollen from the Giant's backhanded slap. Seeing smoke rise from the Winchester's barrel, he stirred his finger around in it, watching it swirl.

Chapter 25

As soon as the fighting started, Rochenbach had rolled away from the tree onto all fours and crawled over to Casings. Stray bullets whistled overhead, thumped into pines and ricocheted off rocks.

"We're heading straight down this path," Rochenbcah said, nodding toward a thin break in the trees. "The horses are hidden down there."

"You've got to be crazy, Rock, staying behind with this going on," Casings said as Rochenbach unlocked his handcuffs and dropped them to the ground. "Change your mind, before somebody lands a bullet in your head."

"Forget it, Pres," Rochenbach said as bullets zipped overhead. "We're not going through all the reasons again. Both of you need to get to a doctor, before you start bleeding out again."

"Want me to backhand him, Pres, carry him over my shoulder?" said the Giant. His big eyes widened as he saw Rock stand crouched before him with a long boot dagger in his hand. "Just joking," he said.

"I know," said Rochenbach. Leaning in, he slipped the blade under the rope holding the huge man to the tree. One slice and the rope fell away.

"Jesus!" said Casings. "You've been carrying that around? Didn't anybody search you?"

"Yes, but not that good," Rochenbach said.

"When were you going to use it?" Casings asked, seeing Rochenbach run the blade under the rope on the Giant's wrists and make one swipe through it.

"When it came time to cut somebody loose from a tree," Rock said, hefting the knife on his palm, then slipping it down his boot well. He stared at Casings as he turned to the hidden path. "Now come on, follow me, get yourselves out of here. I'll meet you at the doctor's in Dunbar."

"The doctor in Dunbar is a drunkard and an opium smoker," the Giant said.

"So?" Rochenbach responded.

"Nothing," said the Giant. He shrugged. "Just thought I'd mention it."

Casings shook his head and fell behind Rochenbach on the narrow path.

"Come on, Giant," he said, "I know when I'm not wanted." He grinned, holding the bandanna to his wounded side.

"Me too," said the Giant, turning to follow Casings. A stray bullet zipped past and opened a seam on the shoulder of his coat. The impact of the shot startled him. "Whoa, let's get out of here!"

When they'd reached the horses, the Giant looked back and forth, deciding which horse would be strong enough to carry him down off the trail and into Dunbar. Bullets continued to slice through the treetops.

"Take two, Giant!" Casings said, getting impatient. As he spoke, he pulled the reins to three horses loose from a rope hitch line tied between two trees. He handed two sets of reins to the Giant.

"I want to leave a good horse for you, Rock," the Giant said.

"Don't worry about me, Giant," Rochenbach said. "My horse is standing right there. You're the one needs medical attention."

Climbing into the saddle, Casings spun his horse toward Rochenbach and pointed a finger at him.

"Dunbar, Rock," he said. "Don't make us come back looking for you."

"I'll be there before you are if you don't get going," Rock said. He slapped the horse's rear. Casings galloped away, the Giant right beside him, leading a spare horse for himself.

Halfway down the trail, both men slowed their horses a little and looked back toward the raging gunfire.

"What the hell is Rock up to?" the Giant asked.

"I have no idea," said Casings. "Whatever it is, he wants to handle it himself." He shrugged and booted the horse forward. "He's been straight with us. This is what he wants, this is what he gets."

"Dang it, I'm starting to bleed all over again," the Giant said.

Casings looked him up and down, seeing fresh blood on his wide chest, his sides, running down the back of his hand from under his sleeve.

"So are you, Pres," the Giant said, gesturing toward the fresh blood soaking through the shoulder of Casings' coat.

"Yeah, I know," Casings said. "Got to get to that doctor in Dunbar. . . ." He booted his horse forward, back up into a gallop. . . .

With the two wounded men out of sight, Rochenbach jerked his horse's reins free from the hitch line and stepped up into his saddle. The big dun grumbled and chuffed and slung its head back and forth before Rock collected it with a strong draw of the reins.

"I've missed you too," he said wryly to the horse. He booted the big, restless dun onto another thin path leading diagonally up the hillside toward the fighting.

As he neared the edge of the trail, he swung the dun wide to his left, avoided the fighting and climbed up a steep rocky path as far as the spirited horse could take him.

Jumping down from the saddle, he wrapped the dun's reins around the saddle horn and slapped its rump, sending it back down the steep path toward the trail. He reached down and jerked the knife from his boot well.

Ten yards to his right, slightly above him among a stand of rock, he saw gray looming smoke and heard steady rifle fire raining down on the soldiers below.

A good place to start, he told himself.

Shoving the knife down behind his belt, he stepped over onto a foothold in the rocky hillside and climbed hand over hand until he reached the edge of a cliff.

He rolled onto his hands and knees on a narrow ledge and stopped for a moment to look around quickly.

Twelve feet away, at the far end of the ledge, he saw Lyle Myers staring down his rifle barrel, firing round after round, the rifle bucking repeatedly in his hands.

Rochenbach snatched the knife from his waist and sprang forward, coming up off all fours like a mountain cat. Myers saw his attacker coming from the corner of his eye. He swung his rifle around to meet him, but he was too late. Rock blocked the rifle with his forearm as he brought the steel point of the blade up between Meyers' ribs and buried it in his heart.

Myers' rifle fell from his hands at Rock's feet. He rose onto his toes as if to get away from the sharp bite of the blade, but there was no escaping it. His mouth and eyes opened wide. Rochenbach's arm slipped around his shoulders and embraced him like an old friend. He held Myers in place until the weight of him fell forward, lifeless against him.

Jerking the blade from Myers' chest as he fell, Rock stepped back and to the side. Then he wiped the blade across the dead man's back and quickly picked up the smoking rifle. He checked it and looked farther along the ridgeline as he slipped a big, bone-handled Colt from Myers' hip and stuck it into his empty belly holster.

Standing in a crouch, he picked up a bandoleer of ammunition and slung it over his shoulder. Below him the fighting raged. Along the ridgeline stretched out before him, he saw two separate clouds of looming gray smoke. He heard the endless explosions of gunfire.

"One down, two to go," he murmured to himself.

He climbed a steep footpath to the spot where Lyle Myers' horse stood hitched to a scrub juniper. He snatched the horse's reins free and slipped up into the saddle. Rifle in hand, he booted the blaze-faced chestnut out along the rocky ridgeline.

When he got to the next gunman's position, he saw the man's horse reined to a stand of rocks. While the gunman stood looking down over the edge of the trail, his full attention focused on firing madly down at the soldiers, Rock slipped from his saddle and reined the chestnut next to the other animal. As the two horses nosed each other's muzzles, Rock slipped over to the edge in a crouch and stared at the gunman from twenty feet.

As if suddenly realizing someone was watching him from behind, Frank Penta turned around, smoking rifle in hand, and looked at Rochenbach through a haze of gun smoke. Seeing that Rockenbach had him cold, the rifle in Rock's hands pointed, aimed and cocked at him, Penta gave him a strange, tight grin.

"Some fight, huh, Rock?" he called out above the roar of gunfire, sounding as if the two of them had been close friends.

"Yes, it is," Rock agreed. His right eye fixed down the rifle sights, he squeezed the trigger. Penta dropped his rifle and clasped his chest with both hands as he staggered backward. He caught himself at the edge of the cliff for just a second. Then he fell off the cliff and bounced down the steep, rocky hillside.

Rochenbach looked toward the next looming cloud of smoke thirty yards away. He levered a fresh round into his rifle chamber and walked back to the horses. Before stepping into the saddle, he dropped the saddle and bridle from Penta's horse and slapped its rump. As the horse bolted away, the chestnut tugged at its hitched reins, trying to run alongside the freed animal.

"Not you," Rock said to the chestnut. "Not yet anyway."

Looking along the ridgeline, he heard one shot fire at the trail below. Then he saw Dent Spiller scramble over the edge of the cliff and run to his waiting horse. The gunman grabbed his horse's reins, jumped into his saddle and raced away, not giving Rochenbach so much as a glance.

Rock raised his rifle to take aim, but Spiller disappeared over a rise on the hilltop and thundered down the trail. Lowering his rifle, Rock turned and stepped up into his saddle. Noting that the firing below had waned over the past few minutes, he gave the chestnut a tap of his boots and rode away.

Realizing they'd been caught in a trap, Grolin and Swank leaped atop their horses and fled the trail as soon as the rifle fire from their men above the trail came to a stop. As they beat a hasty retreat around the turn in the trail, Swank looked at the reins to Bobby Kane's horse in Grolin's hand, Kane riding along close behind him.

"Why are you keeping that idiot alive?" Swank shouted at him.

But Grolin didn't answer. He kept his head down and rode hard toward Dunbar.

Silas Dooley and the Dog fought on fiercely for a few minutes longer, until they saw Dent Spiller ride down a thin path and across the trail twenty yards away and keep on riding.

"What the hell was that?" Dooley cried out as shots still whistled past them.

"That was the last of our rifle cover running out on us!" said the Dog.

"Damn it!" said Dooley. He looked down the trail toward the empty wagon, then back to the Dog as two more bullets sliced past them. "What the hell are we waiting for?"

"Beats me," said Lou. "I've been ready." He turned and ran in a crouch in the same direction their spooked horses had taken toward the turn in the trail.

"That bastard Swank!" said Dooley, running right beside him. "He led us right into this—made it sound easy, talking about taking the gold away from Grolin and his men!"

"He shoulda hit a little harder on what we'd have to do to get it from these fellows *first*!" shouted Lou.

The two continued running away even as the firing slowed to a stop behind them.

Chapter 26

———

Rochenbach caught sight of the two fleeing gunmen as he rode from the ridgeline back down onto the trail. But he didn't have time to raise his rifle and fire at them before they'd disappeared out of sight around the turn to where their horses stood beside the trail. Instead, he booted the chestnut on to where his big dun stood at the foot of the path he'd sent it running down.

"Glad to see you made it," he said to the waiting horse.

He picked up the reins from around the dun's saddle horn and had started to lead the animal away when he saw Trooper Lukens spring out of the brush on the other side of the trail with a rifle pointed at him.

"All right, Smith, drop the gun! Drop it now!" the young soldier said, his voice sounding nervous and uncertain. He stood pale-faced and covered with fresh blood. But upon closer look, Rochenbach saw no signs of a wound on him.

"Do you hear me, Smith?" the trooper said. "Drop that rifle before I shoot!"

Rochenbach ignored his order and let out a breath.

"Where's the captain, Trooper?" he asked, seeing the young soldier squeeze his hand tight around his saddle carbine.

Lukens' strong demeanor appeared to almost melt at the mention of the captain. His face took on a worried look.

"He's—he's down off the side of the trail with the horses," he said. "He's been shot *bad*."

Oh no. . . .

Rochenbach winced and swung down from his saddle and led both horses toward the edge of the trail.

"How bad?" he asked as he led the two animals into the cover of rock and brush.

"I told you to drop that rifle, Smith!" Lukens shouted suddenly, trying to take charge. He looked all around, frightened.

"Well, I'm not going to, Trooper," said Rock, "so shut up about it and let's see about the captain. How bad is he?" he repeated.

"As bad as ever I've seen, Smith," Lukens said, swallowing a knot in his throat.

"You know there's a doctor in Dunbar," Rochenbach said, gesturing the young soldier in front and following him down the hillside.

"I'm thinking he's past doctoring, to be honest with you," Lukens said.

Rochenbach winced again.

In the small clearing where the soldiers' horses

stood, the wounded captain raised his head and looked up from where he lay slumped back against a tree. The center of his chest was covered with dark blood. His right hand held a blood-soaked bandanna against the wound. An open canteen rested against the side of his leg.

"A soldier . . . should not die . . . out of uniform," he rasped, seeing Rochenbach walk toward him.

Rochenbach stooped down beside him. He lifted his hand and the bandanna a little and examined the wound closely, seeing the severity of it.

"You're a soldier, Captain, uniform or not," he said. "There's no doubt about that."

"I—I saw you," Captain Boone said, clutching his forearm with his other bloody hand. "You were up there . . . shooting at them. You were on our side."

"Don't tell anybody," Rochenbach said. "You'll ruin my reputation."

"Who are you, Smith?" the captain said. "I know there's more to you . . . than you told me."

Rochenbach saw the man was dying. He tossed a glance up toward Lukens. Captain Boone caught the look.

"Trooper . . . go look the wagon over good," he told Lukens. "We've got . . . to load the gold when the others arrive."

Lukens looked hesitantly at Rochenbach.

"Go on, Trooper," urged the captain. "This man is no longer a prisoner."

"Yes, sir," said Lukens, looking a little relieved. Turning on his heel, he hurried away through the brush and toward the trail.

"You're hauling that gilded junk out of here, are you, Captain?" Rochenbach asked as soon as Lukens was out of sight.

"Of course . . . we are," said the wounded captain with a crooked, bloody smile. "That's the mission." He coughed and looked back at Rochenbach. "Now, who are you, Smith? I don't want to die wondering."

"Remember the identity code you asked me for? I told you I'd forgotten the four numbers?"

Boone nodded his head weakly, a knowing look coming upon his pale face—a look of satisfaction.

Here goes . . . , Rock told himself.

"My name is Avrial Rochenbach, Captain," he said in a low voice. He glanced around, then leaned in closer and whispered the four numbers into the captain's ear.

Boone gave a smile of recognition. "I knew it. I was right . . . you're the *government man.*"

"*Shhh,*" said Rochenbach. "My reputation."

"Yes, of course, your reputation . . ." Boone managed another bloody smile. "Tell me, Avrial Rochenbach. Did we do . . . this right, all of us, together?" Boone asked, his voice fading fast.

"We did it all the best we could, Captain, under the circumstances," said Rochenbach. "We always do, folks like you and me. We're fellow countrymen."

"Fellow countrymen. That's good . . . to hear," said Boone. His grin turned to a faint smile as more blood seeped from his trembling lips. "I'm going on now . . . ," he whispered.

"Captain?" Rochenbach started to shake him a

little, but he stopped himself, seeing it would do no good.

Captain Boone's eyes glazed over. His hand fell away from Rochenbach's forearm.

Adios, Captain. . . .

Rochenbach wasn't about to tell the dying captain how foolish he thought this had been, men dying over worthless plated gold. All this just so he could ferret out the name of one man—a man in a position of public trust, who used his position to steal from the very people who had bestowed that trust upon him.

Shame on you, Inman S. Walker.

He reached out and closed the captain's eyes.

"He was felled by the last shot fired from up on the ridgeline," Trooper Lukens said, walking up quietly behind Rochenbach.

Rochenbach considered it, picturing Spiller running to his horse, his rifle in hand. He reached down and pulled his Remington from the captain's belt and stood up, letting the gun hang down his right side. In his left hand he held his rifle.

"I'm leaving," he said flatly, giving Lukens a flat, determined stare.

"Go on, then," said Lukens. "Captain Boone said you're not a prisoner anymore. That's good enough for me."

Rochenbach turned to get his horses.

"You best hurry on, Smith," said Lukens. He gestured a nod upward toward the trail. "I saw Sergeant Goodrich and a couple others limping along the trail, headed this way. They're chewed up, but they might shoot you on sight."

"Obliged, Trooper," Rochenbach said. He walked back through the brush to where the two horses stood waiting. He left the blaze-faced chestnut where it stood, stepped up atop the big dun and rode away, down through the trees toward the trail leading to Dunbar.

Pres Casings lay on a gurney in the surgery room of the doctor's office in Dunbar. Afternoon sunlight spread slantwise across the floor through an open window. The Stillwater Giant, being too large for a gurney, was stretched out on two dinner-sized tables standing along the wall to keep from blocking the whole room. The doctor stood over his massive chest with a pair of long, tapered surgery tongs.

"My goodness," the bald, middle-aged doctor said, staring at the round stone he'd pulled out of the Giant's chest with the tongs. "This is most unusual." A long, dark strand of congealed blood hung from the stone.

"What is, Doc?" the Giant asked, raising his head a little and staring along with the doctor.

"I probed for a bullet, but I pulled this stone from between your ribs.

"Oh, that . . . ," said the Giant, laying his head back down. "I stuck it there."

"You stuck a stone in your chest wound?" the doctor asked in disbelief.

"I just wanted to see if it would stop the bleeding,"

the Giant said with a big-toothed grin. "It stopped it, huh?"

"Well . . . yes, it appears that it did," the doctor said. He dropped the stone into a pan.

From his gurney, Casings listened and smiled to himself.

"Doc, he stuck rocks in his wounds when we stopped to water our horses at a creek. That's why he wanted you to attend to me first. Right, Giant?"

"Yep," the Giant said proudly. "I was in no hurry once the bleeding stopped."

The doctor looked at the Giant's other wounds, bullet holes crusted over with dried blood.

"So, am I to believe I'll be finding more of these stones inside you, Mr. Garth?"

"Yep," the Giant said. "There's one stone per bullet hole. I didn't stick them in too deep, but riding might've stuck them deeper." He grinned. "I thought about sticking more than one in a couple of the holes. But I was afraid it might be harmful."

"*Harmful . . . ?* Yes, I understand why," the doctor said. "Good thinking, sir." He shook his bald head a little and wiped crusted blood from another wound with a wet cloth.

"Ready, Doc?" the Giant asked.

"Yes, hold on to the table edge, Mr. Garth," the doctor said. "Here we go again."

The Giant's huge hands gripped the tables' edges tightly. He took a deep breath as the probe went inside the nearly bloodless bullet hole and slid deeper until the doctor felt it clink against a stone.

"Oh, I felt *that*!" the Giant said through his big clenched teeth.

"I bet you did," said the doctor. He laid a folded patch of gauze on the wound and pressed it gently but firmly until a thin seepage of blood held it in place.

Casings lay back on the gurney and stared up at the white ceiling, exhausted from the loss of blood, but feeling better already now that his wound had been attended and bandaged.

As the doctor probed, he spoke to both men.

"Not meaning to pry, gentlemen," he said, "but were the two of you involved in the shooting that went on along the high trails earlier?"

"What if we were?" Casings asked.

"If you were, then I feel it only fair to warn you there's an angry teamster roaming the range with a shotgun. He's looking for the men who knocked him unconscious and stole his freight wagon."

"Obliged for the warning," said Casings, "but that wouldn't be us. We just arrived in town a few minutes ago—came here first thing."

"I see . . . ," the doctor murmured, concentrating on pulling out another creek stone and dropping it into the metal pan. "There was a train robbery not far from the high trails," he said, wiping the wound with the wet cloth and inspecting it. "The robbers managed to steal an engine and three railcars. One was a shipment from the Denver City Mint."

"You don't say?" said Casings. He and the Giant looked at each other.

"The telegraph came in this morning," the doctor

said as he set another gauze patch into place and pressed on it. He shook his head. "This modern world we're living in, you hear of these things every few weeks, sometimes more frequently. . . ."

"It's amazing," Casings said, relaxing, "no doubt about it."

When the doctor finished removing stones and bullets from the Giant's wounds, he dressed the wounds with clean cotton gauze and wound his huge body with strips of cloth to hold the gauze in place. As he finished, he looked down at the Giant's trousers and noted that two large pairs of trousers had been sewn together into one. As he helped the Giant put on his shirt, he saw it had been made out of a large wool blanket.

"If you don't mind my saying so, Mr. Garth, you are the biggest man I have ever seen," the doctor said in amazement.

"I don't mind," said the Giant, his huge fingers buttoning the bib of his shirt. "I'm glad to hear it since I was the runt of my family."

"My God," said the doctor, "you can't be serious!"

The Giant grinned and didn't answer.

"I am the *biggest* man in the world, Doctor," he said.

"How do you know that to be true?" the doctor said.

"I've asked around," said the Giant.

Casings chuckled under his breath, drew coins from his pocket and placed them on the doctor's desk. The doctor looked at them and nodded his approval.

As the two left the doctor's office and walked to the hitch rail out front, each with a rifle in his hands, they slowed to a halt, seeing Andrew Grolin, Heaton Swank and their remaining men standing in a wide half circle around the front of the doctor's white clapboard-sided house.

"Well, well, *well-well-well!*" said Grolin, with a wide, menacing grin.

A few feet from Grolin, Dent Spiller had his rifle aimed at the two gunmen. Silas Dooley stood flanking Spiller with ten feet between them. Swank was a few feet from Spiller on his right. Bobby Kane stood off to the side, still looking confused, but appearing to be a little more aware of what was going on around him.

Grolin's left fist rested on his cocked hip, while his right hand wrapped around the butt of a big holstered Colt.

"Tell me something, Pres," he said. "How many times do I have to kill you two before it's going to stick?"

Chapter 27

Casings and the Stillwater Giant stood four feet apart in the dirt street, their shadows stretching long in the afternoon sunlight. Grolin looked them up and down, noting the bandage on Casings' head. Neither of them had offered an answer to his question moments ago. They had no doubt he would kill them this time.

Spiller took a step forward, his rifle aimed and cocked toward the two wounded gunmen.

"Don't talk to these two poltroons, boss," he said to Grolin. "Give me the word, I'll chop them both down right now where they stand."

"Not before I wring your head off like a chicken!" the Giant growled at Spiller. He stepped forward; rifles cocked. Casings grabbed him by the tail of his coat.

"Take it easy, Giant," Casings said loud enough for Grolin to hear. "Don't do it. This is what they want us to do!"

"Try me, Giant!" said Spiller, taking a stance with

his rifle toward the big man. "I'll kill you quicker than—"

"Relax, Dent, we're talking here," Grolin ordered, cutting Spiller off. He chuckled a little. Knowing the two wounded gunmen were outnumbered, he was in no hurry. This time he had them. They weren't leaving here alive. He looked at Casings.

"Believe me, Pres," he said, "if I wanted you both dead *right now*, you'd both be lying bloody in the street *right now*." He looked past the two, his eyes searching the doctor's porch, the front door.

"What do you want, then?" asked Casings. Both he and the Giant stood with their right hands on the butt of their Colts. Rifles hung ready in their left hands. Still, they both knew the odds were against them.

"I want the son of a bitch who fouled everything up for me!" Grolin said angrily. *"That's* what *I want!"*

"Then you're out of luck," Casings said. "Rock's dead."

"You're lying, Pres," Grolin said.

"Hell yes, he's lying," said Spiller. "Let me blow his head off."

"Wait, damn it to hell!" Grolin said to Spiller, losing patience, giving him a scorching stare. He shot a look back at Casings and said, "What do you mean he's dead? Didn't he kill Shaner when I left him to take care of him?"

"Yeah, he killed Shaner," said Casings. "But we found him dead on the trail. Evidently the posse made quick work of him."

Grolin chuffed and relaxed a little. He let out a breath.

"Hell," he said, "I never thought I'd be this happy to hear about a posse killing a long rider." He let his hand come off his gun butt, go inside his coat and come out with a fresh cigar.

Around him, the men eased down a little, except for Spiller. Itching for a fight, he kept his rifle aimed and cocked.

"Who the hell were they anyway?" he asked Casings. "Railroad men or what?"

Casings only shrugged. He and the Giant kept their right hands on their holstered Colts and watched as Grolin bit the tip off a fresh cigar and blew it away.

"I don't know *what* they are," Casings said. "But I see you didn't get all the gold from them."

"Not all," said Grolin, "not yet anyway. But I *will* get it all. Swank and I are partnered up on it." He gestured a nod toward Heaton Swank, who stood watching, listening, his hand also resting on his holstered gun butt. "We'll get it *all* before it's over."

"Yeah? Well, we've got news for you, Andrew," said the Giant, a wide grin coming to his big face. Knowing he was going to die anyway, he couldn't deny himself the satisfaction of seeing the look on Grolin's face when he found out the ingots were not real gold at all, only cheap gilded metal. "Tell him, Pres," he said, turning it over to Casings.

"Keep quiet about it, Giant," said Casings. "We don't need to tell him anything."

"Tell me what, Pres?" Grolin said.

"Nothing," Casings said. He stared hard at Dent Spiller, the man who used to be his close friend. To the Giant he said, "Let them all find out for themselves."

From inside his coat, Grolin took out a match, struck it and lit his cigar. He puffed on it, shook out the match and held the cigar between his finger and thumb.

"If there's something you want to tell me, Pres, get to it," Grolin said. "If not, I see no reason in standing here just to watch the sun go down." He gave Spiller a nod and flipped the spent match away.

"It's about damn time," Spiller growled under his breath. He raised his rifle, ready to fire.

"Grolin! Look at this!" said Silas Dooley.

Grolin, Spiller and the others all turned as one, seeing Rochenbach ride slowly toward them right up the middle of the dirt street.

"Well, I'll be damned," said Grolin.

The Giant grinned and said to himself, "Ol' Rock! Right on time!"

As the Giant spoke, he and Casings drew their Colts instinctively while the others' eyes were turned for a second toward Rochenbach.

Grolin clenched his teeth tightly on his cigar.

"This son of a bitch!" he growled. He swung back toward Casings and the Giant. "Don't think—" His words stopped as he saw their guns out, leveled and cocked. But then he continued. "Don't think this is going to help you any. We'll kill him too. In fact, it will be a pleasure"

"It's already helped us some," Casings said, ready to start squeezing the trigger himself.

Grolin and the others stood in silence as Rochenbach rode up, stopped fifteen feet away and turned his dun to them in the street. He held his big Remington resting along his right thigh. As soon as the dun had settled, Spiller stepped closer with his rifle half raised, his finger on the hammer.

"Rochenbach!" he shouted. "I can't tell you how long I've waited for you and me to stand off toe-to—"

His words stopped short beneath the sound of Rochenbach's big Remington resounding along the empty street. The shot nailed Spiller squarely in the chest and sent him flying backward through a heavy mist of blood. His rifle flew from his hands and landed at Bobby Kane's feet. Kane stared down at it as if he might or might not know what it was.

For the captain, Rock told himself. The big Remington stood smoking in his hand.

The gunmen aimed their weapons toward Rochenbach. But then they froze, tense, waiting. Rochenbach calmly lowered the smoking Remington and stared at Grolin before he pitched an ingot to the ground at Grolin's feet.

"What the hell?" Grolin managed to say. Swank stepped over, stooped down, picked it up and looked it over in his hand.

"Well . . . ?" Pres Casings called out to Swank, liking this sudden turn on things. "Tell him what it is, Heaton," he said as Swank looked at the cut corner of the glittering ingot.

"Casings is right, Grolin," said Swank, a sour look coming to his face. "This is a damned phony—a chunk of lead, *pig iron* . . . something. It's sure as hell not gold!" He shoved the ingot to Grolin, again fixing his angry eyes up at Rochenbach.

Grolin looked at it, his face twisted and confused.

"I don't know where you got this, Rochenbach," Grolin said, "but it's got nothing to do with the ingots we took from the train—"

Rochenbach cut him off, saying, "I got it from one of the ingot crates you've got stashed in the stall with the Belgium," he said, gesturing a nod toward the livery barn a block away.

"No, you didn't! You're lying!" said Grolin, gripping the ingot tight in his fist. "Lou the Dog is guarding that gold!"

"He *was*," Rochenbach said calmly. "Maybe he will be again when he wakes up."

Grolin gritted his teeth; his thick hand tightened on the butt of his Colt, the only gun still in its holster. But he dared not draw the Colt, not now—not with Heaton Swank's eyes burning a hole in him.

"Rochenbach, you son of a bitch!" he shouted. "You've done nothing but mess up everything I've tried to do since you've been here!"

"What'd he do?" Swank asked pointedly, staring hard at Grolin.

"He did what he was *supposed* to do," Casings called out. "He did what Grolin told him to do, just like the rest of us always do. Hell, he's the best safe man we've ever seen."

"Shut up, Casings," said Swank. He turned back to Grolin. "Well, Andrew? What did he do?" he demanded.

Grolin looked stuck for an answer. He stalled, threw his cigar to the ground, grabbed his temples with his thumbs and fingers as if suffering from a terrible headache.

"Damn it, Swank! I can't pinpoint every least little thing he did. He's been . . . unruly, undermining, divisive!"

Swank gave him a look of disbelief.

"*Unruly? Undermining . . . ?*" he said. "What the hell is this, a school yard? The man's an outlaw. Didn't he tell you?"

"I told you it's hard to explain!" said Grolin. "But he's ruined this whole big job for all of us—ruined it from the start!"

"You're losing your damned mind, Andrew," said Swank. "I'll tell you something he *didn't* do. He didn't get none of my men shot up over a damn load of fake gold ingots!" he snarled. "You didn't have the sense to check the load, make sure it was real gold?"

"Don't crowd me on this, Heaton, I'm warning you!" Grolin shouted.

"Crowd you, Grolin? You're lucky if I don't kill you!" Swank shouted in reply.

Rochenbach watched calmly from his saddle. Casings and the Stillwater Giant stood pat, their guns drawn, cocked, ready for anything, rifles in their other hands.

They're good.

Swank snatched the ingot from Grolin's hand, threw it to the ground and shot a hole through it. It broke in two. Both pieces of metal bounced ten feet in the air. Bobby Kane watched with a half smile as the pieces spun and glittered in the afternoon sunlight.

When Swank turned back to Grolin with the smoking Colt in his hand, Grolin mistook the move. Thinking Swank meant to shoot him next, he jerked his Colt up from its holster and fired at a distance of less than three feet.

Swank rose onto his boot toes as the bullet ripped through his belly. He staggered back a step, but caught himself and returned fire. Grolin took the bullet in his chest and wobbled on his feet, but he continued firing. Rochenbach watched intently; so did Casings and the Giant—two gunmen shooting each other back and forth repeatedly on the dirt street.

Jesus . . .

Rochenbach shook his head a little, seeing Heaton Swank go down beneath a gray rise of smoke. Grolin staggered back another step and wobbled back and forth, waving his Colt, gripping his belly, blood spewing from his lips.

Seeing Swank dead, knowing the gold ingots were worthless, Silas Dooley murmured to himself, "To hell with this!" He backed away a few feet, then turned and ran off while all eyes were set on Grolin.

"Don't nobody . . . try to stop me!" Grolin warned mindlessly, no longer interested in Rochenbach, the gold or anything else. He turned and staggered off toward the livery barn a block away, leaving a bloody trail behind him.

Rochenbach, Casings and the Giant stood watching.

Grolin had made it fifty feet up the center of the empty dirt street when suddenly a loud shotgun blast exploded from an alleyway and hit him from the side. The buckshot lifted him up like a rag doll and flung him sidelong ten feet. He landed dead and bloody in the dirt.

A big bearded man in buckskins walked out from

the alleyway carrying a smoking double-barreled shotgun. A bloodstained bandage covered his otherwise bare head.

"Steal my wagon *now, you son of a bitch!*" he growled down at Grolin's mangled body. Then he looked down the street at Rochenbach, Casings and the Giant. He half raised his shotgun toward them.

Rochenbach raised his hands chest high in a show of peace, and the buckskinned man backed away warily for a few steps. Then he turned and stomped back into the alley, still grumbling under his breath.

"Where's the sheriff of this town?" Rochenbach asked Casings as he and the Giant walked over and stood beside him.

"The doctor said he's gone fishing," Casings replied. "Said he's been gone all day."

Rock looked around at the dead men on the ground, then up at the fading afternoon sky.

"This would've been a good day for it," he said. He stepped down from his saddle and looked the two up and down. "I don't know how some folks find the time."

"Me neither," the Giant said.

Casings chuckled and shook his head. "Rock, I got to say, Grolin was right. You're a hell of a safe man. But things do seem to get crazy when you're around."

"What if it rains, Pres?" said Rock. "Are you going to blame me for the weather too?"

"I'm not blaming you for anything," Casings said. "I want to rob trains, open safes with you, get to be rich desperadoes."

"Hey! What about Bobby there?" the Giant asked.

They looked over and saw Bobby Kane standing with Spiller's rifle in his hands, a blank look on his face.

"Bobby, put the rifle down," Casings called out.

Kane looked at them, confused for a second. Then he nodded and tossed the rifle away. He stepped back and wiped his palms on his trousers. The Giant walked over to him.

"Are you doing all right, Bobby?" he asked in his deep powerful voice.

"Just fine," Bobby said with a dazed grin. "How's everybody here?"

"Come on with us awhile, Bobby," the Giant chuckled. He patted a huge hand on the gunman's shoulder. "I'm sorry I smacked you so hard."

"Me too," Bobby said, still wearing the same dazed grin.

"What now, Rock?" Casings said, the four of them turning, walking along the middle of the dirt street, seeing faces appear in windows and shop doors now that the shooting was over. "You got anything lined up?"

"Not right now," Rock said. "It's a good time to lie low awhile, I think, until the dust settles over this job."

"Are you sticking with us, me and the Giant?" he asked.

"Right now I've got to send a telegraph, report in," Rock said.

"*Report in*?" Casings said. He looked puzzled, but only for a second. "Oh, I get it. You've got a woman you're stuck on somewhere."

"Something like that," Rock said, walking on, leading the dun behind by its reins.

"Something serious, is it?" Casings asked.

"Yeah, you could say it's serious," Rock replied. "I keep in touch every chance I get."

He spotted the town telegraph office up the dirt street. He would go there, send a wire to his field office in Denver City, give them Inman Walker's name and call this case closed. That was that, he told himself.

"Why don't you and the Giant get out of here, before the sheriff gets back from fishing?" Rock said. "If you get something that looks good, I'll be in Denver City for a while. You'll find me there. Ask around at any of the saloons. Meanwhile, I'll see what I can come up with for us."

"We could ride there with you," Casings said.

"No, you two need some rest tonight," said Rochenbach. "Get your blood back to where it should be. I'm going to take care of my horse, clean my guns and ride out come dark." He smiled. "Ride *all night*. Nothing stops me. I'll be onto something tomorrow."

"Sounds good to me," Casings said, he and the Giant walking on along the empty dirt street in the waning sunlight.

Arizona Territory

Wildfire raged.

The young ranger Sam Burrack sat atop a rust-colored barb on a bald ridge overlooking a wide, rocky chasm. With a battered brass-trimmed telescope, he scanned beyond the buffering walls of boulder and brush. Long rising hillsides ran slantwise heaven to earth, covered by an endless pine woodlands. He studied the blanketing fire as it billowed and twisted its way north to south along the hill lines. He watched flames the color of hell lick upward hundreds of feet, drifting, blackening the heavens.

Through the circle of the lens he spotted four wolves sitting next to one another along a rock ledge, winded and panting. Their pink tongues lolling, they stared back at the wall of smoke and fire as if numbed, overpowered by it.

At the bottom of the hills, where the woodlands came to an end at the chasm, Sam saw a large brown bear stop in its tracks, turn, and rise on its hind legs. The beast stood erect with its forearms and claws spread wide and raged back at the fire, ready to do battle. Yet even so powerful a beast looked helpless and frail beneath that which lay spoil to its domain. At the end of its roar, the bear dropped back onto all fours as if bowing in submission, and loped on.

The ranger shook his head, noting how little caution the other fleeing woodland creatures paid it as they darted among dry washes and gullies, and bounded over brush and rock with no more than a reflex glance in the roaring bear's direction. Even the barb beneath him paid no mind to the bear's warning until a draft of hot smoke swept in from behind. Then the horse skittered sideways and chuffed and scraped a nervous hoof.

"Easy now . . . ," the ranger murmured, tightening his hold on the reins, and collecting the animal. "We're not going to get you cooked." He patted a gloved hand on the barb's withers. "Me neither, I'm hoping," he added, closing the telescope between his hands. He looked down at the sets of hoofprints he'd been tracking for three days and gave the barb a tap of his bootheels.

But the barb would have none of it. Instead, the animal grumbled and sawed its head and stalled back on its front legs.

The ranger picked up his Winchester from across his lap. He gave another, firmer tap of his bootheels, this time reaching back with his rifle and lightly striking the barrel on the barb's rump.

"Come on, pard, we know our jobs," he said.

This time he felt the barb take his command and step forward onto the path winding down toward the rocky land below. But even as the animal did as Sam asked, he gave a chuff of protest.

"I know," said Sam. "I don't like it either."

Four hundred yards down, the meandering dirt trail hardened into rock and left the ranger with no sign to follow other than the occasional broken pine needles where one of the four men's horses had laid down an iron-ringed hoof. But that gave him no cause for concern—the old, overgrown game trail lay down the rocky, deep-cut hillside. And now that the fire had moved in across the thick woodlands, there would be no other logical way north except to follow the chasm to its end.

He knew the bottom trail would stretch fourteen miles before coming to water—twenty-six miles farther before reaching Bagley's Trading Post. By then the men he followed would need fresh horses. They wouldn't rest their current horses before riding on. *That would take too much time*, he told himself. Men like Royal Tarpis, Silas "Red" Gantry, and Dockery Latin never wasted time when they were on the move. Out in the open this way, these men moved instinctively as if someone was on their trail, whether they knew it to be a fact or not.

Men with blood on their trail . . . , Sam told himself, knowing there was a younger man leading the gang these days. That man was the Cheyenne Kid, and he was known to be ruthless. But now the Kid was wounded and bleeding. He'd shot and killed two men, a bank teller and the town sheriff, in Phoebe. The sheriff had managed to put a bullet in the murdering young outlaw before falling dead in the street. Sam had picked up the men's trail the following day, and he'd been on it ever since.

Sure, they know someone is coming . . .

Sam drew the barb to a halt at a break in the trail and looked to his left, across the chasm where the fire roared, smoke filling the sky. He took off his left glove and felt the barb's withers. The horse's coat was dry—hot to his touch. So was his own left cheek, he thought, raising his palm to his face, feeling the prickliness of his beard stubble, noticing the stiff, scorched sensation along his cheek line, the dryness in the corners of his eyes as he squinted them shut for a second, gauging the heat.

Untying the bandanna from around his neck, Sam used it to fashion a curtain beneath the brim of his sombrero, which draped his left cheek. It would help some, he thought.

"I hope I didn't lie to you, pard," he said to the horse, recalling his earlier words to the animal.

He picked up his canteen that hung from his saddle horn, uncapped it, swished a mouthful of water around in his mouth and spit the water out along the left side of horse's neck. He leaned forward in his saddle and poured a thin stream of water down the horse's muzzle and along its left side, taking in his own leg and back along its flank. The horse shuddered and chuffed and reached its tongue around to lick at its side.

"That's all for now," Sam said.

He capped the canteen and rehung it. All right, it was hot, but he'd expected that, he reminded himself. Three miles ahead of him, give or take, he saw the fired had waned on its push southward. In the wake of the billowing inferno stood a few bare and blackened pine skeletons.

But he and the horse were safe. He had calculated the risk before putting the horse forward onto the trail. Had the wind made a sudden shift and blown straight at them before they'd reached the trail's halfway point, he would have turned back and raced to the top again before succumbing to the heat. Halfway down the trail, he'd realized there was an end to the fire a few miles to the north—the direction he was headed in. From that point, had the wind changed suddenly, he would have raced down the trail.

Whichever way, they'd make it.

And oddly enough, he thought, owing to the rise of heat, it had been hotter atop the trail than it was here below. Still, it had been risky, said a cautioning voice that often admonished him at times such as these.

Yes, it had, he admitted. *But . . .* He let out a breath of relief.

"*Life is naught without its risks . . . ,*" he quoted to himself.

Who had said that? He shrugged as he nudged the horse forward. He didn't know. Probably some obscure penny dreadful author who had stood—or had *imagined* himself to have stood—on just such a trail as this.

He started forward along the lower end of the trail,

where he knew the heat would be less intense. As he rode he shook his head. Leave it to men like these to ride into a wildfire, he thought.

Why did they do that . . . ?

But as he asked the question, he had to remind himself that he had followed without hesitation—so closely that he'd had to water both himself and his horse down to keep up his pursuit. What did that say about him? He didn't want to think about it right now.

He rode on.

Four miles farther down along the chasm trail he felt the heat on his left begin to wane. A mile farther the temperature had subsided enough that he was able to take the bandanna down from his face. Beneath him the rusty barb rode at a stronger gallop. Along their left, beyond the buffer of boulders, dirt and shale, the woodlands lay blackened and ruined, smoke still rising. The smoke was slower now, less intense, but nevertheless engulfed them in a gray, suffocating haze.

Now he had another problem.

He stopped the horse and stepped down from his saddle. He listened to the barb wheeze and choke, its labored breath rattling deep in its lungs.

"Easy, boy," he said, rubbing the horse's muzzle. He stepped back to his saddlebags, rummaged a shirt, and shook it out.

He tied the sleeves up around the horse's head and made a veil of the shirt. The horse resisted a little and whipped its head until the ranger took the canteen and poured water down the horse's face and threw the shirt onto its parched muzzle. He held the wet shirt in place, letting the animal breath through it. When the horse felt the good of what the ranger was doing and settled, Sam took his hand off its muzzle.

"Good boy . . ."

He poured water onto his bandanna and tied it across the bridge of his nose. He led the horse forward by its reins, feeling the thickness of the smoke with every step.

"I make it . . . seven, eight miles to water," he rasped, as if the winded horse understood his words and took comfort in them.

Three miles farther, he noted that the smoke had let up, enough that he could make out the blue of the sky. Underneath him the horse breathed easier; so did he. Stopping, he took down the warm canteen and lifted the shirt from the horse's muzzle. He kneeled in front of the horse and took off his sombrero like a man given to a vigil of prayer.

"You need this worse than I do," he said, pouring the water into the upturned hat.

The horse lowered its muzzle into the sombrero and Sam let the wet shirt fall around the ensemble.

When the horse finished the water and tried chewing at the hat brim for more, Sam stood and pulled his wet sombrero away and placed it atop his head. Canteen in hand, he climbed back into the saddle and gave the horse a tap of his heels. On their left, among boulder rocks and dry washes, antelope, deer, coyote, and an assortment of smaller creatures still skirted in the same direction, slower now that the threat of death inched farther into the distance.

"It's up to you now," Sam said to the horse as the

barb galloped forward, the air, the ground, and the atmosphere already turning cooler around them.

For the next five miles he gave the barb its head, the barb keeping up a strong, steady pace, moving farther away from the raging fire. With the wind in their faces, even with the lingering odor of pine char and brimstone in the air, Sam felt the horse surge with a renewed energy when the scent of water managed to reach into its nostrils.

In the last few hundred yards he had to rein the barb down to keep it from bolting toward the rock runoff tank lying below a steep hillside to their right. The barb muttered and blew and shook its head in protest; but it followed the ranger's command.

As the ranger scanned the rock tank from fifty yards, a young bear stood up on its hinds and looked at him and the horse, then dropped and turned away. When he was thirty yards away, Sam saw a panther and two cubs begin to slink back from the water's edge. Grudgingly, with a large-fanged growl, the big mother cat crept backward to the shelter of boulders as the ranger stepped the horse forward. He noted the upper half of the mother cat's left ear was missing. Dried blood caked down her neck and shoulder. Mimicking its mother, one of the cubs raised its back toward him and let out a hiss—showing its small and helpless fangs. The ranger smiled sadly, nudging his horse forward.

Across the water Sam saw the rumps of a small herd of elk move away into the growth of pine and juniper mantling the rock chasm still running alongside the trail. Odd, he thought, elk, mountain lion, and bear, all watering within less then thirty feet of one another. Yet odder still was that all three species had cut short sating their thirst at the glimpse of man. The only animals to remain as the ranger rode closer were birds of all sizes and varieties. They sat along the water's rocky edge, preening themselves of the smell of smoke, and drinking fearlessly, as if knowing that in an instant they could be up and gone should man try any of his dark shenanigans.

A few of the smaller birds fluttered up and away as the ranger and the horse filed past them at less than fifteen feet. But the larger birds only stared and squawked and continued attending themselves.

"Don't mind us," he murmured, riding past.

When he had looked all around the water hole and satisfied himself that he and the horse were the only ones there representing their species, he swung down from the saddle, rifle in hand. The larger birds sidestepped away from him, making room, but giving up no more of their spot than they had to.

As he stepped down from his saddle he saw the hoofprints of the four horses in the sandy dirt among the rocks. On one of the half-sunken rocks he saw spots of dark blood, and he stooped, took off his glove, and touched his fingertips to it while the horse lowered its muzzle and drank.

All right, Cheyenne Kid, how far ahead are you? he asked, rubbing his fingertips on the spots, then examining them for any sign of red moisture.

"Bone dry . . . ," he murmured aloud, as if any of the creatures of the wilds were interested. He stood and looked back and forth along the trail, first at the smoky distant trail behind, then along the rocky winding trail ahead. Now to the earlier question he'd asked himself: Why had they ridden into the fire?

Because they had laid out their escape route before ever riding into Phoebe, he realized. Somewhere up ahead, they had fresh horses waiting for them. That was all it could be. When he worked out the miles from here to Phoebe in his head, he knew that they wouldn't have attempted to make it as far as Bagley's Trading Post without a change of horses. The trading post was still a twenty-six-mile ride from here, most of it over dry, rocky, leg-breaking terrain.

Fresh horses? Good enough . . . He'd stick with that notion until something proved otherwise, he decided, staring up along the rocky, winding trail. He had their tracks. He'd catch up to them and take them down. He only hoped none of the fire had jumped across the chasm and rekindled among the pine woodlands in front of him. It was the season for wildfires, he thought. *Dry, hot, deadly.* There was nothing he could do about that. His work had to go on, wildfires or no. He cradled the rifle in his arm while the horse stood drawing water beside him.